OUTSIDERS
2

Unfinished Business

TAMMY FEREBEE

Outsiders 2
Unfinished Business

Cover Design by Ilsie Omareva
Book Interior by The Book Khaleesi
www.thebookkhaleesi.com

ISBN-10: 0-9966292-1-1
ISBN-13: 978-0-9966292-1-8

www.tammyferebee.com

First Edition
First Printing, May 2017

You were like a parent to me.
You were one of my best friends.
You were my mentor.
Now, you're my angel.
I will forever love and miss you.
My sweet Evelyn

Chapter 1

S ilence screams the truth. Right now, it's loud and clear there's no time for us to casually sit around. We graduated just a couple of hours ago. The joy of such a happy occasion has already faded. We must figure out what to do now.

I stare out the passenger side window as Michael drives us toward a place neither of us wants to go. We had been looking forward to settling into my home in Hopewell, New Jersey. I was anxious to show my boyfriend where I grew up, to show him the place my mom had covered in love and comfort. Instead, we're on our way back to West Virginia, to Ethan and Ms. Housley's home. We're supposed to be putting our heads together and trying to determine how to put this Indigo situation to rest. It's something none of us wants to think about or act upon, but unfortunately, we have no choice.

Something had snapped inside of my ex-best friend's mind. Granted, we started off rocky. After rejecting Indigo's kiss mere hours after meeting her, I wasn't sure we could even remain friends. But we had. We found a place for each other. We had enjoyed our closeness, though there was something weird between her and Michael that almost everyone could feel. Come to find out, that awkwardness had only surfaced

1

after they'd slept together. But, as hurt as I was, I could still understand her anger toward him. What I couldn't make sense of was her controlling personality. Michael and Indigo were equally wrong in keeping their secret from me, but Michael had never tried to stop me from being friends with Indigo. He never butted into our friendship. He never tried to hurt her. As much as I wish I could, I can't say the same about my former best friend.

Indigo stalked us on our prom night, found us after a brutal animal attack, and after barely escaping with my life, she helped me in my weakened state. Sadly, and still unbelievably, she had abandoned Michael while he was helpless. Even if she couldn't offer her hand to him, even if she had been too angry to help him to his feet, she could've simply handed him that bottle of water. She could've given him what he needed to survive. Instead, she had poured it out. She had left him to lie there and suffer, to feel his insides painfully dry out, to die. If it hadn't been for Michael's mother, he wouldn't be alive today. If Indigo had just given him that damn bottle, none of us would still be thinking about her. I'd never have attacked Indigo and tried to kill her, Indigo's aunt wouldn't want to kill me in her niece's defense, and none of us would be spending the day of our high school graduation worrying about this insanity.

An icy tremor runs through my entire body. My fingers and even my toes tingle. I grab a water from one of the middle cup holders and take a few sips. "Want some?" I offer Michael with the bottle held out.

He takes it and downs the rest before placing the empty bottle back in the cup holder.

"Wanna talk?" I ask.

"About what?"

I reach over and place my hand on his thigh. "Whatever's on your mind."

"You know what's on my mind. This is bullshit! I don't

want to go back to West Virginia. We had a plan, Jaylen. This isn't it. This girl is still controlling every move we make. I'm tired of her."

"I don't want to be in West Virginia either, but if being together will make your mother more comfortable, then why not? It's only temporary. This *is* frustrating, but remember, we aren't moving to West Virginia. This is just temporary."

"And it makes absolutely no sense. My mother wants us all together because she thinks that's how we'll all remain safe, right? But Indigo doesn't know where your house is in Jersey. How are we not safe there?"

"Being together in West Virginia allows us to collectively come up with a plan. Not only that, but I really think your mother needs to keep an eye on you. For her own sake. We could see you getting heated after the ceremony."

"Why wouldn't I get heated? You know what Indigo tried to do to me! I should've been the one with the mean mug. Not her and her evil, Amazonian aunt. Don't stare at me like you wanna do something to me and not expect me to get pissed off."

I rub Michael's thigh. "We were all looking at each other that way, Michael. No one knows what the other plans to do. Not to mention, they thought you were dead. Her aunt wants to protect Indigo and we want to protect you."

He quickly switches lanes. "I don't need protection."

I release a loud sigh. "Like I said before we left the school, I think we should all talk. Us and them."

"Why do you keep suggesting that? Let's say Indigo does tell us that she'll leave us alone. What if she does promise to stay on her campus, to not find out where you live so she can sneak around and do whatever else nutty ass people like her do? Can we really believe her? If we tell them we have no interest in taking this further, do you really think her aunt is going to believe us? She's probably going to think it's a setup."

I snatch my hand from his leg. "Maybe it will take a lot of

convincing, but a talk needs to happen. I'm still not with creating some top secret plan and attacking her. We're not killers, Michael!"

"Why are you yelling at me? I didn't start this!"

I scoff, taking the other bottle of water from its cup holder and gulping some down before turning back toward the passenger seat window. As we pass by exit signs, my mind goes to Ethan. He seems like a rational person. Maybe I can get him to talk to Indigo and her aunt with me. I understand Michael's anger. I understand why he's so frustrated. But killing is the ultimate crime. There's no coming back from death. Not even for our kind. Allowing my boyfriend to retaliate out of anger when I'm certain he'll regret it afterward would be a mistake. There's another way to end this situation. I'm sure of it.

His hand reaches over and covers mine. "I'm sorry I yelled."

I exhale and turn slightly in my seat. "I apologize too. I just want you to understand I'm not your enemy, Michael. I'm trying to be your partner and save you from making a mistake you'd have to carry with you the rest of your life. You need to find a way to release some of that anger so you can think clearly. Think about how this feels for me, someone who loves you."

"For the millionth time, I'm not asking you to take part in this."

"Are you kidding me? You're leaving me no choice!"

The car becomes silent again. The tension is palpable. I've never had my life and well-being completely disregarded while in a defenseless state, so I can't fully comprehend how unsafe, hurt, and furious he truly feels. I do know what it feels like to want to kill someone, though. I wanted to kill Indigo, too. Almost did. While I had her neck firmly gripped in my hands, I saw her life slowly leaving her body. It was painful seeing her suffer, but anger and grief were fueling me. It's not easy to take a life. Michael would understand that if he could see past the hate and his vengeful thoughts.

I pull my cell out of my bag and begin scrolling through my text message feed.

"So I guess you're done talking to me, huh?"

I don't respond. I keep my eyes on my cell's screen. Yeah, I'd rather spend this ride talking to my boyfriend, but I don't want to argue. I want him to see my point, let it sink in, understand the horror I see in our futures should we let this mess go on and grow to uncontrollable heights. He wants me to hear him, to keep my guard way up, and to not trust there's any good in Indigo. While I can't trust there's still good in her, I don't want to make any assumptions. I don't know for sure that there isn't. We're talking about lives here. All our lives. All I want to do is talk to them. No one has lost a life, and I'd like to keep it that way. If we make angry decisions, we'll see stupid, senseless, regrettable results. I want to avoid that.

Michael eases over onto the shoulder of the highway. After shifting into park, he slowly turns to me. "I can deal with anybody else being mad at me. Anyone. But not you."

I stare into my boyfriend's eyes.

"This fight isn't ours, Jaylen. Let's not take this out on one another."

"I don't wanna lose you, Michael," I say hastily, almost speaking over him.

"You won't."

"You don't know that for sure. That's what I want you to let sink in to that concrete brain of yours. You can't see past the fact that she wanted you to die that night. Yes, what she did was wrong. No doubt about that. But what happens after you retaliate? If you do kill Indigo, do you think her aunt will call that an even score? No. She will come for you. For us! That's what you need to open your eyes and see. Getting rid of Indigo won't end anything. It's gonna open a floodgate." I softly touch his cheek. "Think about it, Michael." I soften my tone. "We won't even be living in Virginia anymore."

"My mom will still be there. Our house is still there."

"I don't think she's gonna do anything to your mom. Your mom has nothing to do with this. We can let this go. Michael, please," I beg. "Let this go."

Michael holds my hand in between both of his. "I don't want her sneaking in my house ever again. I don't want to think about my mom there alone and that girl being anywhere near her. I don't trust Indigo." He shakes his head. "I'm never going to trust her again. You are trying too hard to convince yourself that she's someone who just made a horrible mistake. I can't see her that way. Maybe because it was me she tried to get rid of." He shrugs. "Maybe it's my gut talking to me. The point is, Jaylen, I can't convince myself that a talk is going to solve anything."

I look away from my boyfriend's eyes. I'll never forget how good it felt when I realized Michael hadn't been taken from me. Words can't explain that kind of relief. I don't ever want to feel as lost as I did those three days when I had nothing else to believe except that he was no longer with me. That emptiness was soul-ripping.

His volume is low. "Look at me, Jaylen."

My eyes find his.

"I can promise you I won't do anything today, and I probably won't do anything tomorrow, but my mental wheels are turning. I don't feel like this whole situation is going to disappear even if we do all sit and talk."

I don't respond. Again, the car becomes silent.

He caresses my face. "I know you're angry with me."

I shake my head. "I'm not angry. I'm scared."

He leans in closer to my face. "We're gonna get through this."

As I stare at my boyfriend, my mind goes to Indigo. I saw her face at the ceremony. She was terrified. The scorned, vengeful teenager had become a fearful child. If I can get her to believe that we'd prefer to take a peaceful route as opposed to a violent one, maybe I could end this myself.

"I was happy to see you graduate today, brainiac."

His words pull me from my thoughts of Indigo and momentarily distract me from the nasty situation at hand. I smile. "I was happy to see you walk the stage today, too, slacker."

He chuckles. "Ms. Ward was crazy loud."

"She made me feel so special."

"You are." His voice is almost a whisper.

My smile widens.

"See, that's what today is supposed to be about." He gently glides his thumb across my bottom lip. "We just graduated. Let's enjoy this. We have to stop giving Indigo so much power."

His lips press against mine. Usually, his kisses can stop my thoughts in their tracks. Normally, when our lips meet, the world around me feels as though it's frozen. Not today, though. I can't stop believing there's another way out of this situation. A non-violent way that will bring peace back into my world.

"We good?" he asks.

I force a dishonest smile and nod. "We're good."

As Michael merges back onto the highway, I locate Kennedy's name in my contact list. Quietly, I text her, *This is not a trick. This is not some sort of trap. I wanna talk to Indigo, in person, preferably today. I just wanna squash this beef before things get any worse. Can you assure her that this won't be an attack, and ask her to meet me somewhere public? She trusts you. She'll believe this coming from you. And I promise, I just wanna talk.*

"Who are you texting essays to?"

"Kennedy," I answer.

He releases a soft grunt. "Be careful who you trust, Jaylen."

I look straight ahead as I wait for Kennedy's reply. I think about my home in New Jersey. I was so looking forward to spending the night in my old room. I was hoping to settle back into a house filled with my mom's love. Because of my mom, our home always felt secure. I could use that feeling right about now.

I take a sip of water. "I thought you liked Kennedy."

Michael shrugs. "I mean, she seems nice. She seems to care about you. But liking and trusting are two different things."

"I know that, but what does your gut tell you?"

"To be careful," he replies in a hurry. "And yours?"

"That she's okay. I wouldn't totally let my guard down with anyone right away, but something tells me she's not a malicious girl who wants this situation to get any worse. True, she was Indigo's girlfriend, but that doesn't mean she's demented like her. In all fairness, I was Indigo's best friend, and I'm nothing like her."

He checks both mirrors before merging into a new lane. "All I'm saying is, be careful. I haven't accused her of anything."

"I hear you, Michael," I say as I rest my phone in my lap. "So are we going straight to Ethan's?"

"Moms wants to take us to celebrate."

"Where?"

"Some top-notch steakhouse Ethan and Ms. Housley go to for special occasions. It's not too far from their house."

"Our kind goes out to eat?"

Michael lets out a short laugh. "We may not eat as often as humans, but I grew up on more than just water. I didn't live like a plant."

"Ha ha," I say sarcastically. "I eat, too. You've seen me nibble. I just feel as though I'm forcing it when I do. It seems so natural for you."

"We can survive on water alone, but as you already know, salt helps us retain the water, and Moms has been told that food strengthens us. Of course, there's no proof to back that for our kind, but I'm used to eating at least once a day. It's a habit at this point."

"I get it. And, hey, there's still time for it to become a habit of mine, too. I just need more…"

"What the hell?" Michael interrupts, throwing his arm across my chest and stomping the brake. Both of our bodies are thrown forward as we suddenly stop only inches from the car in front of us.

Michael honks repeatedly at the car that abruptly stopped. "Sorry about that, babe. I wasn't speeding. I don't know why this asshole slammed on his brakes like that."

While trying to control my sporadic breathing, the red Civic in front of us quickly changes lanes. Ahead, we see a huge hunk of retread lying in the middle of our lane. As Michael continues forward, the large piece of rubber levitates and flies to the side of the road.

We continue in the now unobstructed lane, and I eye my boyfriend in envy. Had I been driving alone, I would've been forced to hit my brake and make a quick lane change just as the red Civic had to do. Michael is lucky. All he has to do is need or want something and then tell his mind to make it happen. He can say and believe whatever he wants. Telekinesis beats the hell out of my physical strength. I still have to make physical contact with things. He never has to move if he doesn't want to.

He chuckles. "Stop staring at me, hater."

"You're lucky as hell, Michael. I would love to be able to sit back and move things."

"Since you can't, just let me move things for you. A long time ago, I learned that my telekinesis can do more than just move objects. I can push, pull, even hurt a person if I have to." He throws me a quick look. "Learned that when I witnessed bullying for the first time in second grade. Saw a kid getting picked on, pushed around, mushed in the face, victimized. Mean shit just for laughs, you know? I felt like I was too small and skinny to take on Jeremy by myself, so in my head, I would whoop his ass. One day during indoor recess, I watched him picking on Little Davey, this kid with some speech issues and a nervous tic. The substitute just kept telling us to quiet down but wasn't doing anything to end the situation." He shakes his head as he continues. "I just wanted to get Jeremy away from him. I mean, Davey couldn't help how he was, and even if he could, leave him the hell alone anyway. I just hate when people are taken advantage of or punked. So," he says, dragging out the word, "in my head, I pulled Jeremy's hands behind his back, twisted his wrists, and ran him head first into the chalk board. All I did was look at him and really think it, really want it, and it happened in front of everyone. He fell on the floor, crying hysterically. I sat in my seat, had some water, and colored. The other kids laughed because it looked like he did it to himself."

"He left Davey alone after that?" I ask.

"Nope. I think the parents had to get involved, but that's how I learned I could use my mind to move or contort just about anything. Point being, if you don't want to move to get something, or put something somewhere, let me and my mind handle that for you. Want someone knocked out? I can handle that, too."

"When I'm around you, you'll be handling just about everything, then. I'm not getting up to get the remote, my water, anything. If someone pushes the wrong button with me, I'll let you know so you can handle that for me, Carrie White."

He releases a short laugh, and I recline my seat.

"Going to sleep, woman?"

"No. I'm thinking about Ms. Ward. I mean, it'll be nice to celebrate, but I feel weird not celebrating with her. She begged me to let her throw me an after graduation party."

"Call her. Invite her."

"No, because then we'll have to wait for her to drive to the restaurant." I shrug. "It's no biggie. Ms. Ward will do something for me, even if it's a year from now."

Michael laughs. "I believe that. She feels like you're her daughter."

"I really hope she has kids. That woman is a rock star. She's queen of the foster mothers. Any kid would be lucky to have her."

My cell alerts me of a text. Silently, I read Kennedy's response. *Are you sure, Jaylen? You want to meet with her alone? I'm not so sure that's a good idea. That doesn't sound safe.*

I reply, *I'm sure. We need to come to some sort of agreement. I can't allow this to get violent. I don't want Michael's family to get hurt. I don't wanna get hurt.*

"What are you guys talking about? Ethan?" Michael guesses.

"Maybe," I answer.

"You're hooking them up?"

"No. They have each other's numbers. They don't need my help."

"He's really feeling her."

I dig. "What has he told you about her?"

"None of your business, nosy."

I scoff. "Fine. Keep your secrets. Just know that I'm gonna respond to you the same way when you wanna know the details Ethan chooses not to share with you."

"Yeah right. Like you could keep a secret from me."

I reply coolly, "I already have."

Michael's silence tickles me. I know what he's waiting for. He's waiting for me to tell him that I'm joking.

My text alert pulls my attention from Michael. Kennedy's response reads, *I still don't think this is the safest idea, but at least you're meeting her in public. I sent her a message for you. I'll let you know what she says, and as a friend, I suggest that you take someone with you. Not Michael!*

I send her back, *I really appreciate it, Kennedy. And don't worry, I wouldn't dare take Michael. I'm gonna ask Ethan. Please know that*

I'm just trying to clear the air. I'm not looking for trouble.

"So…" Michael pushes.

"So, what?"

"This secret you've supposedly kept from me."

"If you haven't figured it out yet, then it's not important."

"Important or not, tell me."

"It's not a big deal, Michael," I say, fully aware that there's no secret, no bomb to drop on him.

"Tell me."

"No."

He sucks his teeth. "Tell me," he again demands.

"You don't need to know."

"Jaylen!" His volume is much louder, his frustration is painfully clear, and I'm really enjoying this.

I exhale loudly. "Fine. You really wanna know?" I ask as I try to think of something to say.

"I asked."

"Promise you won't get mad?"

He keeps his eyes on the road. "No, but I'll try not to."

I allow seconds to pass. I wait for him to ask one final time.

"Spit it out, Jaylen."

"I used to be a man, Michael. I'm sorry I kept this from you, but…"

His burst of laughter interrupts my false apology. I laugh, too.

"So I slept with a man?"

I nod. "Twice."

We laugh together. My bad sense of humor did two very necessary things. One, it briefly took my mind off Indigo. Two, it got rid of what was left of the uncomfortable tension between Michael and me. If there's anything I need right now, it's for Michael to be relaxed. If he's worried about me and how I'm feeling about him, he'll spend so much time trying to make me comfortable and happy that I won't have an opportunity to sneak away and meet with Indigo. With him thinking I'm okay, I can get away, and possibly end this madness today.

Chapter 2

*A*s the waitress takes our menus and rushes off to enter our orders, I text discreetly beneath the table. According to Kennedy, Indigo is willing to meet me, but only with her aunt present. I agree, but now I need Ethan to accompany me more than ever. As Kennedy plays the messenger and helps us to set up a time and place to meet this evening, I text Ethan asking him to meet me by the bathrooms so we can talk.

"So how does it feel to be high school graduates?" Ms. Housley asks.

As Ethan reads my text, I answer Ms. Housley. "Feels great. I'm excited about college."

She smiles broadly. "You should be. This is an exciting time in your young lives. What about you Mike?"

"I'm just happy high school is over."

"What are your plans? Your mom told me that you're not interested in heading right off to college."

"Oh, he's going to college," Ms. Reed makes clear.

"Yeah, I'm going," Michael says. "I'm just taking a little break. I'm thinking about working and maybe interning for a year."

Ethan makes eye contact with me before scooting his chair back. "Excuse me, everyone. I need to go wash my hands."

"I was just about to say that I need to excuse myself as well. I need to call Ms. Ward back," I say dishonestly.

Together we stand and head for the front of the restaurant. Because the bathrooms are so close to the restaurant entrance, Ethan and I are able to slip outside without those left at the table noticing.

"You okay?"

I nod. "I'm fine."

"What's up?"

"I'm meeting with Indigo tonight."

His eyes widen.

"I know it sounds crazy, but we're gathering at your house to plot, to discuss possibly taking her life, Ethan. Don't get me wrong, I'm still disgusted and hurt that she left my boyfriend to suffer and die, but we're not those people. We don't take lives and go on about ours like nothing ever happened."

"What do you think this meeting is going to do, Jaylen?"

"I wanna talk to her and her aunt. I wanna come to some sort of an agreement. Trust me, I know Indigo. She doesn't want this fight."

"What could they possibly agree to?"

"If we can convince them that we're moving out of state and on with our lives, maybe we can get them to leave us be. If they don't feel threatened, they have no reason to hurt us. We just need to assure them that we're not going to come for them. Any of them. I mean, I understand Indigo's aunt. She wants to protect Indigo, who she raised as her own daughter. No one is going to stand around and let their kid be harmed. She's involved simply to protect her child. That's why we need to make sure she understands we're seriously not interested in hurting Indigo. I'm sure this grown woman has no interest in hurting a bunch of teens, but I'm sure age doesn't matter to her when it comes to someone trying to kill her child. She needs to hear, especially from me, that we want to squash this before it goes any further."

Ethan releases a mouthful of air. "And you want me to go?"

"Only if you feel the same way I do."

"From day one, I was hoping we wouldn't have to fight this out. My mom is not going to let me step in the middle of a fight like this if she's not right there beside me. And once she had me, she passed her abilities on to me, so she'd literally be setting herself up to get hurt."

"Not hurt, Ethan. Killed," I correct. "We're all putting our lives on the line. Yes, Indigo started this, but if they have other family members with abilities we don't even know of, we could lose this fight *and* our lives."

Ethan places both of his hands on his head and looks to the ground.

"I'm sorry, Ethan. I know I'm putting you in an awkward position."

He shakes his head. "You're not. You're making perfect sense." He looks up at me. "So what do you have in mind?"

"We go back to your house, sneak out while Michael's in the shower, take the drive to the meet up place, and we talk."

"Where's the meet up place?"

"Kennedy's gonna text me and let me know. She's been doing the talking for me."

He nods slowly. "Okay. Eat then, Jaylen. And drink all your water. If this girl wants to do more than talk, you need to be ready to defend us. If you're as strong as Michael says, and her aunt can still overpower you, I won't have a fighting chance."

"I'll be ready, Ethan. If anyone gets hurt tonight, it'll be me. This is my idea."

"I'll do my best to make sure that doesn't happen. I might not be able to take her aunt on in a fight, but I have a way of getting out of situations pretty quickly. Still, just to be safe, drink up."

My cell vibrates in my hand.

"Check it. It's probably Kennedy."

I quickly unlock my phone and swipe to locate the message. It is from Kennedy. I read it silently.

"Well?" he asks impatiently.

"They want to meet at some park."

"Hell no," Ethan rejects immediately. "Why a park? We're supposed to be talking. Why not a diner or a McDonalds?"

I text back, *We were hoping to meet at a restaurant, or somewhere else public like that. An open park gives them an opportunity to attack. We need to be surrounded by humans. We need eyes surrounding us. It'll keep us all in line.*

Ethan shakes his head. "I don't like the idea of a park."

"In their defense, it's still early. We left the school at about one. It's only two something now. After we eat, we'll head to your place, and then head out from there."

"The drive is over an hour. And don't forget, you're trying to get away without Mike finding out. Factor that time in, too."

The door swings open. "What are you guys doing out here?"

I put my arm around Michael's waist. "Just playing messenger for Kennedy."

"Are you gonna invite her out to the house?" Michael asks Ethan.

"Yeah, but she probably won't be able to come out today. She just graduated. Her dad is probably doing something for her."

"So what's the move for tonight? We should go somewhere."

I eye Ethan.

"We should." Ethan nods. "I'll call around to see what's poppin'."

"I don't wanna party in West Virginia," Michael declines.

"I'll hit up my man Warren. It's graduation night. He's getting into something for sure. I'll find out and then we should go."

"Sounds good," I say unenthusiastically.

The three of us head back inside. As we rejoin Ms. Housley and Ms. Reed, my cell alerts me twice. I sip from my water before discretely checking the messages. Kennedy's message reads, *They still want to meet at a park. Indigo swears they aren't looking for trouble. It'll still be daylight. People will still be around.* The second message reads, *They said take it or leave it.*

I forward the messages to Ethan. I wait for him to agree to their terms before I reply.

As Ethan reads over the forwarded messages, I listen in on the conversation Michael is having with Ms. Housley and his mom.

"There are paid internships, though," Michael argues.

"Yes there are," Ms. Housley says. "But money isn't everything, Mike. Don't turn down a position simply because it doesn't pay. Internships are about getting experience. Not about getting paid."

Ms. Reed nods in agreement.

"I get that. I still have to make money, though. How am I supposed to support myself in Jersey?"

"The experience is more important, Mike. If you can't afford to keep a roof over your head in Jersey, then stay home," Ms. Reed tells him. "A job is not a priority right now. Your education is. Your future is."

"And Jaylen is a huge part of my future."

I grab Michael's hand and he immediately turns to me.

"You're not listening to them," I say. "They're not telling you that you can't be with me. They're just trying to rearrange your thinking. You're not focusing on what's most important. You told me and everyone else that you're not going to school yet because you don't know what you want to do. Your mom just wants you to figure that out first. Worry about our relationship and making money later. Focus on your career goals now."

My cell alerts me. I keep my eyes on Michael.

"I get what y'all are saying. For real, I do. I just wanna be where I wanna be. I'll focus more on getting an internship first. I'm still looking for a job, though, and I'm definitely not gonna stay in Virginia."

I take large swallows of my water before taking a look at my message. Ethan's text reads, *Fine. Just finish that water you have, and order another glass. I need you to be at your strongest. Just in case.*

I send a message to Kennedy, accepting Indigo's and her aunt's terms. The moment my finger touches the 'send' button, a feeling of uneasiness covers me. Knowing Ethan could get hurt scares me. I brought him into this. He's only involved because his goal is the same as mine. We want to end this quietly. I'm sure Indigo and her aunt hope to end this as well. What worries me is their methods. What if I meet them, things go awry, and I never make it back to Michael? What if Ethan doesn't make it back home to his mother? So many *what ifs*. I hope I'm doing the right thing. I hope things go according to plan.

"Earth to Jaylen."

I direct my attention to Ms. Housley.

"You all right?" she asks.

"Yeah, I'm fine. Sorry I zoned out. I'm just taking everything in."

"You mean with school? Or our other situation?"

"Both," I admit. "I'm thinking a lot about Princeton and what I have to do to get prepared for the fall. I really want to be more excited, but I can't help but think about Indigo."

"Just don't think about it."

I cut my eyes at Michael. "You can't be serious. How can I not?"

Ms. Reed says, "We're all thinking about it. We just have to try really hard not to let this consume our lives. I know that sounds impossible, because you saw Indigo today at the graduation, but try really hard to remain focused on school, on your achievements, and on your family and friends. We're your support. If you need to talk about it, talk to us."

I look across at Ethan, and then back over at Ms. Reed. "I wish we could talk this out with them."

"Me too, sweetheart," she admits softly.

"I think we can, Ms. Reed. I think if we all really wanted to end this peacefully, we could."

"I don't think her aunt sees that as an option."

"She probably doesn't think it's an option, but we can let her know it is."

I ignore Michael's teeth sucking. So does his mother.

"So, you want to put together a meeting of some sort?" she asks.

I nod. "I really do. I don't want to see anyone at this table get hurt."

"Or killed," Ethan throws out.

Michael's frustration comes out in a sigh. "I just don't see talking getting us anywhere."

"You're too angry to see any other way," I tell him.

"I'm not angry."

"You are, Michael. And even if talking doesn't work, at least we tried doing the right thing first. I just don't want you or any of the rest of us to do something and forever look back wishing we had gone about things differently. We're talking about lives here, Michael."

"I know all about that, Jaylen. I almost lost mine."

"I know that. Almost!" I say loudly. "You're still here, though. If you let that anger start a war, you might actually lose it this time. And you may not go alone."

The table becomes silent. Michael slouches in his seat and crosses his arms across his chest. I make eye contact with his mother.

Ms. Reed's eyes are on mine. "We'll talk more about it

later, okay?"

I nod, though I know I still have every intention of meeting Indigo later.

"At the house, we'll talk this out." Ms. Housley offers a warm smile. "For now, being that we're not in the most private setting, we should just stick to more casual conversation."

I turn to my boyfriend. "Can we talk, please?"

He shrugs once. "Sure."

"I hate to get up from the table so many times. We're just going to step out front and talk for a minute or two."

Ms. Housley and Ms. Reed both smile sweetly.

"Take your time," Ms. Reed says.

Michael and I head for the entrance. He holds the door open for me to walk through. Out front, we sit side by side on a bench. His eyes look straight ahead. My eyes are on him. I feel so distant from him. We were so happy at the ceremony just hours ago.

"I love you, Michael."

He makes eye contact just long enough to tell me, "I love you, too."

I don't force him to face me. I draw in a deep breath and release it slowly. "This is pulling us apart."

"It shouldn't be. If we ever needed to be together on anything, it's this."

"You won't take anything in unless it's what you want to hear."

His eyes meet mine. "That's not true."

"Yes it is, Michael. Because of what she did to you, you feel you have the right to determine how we retaliate."

"Makes sense to me."

"But you're hotheaded. You're angry, and angry people are usually thoughtless. Believe me when I tell you, Michael, you're not thinking about this the right way."

"I just feel like talking is going to force you and Moms to let your guards down. And I think that's when they're going to attack. You're still telling yourself there's some good in Indigo. Who knows? Maybe there is. But her aunt has it in for you, Jaylen."

"That's because she thinks I still have it in for Indigo. I can't say it enough. What Indigo did was wrong. *So wrong*," I emphasize. "But you're here. You're alive. I want to move on. I don't want to fight this out."

Michael sits quietly.

"I feel like talking to you is like talking to a brick wall. You just won't budge."

"I don't feel comfortable taking chances with your safety."

"And I'm trying to get you to see that fighting this out is the perfect way to compromise my safety and your family's."

Michael sits quietly. I want to believe he's at least considering going about things my way.

He reaches over and grabs my hand. No words are exchanged. I look at our palms pressed against one another's. I look at our perfectly interlocked fingers. Then I look up at my troubled boyfriend's face. He claims he's concerned about my safety. I'm sure he is. But I know Michael. I know how he feels about Indigo. I know he wants to protect me and his mother, but just as much as he wants us to be safe, he wants revenge.

I silently tell myself I'm doing the best thing I can by meeting with Indigo and her aunt later. My boyfriend is too stubborn to wait on, and frankly I'm over Ms. Reed and Ms. Housley telling me we'll talk about things later. I want to move on with my life. I want to head back home to Jersey, catch up with old friends, and prepare for college. If I can get Indigo and her aunt to leave us alone with the promise that we'll keep our distance, Ms. Reed will see that I've done what's best for us. In the end, this is the only way to guarantee we all remain safe and alive.

I stand. "Let's head back inside."

He stands. "We okay?"

I pull my boyfriend close in a tight hug. "We're fine. We're just going to have to agree to disagree. For now, at least."

Michael offers me a brief smile as we separate.

"We should change the subject, though. Like you said in the car, today should be all about smiles and celebrating."

He gently kisses my forehead. "Yup. And hopefully we'll find a party to hit later tonight."

I look into Michael's beautiful green eyes.

"What's wrong?" he asks.

"Can I just have another hug?"

He pulls me close once more. I squeeze him tight. I inhale his scent. I tell myself everything will go just fine at the meeting later. But just in case it doesn't, at least I got to hold Michael in my arms one last time.

Chapter 3

On the entire ride back to Ethan's, I sit anxiously in the passenger seat as Michael and Ethan discuss party plans Ethan and I know we won't be following through on. Once Michael realizes we snuck out, regardless of what time we make it back, he's going to be too pissed to do any partying. We'll likely spend the rest of the night arguing, something we only seem to do when Indigo interferes with our relationship or well-being.

"Want some water, Jaylen?" Ethan offers.

I turn in my seat. "No thanks. Drank three full glasses at the restaurant."

"Yeah, I saw that." Michael jumps in. "What was that about?"

"Just thirsty, I guess."

"I actually heard you gulping. You feel all right?"

I let out a nervous chuckle. "I feel fine. You know me, I always do more drinking than eating. I guess I just need to learn how to swallow more quietly."

"Swallow? We haven't gotten to that yet."

I gasp at his slick remark and hit my boyfriend with a fast jab in his right arm.

Michael's left side hits the driver side door. "Ow!" he hollers out in pain. "What the hell, Jaylen? I was just playing."

Ethan laughs at Michael's pain. So do I.

"You better watch what you say, Mike. Your girl can kick your ass."

"Yes, I can." I reach over to rub the spot I just hit. "Sorry to hit you so hard, though. Sometimes I forget how strong I can be."

"You did walk right into that, though, Jaylen."

I turn. "Shut up, Ethan. You can get one too, you know."

Ethan throws his hands up. "I don't want no trouble."

The three of us laugh.

I so needed this—the laughing and joking around. I don't find it easy to lie to anyone, but I find it most difficult to lie to my boyfriend. I'm not sure what's bothering me more, not knowing how this meeting will turn out, or meeting with them behind Michael's back.

As we park in Ethan's driveway, I turn and look back at him. He tries to comfort me with a shaky smile. It's a sweet attempt, but Ethan's clearly just as uneasy as I am.

We head inside the Housley home. Without being told, I head for the unoccupied guest room in the basement with my bag in hand.

Michael stops me on the stairs. "Where are you going?"

"To put my things in the guest room."

"You don't have to sleep in the basement by yourself."

"You wanna switch rooms?"

He shakes his head.

"Are you crazy? We're in your mom's friend's house." I lower my voice. "I know you're not asking me to sleep with you."

"That better not be what you're asking her. My mom would kill both of y'all," Ethan states as he passes us both.

I continue to the basement with Michael only a few steps behind. The basement guest room isn't as spacious as the two upstairs. The temperature is chillier and the windows are much smaller. If it weren't for the cream colored carpet and ivory walls, this room wouldn't look nearly as bright and I'd probably be convincing Michael to seriously consider the switch.

My boyfriend takes a seat on the full bed. I kick out of my heels before sitting beside him.

"No more high school," he says proudly. "Thank God!"

"We're going to miss high school as soon as we start college."

"That's what Moms says."

"It's true. You've been complaining about PowerPoints and writing two page papers. The sizes of the text books are about to double, you're going to have to start writing five and ten page papers, and all the late work you used to turn in that only cost you five points will now probably cost you an entire letter grade."

Michael stares at me through narrowed eyes, "Are you trying to encourage or scare me?"

I chuckle lightly. "I'm just being honest. It's going to take a lot of hard work. You will have to dedicate yourself, and I know you will as soon as you find something you love."

"Yeah, whatever that is." His tone is a defeated one.

I tuck my right foot under my left leg and turn toward Michael. "Real quick, don't think too much about it, okay?"

He nods.

"What are three things you love or love to do? Things, not people. Go!"

Michael sits quietly in thought as many seconds roll by.

I press him. "I said don't think too much about it. Come on. Three things."

"Cars. Basketball." Another few seconds of silence roll by before he adds, "And talking, I guess. I like to make people laugh."

I scoff and shake my head in frustration.

"What? Those three things not good enough?"

"No. They're amazing. It just bothers me that teachers and parents push for their kids to go to college but don't make them understand that they can make money and find success doing the things they really love. You always hear about these really great schools and these six figure careers. All that's great, but not everyone wants to be a doctor, or dentist, or go to law school. Teachers and parents should talk about those overlooked positions that pay just as well."

"Like what?"

"What do you mean, like what? You can do so much with cars."

"Moms did not send me to private school to work as a mechanic, Jaylen."

"That's not what I mean. You could go to school for automotive engineering. Don't think in such general terms. When people think about cars, their minds immediately go to fixing them. There's more out there than that. Don't forget somebody has to make them. You could work in design or development. Maybe even in production. New car parts are produced all the time. Michael Reed could one day be the guy to redesign or create a machine that leads to the groundbreaking car part that makes cars fly."

Michael's head falls in laughter.

"I know that's extreme, but you get my point."

Michael places one of his hands on each side of my face. As his face moves in closer to mine, my stomach drops. He stops when he's about an inch away. "It's really extreme. But yeah, I get it. And that's why I'm so happy you're in my life."

I move in the rest of the way until our lips touch. I get lost in our kiss. Unlike earlier in the car, this kiss brings me back to that place I love being. I'm back in that little world that only consists of me and Michael.

My friendly butterflies have returned and as they dance around inside of me, I can't help but want him. I have a love hate relationship with these feelings. I love how Michael makes me feel, how he can make most of our kisses feel like our first. But I hate how bad they make me want him. Those feelings are too distracting at times. They pull me from my logical thoughts, make me forget my words, make me want to spend every second with him. And even though being with him is the greatest feeling in the world, there are times when I need to remain focused. This is one of those times. Right now, these feelings are an inconvenience.

We slowly ease away from one another. I look into those forest-green eyes as they stare into my chocolate ones. He reveals a closed-lip smile. I don't return the gesture.

His smile quickly fades. "What are you thinking?"

I briefly look away from his face before focusing back in on those eyes. "I'm just feeling really overwhelmed."

He carefully pushes my hair from my face. "Part of that's my fault."

I don't deny his statement.

"I want to get back to where we were," he says.

"We'll get back there." My voice is low. "Once this Indigo nonsense is cleared up, however it gets cleared up, things with us will fall back into place. And really we're not even in a bad place. Things are just stressful right now. Regardless of how we want to go about things, we want the same end result. We want to feel safe and move on with our lives."

"That's all I want, Jaylen. I know a part of you thinks I just want to fight because I'm angry. And I am angry. No point in lying about that. But I want to know you're safe. I need to know you're safe," he states sternly. "I don't want to have to worry about you when I'm not around you. Do you know how much I'd blame myself if something were to happen to you that I could've prevented?"

I don't answer.

"I love you."

"And I love you."

He reveals that smile again. I smile back this time.

"So, are you gonna change and then call Warren about a party?" I ask.

"I'm actually gonna take a shower real quick."

Perfect. I lie and say, "Me too."

"You wanna go first?" he asks considerately.

"No. Take yours upstairs, and I'll take mine down here. We'll call about the party afterward."

"Bet."

Michael heads upstairs, and I waste no time texting Ethan. With my guest room door closed, and my *hurry up and let's go* text sent, I quickly change out of my graduation dress and into a tee, some yoga pants, and my sneakers. Without checking to see if Ethan texted me back, I tiptoe up the stairs and out the front door. Ms. Housley and Ms. Reed must be out back on the deck, their favorite place to sit and swap stories.

I step inside my car and impatiently wait behind the steering wheel. My nerves are at their peak. All Michael has to do is take a quick look out the window, and we're caught.

"Come on, Ethan. Come on," I say aloud as I wait alone in the car.

Minutes pass before Ethan walks out the house. He quickly runs around to the passenger side and hops in. Before he completely closes the door, I begin backing up.

"I went downstairs looking for you."

"Why would you do that? I said get dressed and let's go."

"You didn't say to meet you outside."

I shake my head. "I didn't know I had to be so specific."

He releases a short laugh. I do the same under my breath.

"Did you text Kennedy?" he asks.

"Can you? Let her know we're on our way. Tell her to let them know we're heading straight for the park."

As Ethan types away on his phone, I keep my eyes forward. My eyes are looking ahead at the open road, but my mind remains on Michael, on how betrayed he's going to feel.

"I hope she doesn't show up," Ethan says worriedly.

"Who? Kennedy?"

"Yeah."

"I don't think she will. She doesn't agree with what Indigo tried to do, but being there would still make her feel torn. They were friends for years."

"Whether she feels torn or not, I don't need another person to keep safe. I already have to worry about you."

"No you don't, Ethan. If anyone should be worried, it's me. You're more likely to get hurt than I am."

"Maybe it's just the man in me. Strong or not, though, Jaylen, you're still a girl. I'm gonna do my best to protect you."

"That's sweet of you and all, but if anyone gets physical, push your male ego to the side and let me take care of you. I hope nothing goes down, but like you said before, if anything does, I have a better chance of defending us."

We're silent for most of the ride. The unknown has us both on edge. It seems as though time is never on my side. When I'm looking forward to something, the minutes take forever and a day to roll by. When I'm nervous about something, the minutes tick by feeling almost like seconds. I can't believe we're almost at the park.

My phone sounds off again and just like all of Michael's other calls, I ignore this one too.

"He's probably getting heated."

"If I know my boyfriend, he already is. He doesn't know where we are, what we're doing, why he's purposely being left in the dark. If I were him, I'd be ringing my phone nonstop too. I'd want answers. To at least know things are all right."

Ethan nods in understanding. "If I know anything, it's that I better get you back to the house in one piece."

"We'll be fine," I say as confidently as I can.

I slowly pull into an unoccupied space and turn off my engine. Again, my phone sounds off, and briefly my heart stops. I know my boyfriend is sitting in West Virginia losing his mind. He's probably working his mother and Ms. Housley up as well. Ethan's phone has been going off just as much as mine.

Ethan holds a bottle of water in front of me. "Finish this."

I do as Ethan silences his ringing phone.

"You ready?"

I exhale loudly. "No, I'm not, but let's do it."

We step out on separate sides of my vehicle.

"Don't lock up," he tells me. "Just in case we need to leave in a hurry."

I look away from Ethan and down at my keys. I realize I'm past the state of feeling a little nervous. I'm scared. My trembling hands reveal as much. I don't know what to expect. I want to believe that Indigo's aunt will be level headed, that attacking teenagers is something she really doesn't want to do unless it's absolutely necessary, but you just never know. You never know what people will do, especially people you don't really know.

"Jaylen?"

I look back over at Ethan.

"I said throw me your keys."

"Oh. Sorry. I didn't hear you." I toss him the keys and watch closely as he pockets them. "This is the right thing to do, right?" I ask uncertainly.

"It is, Jaylen. We're here to talk. That's it." He walks around the car to my side. "What's stressing you? Not knowing what they may do or say?"

"Yeah. We just don't know."

Ethan places his hand on my shoulder. "Let's just count on the fact that this girl really cared about you. She probably doesn't want to see you hurt."

I nod, still not soothed.

"And, we're in public, Jaylen. What can they really do?"

That does comfort me. For a brief moment, I forgot that we'll have eyes surrounding us. Kids are still enjoying the jungle gym area, joggers are still pacing themselves along the trails, and there's even a grill letting off the smell of barbequed food. We're not at all alone here. Violence would draw the attention we're all trying to avoid.

Ethan and I walk side by side. We purposely pass by the playground area, as trying to converse near screaming children would be more frustrating than anything else. We head down a trail, expecting to pick up on their presence. We don't. The only presence we both pick up on is wildlife. The squirrels and geese are fleeing as though the sound of gunshots just rang out.

Ethan stops. "We don't wanna walk too far. I don't feel them." He points. "Wanna sit at one of those gazebos and wait?"

I look at the beautiful white gazebos. Each has a generous amount of space in between them. They'll provide enough privacy for us to talk, but aren't spaced so far apart that no one will take notice if something attention-grabbing occurs.

"Yeah," I answer.

We head over to one of the gazebos. The small lake behind us does nothing but bring up bad memories. Though I've never been to this particular park, my memories of Virginia's picturesque bodies of water only remind me of the buck and bear attacks I was forced to endure. I can certainly do without visiting anymore of this state's parks.

As Ethan and I wait, the faint presence of our kind forces us to look around for Indigo and her aunt. As the presence intensifies, we become aware that our presence is leading them to us.

"Stay calm, okay?"

"I am. Do I look uncomfortable?"

"Angry," he points out. "You don't have to be smiley, but you don't want them to immediately jump on the defensive because you look so damn mad."

I release a loud sigh. "I didn't realize I looked that way."

I try to relax my face as much as I possibly can. The powerful feeling of them approaching forces us to turn to the right. I shudder at the sight of four people when we were only expecting to meet with two; Indigo and her aunt.

Ethan releases a loud sigh. "I fucking knew it!"

"We're still in public," I remind him.

As they approach, we step outside the gazebo. We're already outnumbered. Allowing them to trap us inside a wooden enclosure would make me feel like they're in total control. The sight of them already has my stomach doing flips. If those nerves evolve into panic, I need the option of being able to walk away. If I feel trapped, I'm more likely to physically attack in an attempt to free myself from the situation.

My phone sounds off in my hand. I silence it immediately without looking down to verify that it's Michael calling again.

"Give me your phone."

He shoves my phone into his pocket as Indigo and her family stop about two feet away from us.

We stand face to face. Indigo doesn't seem as uncomfortable as she did at the graduation ceremony. Holding eye contact doesn't seem to be as difficult now. Maybe because she realizes that Michael's still alive, that her attempt was unsuccessful, and that we're looking to move on.

My eyes move from Indigo to her aunt. Those large, electric blue eyes can hold the most frightening stare. Without a doubt, she still feels threatened, and she hasn't even opened her mouth to say so.

I look to the left of Indigo's aunt. The platinum blonde's light brown eyes gaze into mine. She came along with Indigo's aunt to our graduation ceremony earlier today. The anger that was plastered across her face earlier hasn't faded even slightly. The Latino guy standing with his arm interlocked around hers doesn't look familiar. Based on his descent, I'm assuming he's an extended family member of Indigo's. His eyes are a deep brown, and his face holds a boyish quality that his thin mustache can't take away.

My eyes find Indigo's aunt's again. I inhale slowly and then release as quietly as I can. "As you already know, I'm Jaylen. This is my friend Ethan," I introduce.

They don't respond. None of them.

"Is there something I can refer to you as?" My eyes are still on the aunt.

She purses her lips the same way I've seen Indigo purse hers so many times before. "Avery," she answers coldly.

"And you guys?" Ethan asks.

Avery points to the platinum blonde. "She's Scarlett."

Scarlett head motions at the guy on her arm. "He's Rafael."

Indigo remains silent.

"I asked you guys here because we'd like to come to some sort of agreement."

"Agreement?" Avery asks.

"To put an end to…" I carefully select my words. "This…" Another pause. "Whatever this is."

"Before you continue, are you guys here alone?"

Of course we are. How could we hide others when we can feel each other's presence?

Ethan and I briefly look at one another before I answer, "Yes. No one's going to jump out or anything."

Avery turns to Scarlett who nods once. She then looks back at me. "Go ahead. I'm listening."

"Should we maybe step off the path? Maybe step inside the gazebo for a little more privacy?" Ethan suggests.

Indigo's family steps inside the gazebo. Ethan and I stand in the entranceway with our backs facing the path.

I continue. "Like I was saying, I would like to put an end to all of this. Michael isn't dead."

Indigo squirms nervously.

"The pain he suffered that night has gone." I continue, my eyes on Indigo. "The pain I caused you the day following the incident has gone." I look back at her aunt. "There's no need for us to fight. No need for this to go on any further.

Everyone's alive. No one's hurt anymore."

Avery's eyes slowly move from my shoes up to my face. "You're a child to me, Jaylen. You were my niece's best friend that I often heard about, but never met. Hurting a child is not something I could do. But the first time I saw you, you had your hands around my niece's neck, and she was seconds from death. Any parent would want to make sure that something like that never happens again."

"It won't, as long as you can honestly say that you'll leave us alone," I tell her.

"So you're telling me you have no intention of attacking Indigo again?"

I make eye contact with my ex-best friend. "If I never see Indigo again, it'll be too soon."

Scarlett nods once.

I'm not sure what these nods mean, but they're of importance to Indigo and Avery. Every time I open my mouth, they turn to her.

"I'm happy to hear that," Avery says. "Now tell me how the rest of your friends feel. Let's talk about Michael."

"Why?" I ask.

"Does Michael feel the same way you do? His mother?"

"We all want to move on. We all want to put this behind us."

"I'm sure. But I'm asking if Michael has let go of his anger. Is he as willing to leave Indigo alone?"

I state dishonestly, "Yes."

Scarlett immediately shakes her head. "She's lying."

Ethan and I both eye Scarlett.

"You're lying," Scarlett exposes.

"How do you know that?" I ask.

"Tell me I'm wrong."

"You're wrong," I shoot back.

"Then call him," Indigo demands.

Avery nods. "I like that idea. Give him a call. I'd like to

hear it from him. From his mother. Understand that as a grown woman, the last thing I want to do is have to hurt teenagers, but from a parental standpoint, anyone who attempts to harm my child will have to deal with me."

"Have you acknowledged just how wrong what she did was? What if he hadn't survived? Your niece tried to kill someone."

"I've dealt with her actions, but as you've said, Michael's alive. She deserves to be too."

"Exactly my point," I say.

"We understand how you feel. I want to hear it from the others. You said they feel the same way. Call them."

I hold my open hand out in front of Ethan. As he slowly reaches inside his pocket for my phone, my heart begins to pound frantically. Not only does Michael want to handle things his irrational way, he's currently furious about being left clueless as to where Ethan and I disappeared to. Calling him is not going to help my case.

Ethan places the phone in my hand. I hesitate to dial Michael. I stare at my display background, a selfie of my boyfriend and me. A boyfriend who's probably going to get me hurt if I make this call.

"Michael is still angry," I confess. My eyes are still on his face on my screen.

"So why lie?" Scarlett asks.

I look at her. "Because I want this to end. We all need this to end. If everyone around Michael has let this go, eventually his anger will subside. And even if it doesn't, he's not going to do anything reckless knowing I could be affected by it."

They all stand silently.

"Plus, if we can reach some sort of peace agreement, I'll let his mother know. She'll help to talk Michael down."

Indigo's head drops forward as she massages the back of her neck.

"What's the problem?" Avery asks her.

"I don't trust Mike," she tells her aunt in a low voice. "And you shouldn't trust her. If Mike wants to do anything, Jaylen is going to stand beside him one hundred percent. I can't overpower her. Against them, I'll lose."

"That's the whole point of me being here, Indigo. To clear the air. To let you guys know we don't want the fight," I re-explain.

She says to her aunt, "Like I said, I just don't trust them."

A loud, ugly scoff escapes me. Like she has been all of this time, Indigo is still leading. We're just marching to her beat.

"Who cares who you do and don't trust?" I question. "You started this. Everything that's happened, has happened because of you."

Indigo eyes me through squinted eyes.

I shake my head slowly. "Don't you dare fault my boyfriend for being angry. You used your vanishing abilities to sneak around his house, to follow us, to invade our privacy. You took advantage of a moment where he needed help. And what did you do? You poured out the water," I remind her. "You didn't just want him to die. You wanted him to suffer, to lie there and feel his insides slowly dry out. So again, Indigo, who the hell cares who you trust and don't trust? I'm here trying to do you a favor. Because honestly, you do deserve some sort of punishment."

Ethan places his hand on my shoulder. I try to keep my cool. I thought if anyone would be fighting for this to end, it'd be Indigo, the culprit. It's becoming more and more apparent that I never knew this girl.

I shake my head. "I don't know what else to say. I'm not going to stand here and beg anyone for anything. I thought peace is something we'd all want."

"It is," Rafael says, putting an end to his silence. "But I think Indigo brings up a very valid point. If this Mike guy really can't be calmed, will you still stand beside him in his choices? If he confronts Indigo, will you do so as well?"

They all watch me closely. Even Ethan turns to me.

Without a doubt, I'd stand beside my boyfriend. Losing Michael isn't an option.

I tell them, "If Michael still wanted to confront Indigo, I'd work even harder to change his mind."

Scarlett shakes her head. "I think we're simply avoiding the most important question here. Let me make clear that I'm not the one you want to lie to, Jaylen." Her tone is almost that of a mother warning their child. "Just how mad is your boyfriend?"

You certainly don't need to know that Michael is sitting in West Virginia plotting to kill Indigo. I'd never reveal that. I say, "He's really angry. He almost lost his life, and right now, he doesn't know what else Indigo might do."

"Mm-hmm. That may be true, but it's also true that you guys are staying in Charles Town, West Virginia and your boyfriend wants to kill Indigo."

I can feel my eyes widen. Slowly I turn to Ethan. Our eyes meet and I think we both realize why Scarlett tagged along to the graduation ceremony and why she's here now. Those head shakes and head nods have significant meaning. She's been reading my mind, so easily revealing my lies, and pulling information from my thoughts that let them in on things I never intended to share.

With one eyebrow slightly raised and her lips forming a half smile, she says, "I told you, I'm not the one you want to lie to."

I should've never come here. I feared a fight with them because I knew that being unaware of the abilities they all hold could have brought harm to those I love. Even though I'm trying to keep the peace, those abilities I never wanted to surprise and hurt me, ended up biting me anyway.

I stand silently, trying so hard not to let my building anger consume my thoughts. I silently recite the lyrics to *Twinkle Twinkle Little Star*, the first song I could think of, giving her no more of an opportunity to steal what's on my mind.

"Ugh. I hate that song."

"Get the hell out of my head!" I yell.

Ethan places his hand over my abdomen and pushes me back softly. "Jaylen, let's just go."

"It's not just Michael now is it? You hate her, too. You want her dead, too."

No point in lying at this point. She'll find out the truth regardless. "Yes, Scarlett," I answer. "I do hate her. She tried to take the only person in this entire world that I need away from me. She's hateful and cruel, and a few weeks ago, I would've ripped her damn head off with no problem. But he's still here, and because there does happen to be a lot of human things about me, I do feel like killing is wrong."

"Let's go, Jaylen!" Ethan pushes.

"I wish I had killed him," Indigo says softly. "I wish he had died that night."

All of our eyes quickly move to Indigo in surprise.

Ethan leans in and whispers to me, "Please, Jaylen. Our eyes have left us."

I look to the left and to the right. Both gazebos are now empty. No witnesses. I get the reason for Indigo's statement. She wants to get me angry so I'll attack her. That'll give her aunt a reason to attack me. I don't know if this is just another way for her to hurt Michael, or if at this point she wants to see me dead too.

I make strong eye contact with her. "Go to hell, Indigo."

Her face reddens. Tears form in her eyes. "I've already bought my ticket."

"We appreciate you guys coming out to listen to what we had to say," Ethan says politely.

"You and your damn boyfriend took everything from me," Indigo continues. Her voice cracks. "I loved you. I don't know why it was you, but it was. You told me we could be friends even if you two were together. You lied."

"Indigo, stop," her aunt orders.

I back up slowly. "I never lied to either one of you."

"Prom night. Remember that? You only forgave one of us. Now I'm the loner. The outsider. You and Michael have each other. What do I have? Y'all even stole Kennedy."

"Nobody stole anything from you. You lost your damn mind, which led to you losing all of your friends. Kennedy would've stuck with you through anything. You know that. But she saw a side of you that nobody would stand by."

"And I guess you're so innocent, huh, Jaylen?"

"None of us are innocent, but in this situation, Indigo, you're wrong! And still you're standing here trying to provoke me. All I'm asking is that you live your life in a way that it doesn't interfere with ours. What the hell is wrong with you?"

"What the hell do I have to live for, Jaylen? Do you remember what life was like for you before you got to Trinity? You think I want that?"

I stand silently with my eyes locked in on who was once my best friend.

Tears fall from her eyes. "I don't have anything, Jaylen. I've lost it all."

Immediately, I shake my head. "No you haven't, Indigo. You still have your family. Look at who came with you today. I'm pretty sure they came out here prepared to take me down if I had come to fight you. That's love, Indigo. Loyalty. Protection. You have a lot. It's just not enough for you. Nothing ever seems to be enough."

Ethan rests his hand on my shoulder.

"What am I leaving here with?" I ask Avery. "Am I leaving here with any guarantees at all?"

She looks at her niece. Her eyes become compassionate. Soft. "Stop focusing on the negative. This is somewhat of a favor to you. End this, Indigo. Let it go. Give them your word."

I wait for Indigo to give in. With Avery prepared to move

past this and leave us alone, all I need now is to hear it from Indigo, and more importantly, for her to mean it.

She shakes her head slowly. "I'm not promising them anything."

In an instant, she vanishes completely. My eyes dart around the area in search of her. Her unpredictability has proven to be dangerous.

"Indigo!" Avery yells.

Suddenly, Ethan releases a loud, agony-filled cry. His knees bend as though someone kicked him from behind and his body caves backwards. As he tugs at something around his neck, I realize she must have him in a choke hold.

Still unable to see her, I grab her invisible frame. As I pull at her, Ethan's being pulled too. Using all of my strength could hurt Ethan. I stop pulling at her body, grab a hold of her sightless arms and pull them from around my friend.

As Scarlett surprisingly moves to Ethan's side, I hold on to Indigo. The rage inside me, I'm not sure I can control. I'm tired of this girl messing with people I care about.

"Let her go," Avery demands.

Still unable to be seen, Indigo chuckles.

Avery walks toward me. The threat is back in that fierce blue stare.

"Don't make a mistake," I warn her aunt. "Don't do something that'll get your niece hurt."

Avery's voice deepens. "Worry more about yourself getting hurt."

Still holding on to Indigo, who isn't fighting for me to release, I say, "She's not going to stop. She wants this. Don't you Indigo?" I ask heatedly. My breathing pattern is short and rapid. "You want this and I'm gonna take your ass out."

Avery moves toward me and immediately I release my hold of Indigo. In a hurry, and with all of my might, I drive my foot into Avery's groin, forcing her tall, thin frame to crash through the gazebo's siding, making a surprisingly large splash when her body hits the water.

Rafael's eyes are wide and on me. I wait for him to move toward me, to defend Indigo, to attack me because of what I just did to Avery. He stands still. The boyish quality in his face is showing even more now as fear overcomes him. His presence must've been a scare tactic. Fighting isn't what he's here for.

Scarlett steps away from Ethan. Mind reading must be her only power. She's not anxious to physically confront me either.

Indigo reappears. My hands immediately reach out for her. Michael was right all along. She can't be trusted, and right at this moment, I just want to get my hands back on her. I want to destroy her now and end half of our issues today. Sure, her aunt will come for us, but Avery can't disappear. The greatest advantage Indigo has over all of us is her ability to become invisible at any given moment.

Ethan grabs my extended left arm and dashes back up the path. I can't get clear vision on anything, can't hear anything but the swooshing of wind in my ear.

The lightening flash speed doesn't allow my feet to fully touch the ground. We pass trees and joggers so swiftly, they're a blur. A blur that can only be seen for a split second because of how quickly he's moving.

He stops abruptly, releases my arm once we reach my Volvo. A car he got me to in seconds it seems. "Get in," he orders.

I step in on the passenger side as Ethan seats himself behind my wheel. In a hurry, he starts my vehicle and races back toward his home.

"Put your seatbelt on, Jaylen."

As I secure myself in my seat, I look over at Ethan. "I'm sorry."

"Don't be."

"I should've walked away when you first told me to."

"She got what she wanted. Indigo has no intention of

42

moving on and that's because she doesn't feel like she has anything to move on to. At least we know that for sure now. We tried to do the right thing, Jaylen."

I massage my forehead. I had hoped we could put things behind us. Things are still completely unresolved. Everything is still a mess. A dangerous mess.

"You okay?" I ask my friend.

He nods.

"Is that all you got? The speed?"

"I'm agile, and really, that's always been enough."

I exhale loudly. "Thank you, Ethan."

"For?"

"For getting us out of there. For stopping me. I stopped thinking after I saw her attack you."

"That's what I came for."

I turn and stare out my passenger side window.

"And thank you."

I don't look back his way. "Thanks for what?"

"For getting that nut off me."

"You're welcome."

I ride silently as my thoughts swirl in circles. One moment, my mind is on what just happened, the next, I'm worrying about what's to come. My stomach clenches at the thought of Michael reacting to what he's about to find out. This was supposed to bring back the peace. But I may have just escalated things even further.

Chapter 4

*A*s we turn onto Ethan's street, I fidget in my seat. My boyfriend has called my phone countless times, and I haven't sent him so much as a text. A warm welcome is one thing I won't be receiving when I see him.

"You nervous?" Ethan asks.

"You're not?"

He shrugs.

As Ethan slowly pulls into his long driveway, my eyes move to Michael sitting on the front porch. I expect him to stand at the sight of the car, to move toward us and demand an explanation. He doesn't move, just lowers his head.

Ethan turns my car off, and we exit the vehicle. As we head for the front door, Michael lifts his head slowly. He doesn't look at Ethan at all. He stares me down. Not through narrowed eyes. Not with an angry gaze. But with a saddened stare. His face looks flushed. Worn.

"Michael," I call out to him softly.

He stands, briefly looks over at Ethan, and then back at me. "Glad to see you're okay," he says in a low voice before turning and walking inside.

Ethan places his hand on my shoulder. We look at one

another and then walk side by side into the Housley home.

"Where the hell have you guys been?" Ms. Housley asks irately. Her eyes are on her son.

"I can answer that. It was my idea."

"What was your idea?" Ms. Reed asks me.

"I convinced Ethan to go with me to meet up with Indigo and her aunt."

Michael stops midway up the staircase. "You *what*?"

"I wanted to end this nonsense, so I planned a meeting, and we met up with them."

"Why would you do something so dangerous?" Ms. Reed's voice takes on a demanding tone.

"Because I think it would be more dangerous to let this play out violently."

Ms. Housley closes and locks the front door behind us. "Go into the living room."

We silently do as we're told. I feel like I'm about to tell my story to the jury just to hear a *you're stupid* verdict.

Ethan and I sit side by side on the loveseat. Michael remains standing, sipping from a water he grabs from the table. Ms. Housley and Ms. Reed sit on opposite ends of the three-cushion sofa.

"What happened?" Michael asks. He folds his arms across his chest, straightens his back. The anger I initially expected is now present.

"We met them at a park, somewhere public to keep ourselves safe. The whole goal was to reach some sort of an agreement."

"Who'd you guys plan to meet?" Ms. Reed asks.

"Indigo and her aunt," Ethan answers.

"I bet money they showed up with others," Michael says.

Ethan and I both remain silent.

"Didn't they?" Michael asks.

I nod. "They came with two others."

"Because this girl cannot be trusted. Why can't you believe

that, Jaylen? Get it through your damn head!"

"Don't yell at me, Michael. And choose your words more carefully," I say calmly. "We can discuss this without disrespecting one another. I may have done something you're not okay with, but don't speak to me like that. Ever. You think you're mad now? Disrespect me again. I'll leave right now, and I won't turn back."

The room becomes uncomfortably silent. I wait for an apology that he's obviously not planning to give.

"Tell us what happened."

I turn to Ms. Housley. "We met with them. I explained that I wanted to reach some sort of peace agreement. They weren't convinced we would all be willing to let this go, but I did get to the aunt. She doesn't want to hurt teenagers. She made that clear."

"She actually asked Indigo to back off," Ethan adds. "But Indigo doesn't want to let this go. She did everything she could to provoke Jaylen."

"What do you mean?" Ms. Reed asks.

Ethan goes on. "Just saying things like she wishes she had actually killed Mike."

"Did you let her words get to you, Jaylen?" Ms. Housley asks.

"I got upset, but I didn't physically attack her because of what she said."

"Did you attack her because of something else?"

I look Ms. Housley in the eye. "Attack isn't the right word. I only grabbed her."

"Why?" Michael asks.

Silence fills the room again and I begin to pick at my nails. Though we're both okay, and things could've been a lot worse, I don't want to say that Indigo attacked Ethan. I don't want Ms. Housley's feelings about me to change because my idea made her son the target of Indigo's craziness.

Ethan turns to me, and then looks over at Michael.

"Because Indigo vanished and attacked me," he reveals.

Shock covers the three of their faces.

Ms. Housley stands. "How'd she attack you?"

"Mom, calm down. I'm here, so I'm fine."

"I asked you what happened, Ethan."

"She kicked me in the back of my knees, and then locked me in a mean choke hold," he answers his mother.

"And I pulled her off," I tell them hastily. "I got her off as quickly as I could."

"The others didn't get involved?" Ms. Reed asks.

"One kind of just stood there. The other actually checked on Ethan while I held Indigo."

"And the aunt?"

"Her name is Avery," I tell Ms. Reed. "She demanded that I release Indigo. I didn't. I was angry. I mean, everyone was willing to walk away from this except her. And because I wouldn't let her go, Avery came at me. I thought she was moving in to hurt me, so I kicked her."

"So you and the aunt fought?" Michael asks concernedly.

"They didn't fight," Ethan explains. "I got Jaylen out of there when I saw her going in for Indigo again because I knew that would start a bigger fight and we wouldn't win."

The room becomes silent except for the pattern of ringing phones. My cell goes off and then seconds later, Ethan's does. It's Kennedy. I'm sure she's dying to know how things went and to hear that we're okay.

"Why did you feel the need to hide this from us, Jaylen?"

"It's just that you guys keep saying we'll talk later. Waiting until later just makes this whole thing last even longer. I want this to go away. I want to move forward with my life without worrying about Indigo or any of this. I didn't go for the fight. I went to make peace. I wanted them to know that we may be angry, but we're not crazy, out of control, violent people."

Ms. Reed exhales, briefly looks over at her son, and then back at me. "I understand. Believe me, I get you, Jaylen, and what you want. If Avery and I have anything in common, it's that neither of us wants to hurt a bunch of kids."

"That's what bothers me about this whole thing. She doesn't want to hurt anyone and neither do you, but you both will to protect your kids."

"That bothers you?"

"Yes, because there wouldn't be any need for protection if the two of them would just leave things the way they are and move on. Indigo is forcing Avery into a fight and Michael's hotheadedness is going to force us into one."

Michael shakes his head. "No, that's not fair, Jaylen. You saw for yourself for the millionth time that Indigo cannot be trusted. Do you need me to remind you of all the things this girl has put us through?"

I don't respond. I refuse to answer him directly until I receive an apology for the way he spoke to me.

"Think back to the day you were attacked by the buck at the lake. This girl disappeared and left you to fight for yourself. She may not be as strong as you are, but she could've hit it with something. She didn't help you at all. This is the same girl who knew you were the only one of our kind at your old school, yet she wouldn't help you understand what you are. She just kept dropping little clues like you weren't confused enough." His hands move crazily as he goes on. "She refused to invite me to your birthday party. We still don't know how often she snuck around my house or hung around us while we were out, just listening to our conversations. She tried to get us locked up with that stolen car bullshit she pulled on prom night." He takes a quick sip of water. "Oh yeah, and let's not forget the doozy. She almost *killed* my ass. What other proof do you need? Look at what she did today." His eyes widen. "Everybody there was ready to walk away from this, but she wasn't. I never knew Indigo was this nuts, but she's always been an impulsive, selfish, control freak. When she wants something, she wants it right then and there. If you can't give her what she wants, you're the enemy. It doesn't matter if your reasons are fair. She loves to control people. She knows Kennedy would've probably liked being friends with us. There's not that many of us, so she could've benefitted from having closer bonds with us. Indigo made it so that wasn't possible. Indigo clung to you and called it love, made me out to be a scumbag who dumped her when we were never dating, and though Kennedy could've had all of us, she only ended up having Indigo. Why? Because Indigo's a selfish psychopath, Jaylen. She's not right in the head."

Everyone's eyes look to me, and mine fall to the floor. They're waiting for a response, maybe for me to find a way to defend Indigo's actions. The truth is, I can't. Every word Michael just spoke is true. Indigo has proven time and time again that she can't be trusted, and that her way is the only way. The aunt she never introduced me to, the one she described as a block of ice, and told me didn't care about her seems to be the complete opposite. Indigo has many sides, and unfortunately, one is dark. Completely black, as a matter of fact.

Michael walks over and squats down in front of me. He grabs both of my hands. "Please look at me."

I look my boyfriend in his eyes.

"My mother raised me to be a man. She didn't raise me to disrespect her or other women. This situation is a lot. It's big. I'm angry. You're scared. My mother is torn. We're all dealing with so many emotions. That's no excuse, though. I shouldn't be raising my voice at you. I shouldn't be cursing at you. You don't deserve that. If anything, you deserve more respect for not being so anxious to hurt somebody." He squeezes my hands. "I'm sorry, Jaylen. I'm sorry I spoke to you that way." He stands. "Actually, I apologize to you, too, Ms. Housley for cursing in your house. And you, too, Ma, for cursing in front of you."

A loud silence covers the room and I don't know what to

say. It's true that Indigo can't be trusted. I have no idea what she may or may not do. I don't trust that she won't hurt someone else that I love. Those feelings stir inside of me. They make me realize that something must be done with her. But what?

Michael sighs. "Jaylen, why is it so hard for you to wrap your mind around what has to be done?"

Because I don't want to be a killer, and I don't want to be with one. When I thought Michael had been taken from me, I told Kennedy I wanted to kill Indigo. She told me I didn't mean that, that I was emotionally driven. She was right. I don't want to kill. I don't want to carry that burden with me throughout the rest of my already complicated life.

I can't take this overwhelming feeling. Running away can be the most cowardly thing a person can do, or the wisest. It's the wisest when it saves your sanity and someone's life.

"I'm going home tomorrow," I say.

Michael exhales loudly as I stand and step out onto the deck. I grab a half-empty bottle of water resting on the table and finish it off. This wasn't supposed to be my graduation night. I should be partying, celebrating my high school achievements, and bragging about my Princeton acceptance to all of my old friends. Instead, I'm here. I'm in West Virginia, completely unsure of how much information Scarlett stole from my overflowing brain, and trying to find a way to save lives when the control is out of my hands.

"Can we talk?"

I turn around slowly, make eye contact. "Sure."

"Let's sit."

Ms. Reed and I sit side by side on the deck stairs.

She takes my hand. "It's okay to be angry. It's okay to be scared. It's okay to feel torn. I feel the same way."

I take a deep breath which does nothing to calm me.

"Say what's on your mind, Jaylen."

I don't hesitate. "I don't want to kill her."

She shakes her head. "I don't want to either. Crazy or not, the child is the same age as my son. And please believe me when I say this, Mike doesn't want to kill her either. He feels like he has to."

"Maybe we should call the police."

"I've considered that so many times, sweetheart, but what do we say? Do we ask for a restraining order on someone who can become a ghost anytime she feels like it? Do we tell them what happened to Mike on prom night? Will an officer believe that pouring out a bottle of water is attempted murder? If we tell them we're not humans, do you think they're going to help us or put us in straitjackets?"

Everything just feels too heavy. Too much. Like there's no other choice and the one on the table is the most unappetizing. Poisonous. Deadly. I growl ferociously as I pound the side of my fist into the deck's stair railing. The vertical bars break upon contact, making a series of clacking sounds as they fall upon each other and scatter on the ground.

Ms. Reed jumps up. "Shit!"

"I'm so sorry!"

"Between you and Mike, my friend is never going to have me over again."

"I'm so sorry, Ms. Reed."

"This is frustrating and scary, but you have to learn how to control yourself. Keep in mind the power you have behind each hit. If you can destroy large items or animals with this small fist..." She grabs my hand. "You need to spend some time practicing better self-control. Get a better hold of your emotions so things like this won't happen. Your strength should only do that when you need it to. You think this is strong?" She squeezes my hand. "Your mind is a million times stronger, Jaylen. Use it. Use your brain to control your strength. Only let fear control it when you need to defend yourself. When you're aggravated, angry because of something small, or you're just in a cranky mood, you should have enough control over yourself to not damage things."

I nod. Emotions can force one to make the most illogical decisions, to make the greatest of mistakes. Thoughtfulness is the best way to prevent those things.

I apologize again.

"This isn't my home, Jaylen. You're damaging another person's property. Learn from your mistakes. You just had a similar incident at school not too long ago. Those doors should've never been broken. You should've been able to control yourself enough to contain that level of strength."

I lower my head, exhausted due to all that's surrounding me and embarrassed by the things I've done in highly emotional moments.

Ms. Reed sits back down. "You and Mike are a lot alike."

I don't look up.

"Good hearts. Hot tempers. Impatient."

I turn to her. "I like to believe I'm patient and that my temper is only bad when I'm forced into situations I've already tried to walk away from."

She shakes her head. "If you were patient, you would've waited, talked to me away from Mike about meeting with Indigo, and we would've worked something out together. You had good intentions, sweetheart, but you're impatient, and you ran off in a hurry because you didn't want us to try to talk you out of going."

I release a loud sigh. "You're right."

"So you're leaving tomorrow?"

"I need to," I answer.

"Why do you need to?"

"Because this is suffocating. I can't do anything without thinking about this situation. Every smile is brief. Every laugh is cut short. I need to separate from this. I need distance."

"This isn't far enough away from Indigo, Jaylen? We're over an hour away."

I shake my head. "Ms. Reed, I need my mom. I need to

feel her, see her everywhere I turn, and be in our home. I feel like if I'm in our house in Jersey, I'll find some level of peace. No matter how alone I ever felt, I always felt safe in that house. My mom did that. She created that feeling for me, and even though she's gone, I know it still exists there."

"The power of being a mom," she says as she touches the charm bracelet wrapped around my wrist. The birthday present she bought for me that I adore.

"You guys leave your marks everywhere," I tell her, slightly turning my body toward her. "You know, she never knew just how different I was. She never realized she was raising an alien."

We both release short laughs.

"But she cared deeply about my feelings and insecurities," I say. "More than once, I told her I felt different, that I'm not right, that there's something wrong with me. She never called me names or made me feel like I was being dramatic or paranoid. She made me look closer at those differences. She bought me random books on self-discovery. She listened to my every word."

"Because she loved you, and deep down, Jaylen, she probably was trying to find those answers for herself, too. She knew you were different."

"I know she knew. That made me love her even more. We didn't have answers, but she didn't make me feel crazy for feeling the way I did about myself."

The sliding of the door forces us to turn around. Ms. Housley, Michael, and Ethan step onto the deck. Ms. Housley's eyes bulge at the sight of her damaged deck railing.

I jump up before she can even speak. "I am so sorry, Ms. Housley. I lost it for just a split second."

"This is enough for one day. You three go get settled in. I don't care what parties you may have originally planned on attending. Keep your asses here."

"Ms. Housley, I will pay to get your deck fixed. I promise."

She puts her hand out and I know not to say another word. "Jaylen, please. Go get settled. Drink. Relax. Whatever. Right now, I just need the three of you to leave us alone. Let us talk."

I nod and slowly head inside. I pass by Michael and Ethan and head straight for the basement. I turned eighteen not too long ago, I graduated from high school earlier today, and I have no living parents, but here I am. I'm punished on my graduation night and confined to a house I don't want to be in.

Chapter 5

With a hair band clenched in between my teeth, I twist my freshly washed hair into a bun. As I secure my hair for the night, I sit on the side of the bed with my eyes on the floor. A hot shower slowed down the swirling of my frustrated thoughts, but it didn't bring the relaxing moment of peace I need.

I so badly want to walk upstairs and apologize to Ms. Housley again. I'm a guest in her home, and regardless of whether or not I intended to damage her property, I never should've hit it. Even if I didn't have this strength, I know better than to strike out at things that don't belong to me.

I stand to open the bedroom door. Before twisting the knob, I stop. With my hand still covering the brass, I think about how my apology could frustrate her more. She did ask to be left alone. Sure, another apology would be nice, but it won't repair her deck. The pieces won't return to their secure positions because of a second, *I'm sorry.*

I slap the light switch off and climb into bed. I stare up at the ceiling, at the blue shadow cast by the small nightlight, with my mind now back on Indigo. Undoubtedly, she wanted things to escalate today, but will she really go out of her way to keep things going? Will I really be in danger when I move back into my home in New Jersey? She doesn't have my address. Well, she doesn't have my address now. That doesn't mean she won't try to find out what it is, and actually succeed at getting it. That's what's so awful about this. Not knowing what Indigo might do, can do, or even wants to do. I hate feeling vulnerable.

Two soft taps against the door pull me from my thoughts.

"Come in," I say, unsure of who's standing outside the door, though I'm positive it isn't Michael.

Ethan opens the door. With two bottles of water in hand, he quickly steps inside, closing the door quietly behind him. I don't move. I lie silently, waiting for him to tell me why he's here.

"I just came to check on you."

"That's thoughtful of you, Ethan. I'm fine. Is your mom pissed at me?"

"She's not happy about her deck. You know how she loves sitting out there, but she'll get over it. She can still sit out there. She just needs to get the railing fixed. Don't worry. Tomorrow morning, she'll give you a hug and treat you the same."

"I hope so. I really want to pay for it, though."

Ethan shakes his head. "I know my mom. She's not going to take your money, Jaylen."

"Then I'll buy wood. She shouldn't have to pay for what I did."

He sighs. "If that's what you wanna do."

"It's what I'm gonna do," I say sternly.

The room becomes silent. Ethan stands at the foot of the bed. I look back up at the shadow.

"Are you sure you're okay, Jaylen?"

"Where's Michael?" I ask, ignoring the question I've already answered.

"Talking to his mom. He wants to go with you when you leave tomorrow."

"I want him to. That was our plan."

"Kind of wish you guys would stay," he says, suddenly sounding almost despondent.

"Did they send you down here to convince me or something?"

Ethan takes a seat on the floor. "Toss me a pillow."

I throw a pillow toward him. He catches it, positions it behind his head, and lies back.

"Nobody sent me down here," he finally answers. "I told you I was worried. I came down here because I didn't want you to feel like my mom hates you now, and I don't want you to feel lonely. You're a guest here, Jaylen. I don't care what mistakes you've made. This shit we're involved in is crazy, and we didn't ask for it. I just want you to know that you've got a friend here."

I turn to my side and prop myself up on my elbow. "I appreciate that, Ethan. You've been awesome about this whole thing." Concerned, I ask, "How are you feeling? Any leg pain? Any exhaustion kicking in after that 300 mile per hour sprint?"

He laughs. A short laugh escapes me as well.

"I don't think I'm that fast, but to answer your question, I feel fine. No pain. Tired, but nothing out of the ordinary. I didn't have to run that far."

I trace the flower patterns on the bedding with my finger. "I'm glad you're okay. Do you regret going with me?"

"Not at all. Like you, I needed to know we tried to do the right thing. And I guess I really didn't think anybody could be that crazy. Well, that's not true. I know there are crazy people out here. I just didn't think a hot chick like that would be so nuts. People get emotional and angry and accidentally do stupid shit, but usually it's in the heat of the moment. That chick is a full-blown psychotic."

"She wasn't always like that, though. Don't get me wrong, she's always been very outspoken, opinionated, and selfish, but I never got an evil vibe from her. I never foresaw Indigo hurting Michael or anyone. Not physically hurting them, anyway. I knew she didn't like us being an item, but I never thought things would turn deadly."

He lies quietly as I continue to trace the flower patterns. Even after what happened today, I still wish I could make Indigo understand that the only person who wants to ruin lives with this completely unnecessary situation is her. She could very well bump into another of our kind while in college. She could meet someone and truly fall in love.

"Are you okay up there?" he asks.

"I'm fine. Did you call Kennedy?"

"Yeah. I told her what happened. I let her know everyone is okay, that things only got physical because of Indigo, and that we're back in West Virginia safe and sound. I told her to check on you in the morning. I didn't think you'd want to talk on the phone after everything that's happened today."

"You're right. I don't want to be on the phone, but I did want her to know we're okay. Thanks, Ethan."

"You don't need to thank me."

"Fine. I take it back."

He chuckles lightly. So do I.

"So?" His voice is suddenly filled with curiosity.

"So, what?"

"What has Kennedy told you about me?"

"Nothing much," I answer quickly. "And even if we spent hours on the phone talking about you, do you think I'd really tell you what she said?"

He laughs.

"How do you feel about her?" I ask.

"She's cool. We've had good conversations. She's pretty. Don't know her well enough to say much else. I've only seen her twice."

"But you felt her presence when you shook her hand for the first time," I remind him.

"Meaning what?"

58

"I can't feel her presence at all, so I thought that meant something. Like maybe you guys had an instant love connection or something."

Laughter escapes him. "I really hope you don't believe that's what happened."

"I haven't really thought that much about it. I just wondered if that's what you thought it was."

"I thought she was hot. Feeling her presence felt normal to me until I realized you guys couldn't feel it at all. I like her vibe, though. She seems cool. And, it doesn't hurt that she had a little thing with Indigo. A hot bisexual who tries to act innocent? What's not to be attracted to?"

I reach over, grab another pillow, and hurl it at his head.

He bursts into laughter and throws the pillow back.

"You're disgusting. *A hot bisexual who tries to act innocent*," I repeat mockingly. "Are you serious, Ethan? Stop being a pervert. Don't look at her as a freak. Whether she likes girls or not, I can tell you, the innocence is not an act. I think Kennedy is a conservative daddy's girl"

"You think so?" He asks in disbelief.

"Bisexual doesn't equal nasty freak. Damn, guys are filthy."

He cracks up. A little laughter escapes me.

"Really, Ethan," I say seriously. "I don't think she's that kind of girl, so whatever you may be thinking, stop. Don't think she's hopping from girl to guy to girl and back again doing who knows what. I think her only relationship was with Indigo."

"I get it, Jaylen. I don't need a lecture. She looks good. I'm a guy. Once you hear that two pretty girls were in a relationship, the mind goes to the dirtiest place. I don't just think of her like that, though. She's a really nice girl. She's talked to me about school, her dad, losing her mom, Indigo. Like I said, she has a cool vibe and can hold a good conversation. So far, I like what I know. But that's it. I like her."

"Got it," I say as I turn on my back.

"Did you fall in love with Mike right away?"

"No, but I was instantly attracted to him," I say. "I thought he was hot right away."

As the statement leaves my mouth, I can feel his presence. In this house, I can feel our kind everywhere. Ms. Housley, Ms. Reed, and Ethan could easily sneak up on me, but when Michael is coming my way, his presence sets itself apart and can be felt more intensely.

He taps on the door softly. I remain quiet. Ethan clears his throat, adopts a girlish tone, and says, "Come in."

As he opens the door, Michael and Ethan both release short laughs.

"You're a fool," Michael says, closing the door behind him.

"What are they doing upstairs?" Ethan asks.

"They're about to go to bed. What are you guys talking about?"

"Nothing really," Ethan answers.

With my eyes on the ceiling, I can feel Michael's eyes on me. He walks over and sits on the side of the bed.

"You're not gonna talk to me?"

"You didn't say anything to me," I answer.

"I'm sorry," he apologizes again.

"You already apologized. We're good."

"Then talk to me."

"Michael, you just came in. You haven't been sitting here for hours being ignored."

"Can I lay with you?"

"Can I lay by your side? Next to you…" Ethan sings, hitting a painfully ugly high note, destroying one of my favorite Sam Smith songs.

We all laugh.

"Ethan, you're a clown," I say as Michael climbs in bed to

lie beside me.

"I just better not hear any moaning up there."

"Boy, please."

"Just playing, Jaylen. I definitely don't wanna get hit with one of your jabs."

Michael immediately lifts up. "About that, I've been thinking about that joke I made in the car. I was really just trying to be funny. I wasn't trying to step out of line. Ethan, you know I'm a jokester. My mouth gets ahead of me sometimes, but I don't want you questioning how I feel about this girl because of that joke or because of me losing my temper upstairs. This is my queen right here."

The butterflies awaken inside me as soon as he calls me his queen. We may not see eye to eye when it comes to this situation we're in with Indigo, but our love is real. We may be young, we may not be a perfect fairytale couple, but our feelings for each other are strong. Too strong and too immutable to be called anything other than love.

I look at my boyfriend. "Michael, I appreciate the level of respect you have for me, but really, I didn't take it seriously. I took it for what it was. A joke."

"Same here," Ethan says. "I didn't even think about you guys' overall relationship. It wasn't that serious."

Michael lies down beside me. "Just wanna make sure."

I lift my head up just enough for Michael to slide his arm beneath it. With my head resting on him and our bodies close, I relax.

"Do you guys ever think you'll break up?"

With my eyes on the ceiling, I wait for Michael to answer Ethan's question.

"Nope. Never," Michael answers.

"Jaylen, what about you?"

I exhale. "I believe I'm with someone I could grow old with, but I sometimes have thoughts."

"Thoughts like what?" Michael asks.

I turn to my boyfriend. "That one day we'll meet more of our kind and things will change. I don't want you to get the wrong idea. I don't want anyone else, but we only know a few of our kind. What if we were amongst hundreds of our kind? Say there were like 50 hot, alien girls right here for you to choose from. Would you still choose me?"

"I think I would. Looks are one thing, but there's more than just beauty to you. I have a lot I want to accomplish in my life. I want to share those successes with you. I want to make you happy and I want to make you proud. You. This hot, alien girl right here."

I chuckle softly.

"The real question is, do you think you'd feel different around me or less attracted to me if you had 50 hot, alien guys to choose from?"

"I think I could be physically attracted to other guys. When it comes to feelings, I don't want to be as close to anyone else as I am to you."

"Feels weird just laying down here while you two talk about your feelings."

We laugh.

"You started it," I remind Ethan.

"I didn't know you were going to answer with anything more than a yes or a no. I don't want to hear about your future church wedding, your future Michael juniors, and all that."

I grunt softly. "Believe me, the conversation was not going there."

"Why? You don't wanna get married?" Ethan asks disbelievingly.

"Sure, I'd like to get married one day."

"I think the *church wedding* part of that statement threw her off," Michael says.

"Oh, you're not a church goer?"

"She's not a believer. She's an atheist," Michael reveals.

The room becomes silent.

I sit up. "Say what's on your mind, Ethan."

He sits up, too. "I have nothing against you being an atheist. I just don't think I've ever met one. I don't think I really understand it."

"A lot of people don't, but I have a lot of respect for those who ask as opposed to just making up ridiculous generalizations, or passing along bullshit they created in their own minds."

"I just don't get it, and I don't want to offend you."

"You won't. Believe me, Ethan, you're not going to ask me anything that I haven't been asked before."

"Do you hate God?" he asks, his volume significantly lower.

That's a new one. I've never been asked that. I'm typically asked by ignorant people if I worship the devil.

I ask him, "How could I hate what I don't believe exists?"

Silence again.

"It's okay, Ethan. Ask me."

"You don't want to go to heaven when you die?"

"I don't believe heaven exists either."

"You don't pray?"

"No."

"Never have?"

"I did the night I thought Michael died. I did once or twice after that, too."

"Because you felt something? You had some kind of change of heart?"

"No. Not at all. I never felt anything. Honestly, I didn't realize what I was doing."

"I don't get it," he says.

"I don't want to sound offensive. I don't play around with religion just because I don't believe in what others do."

"I'm not offended," he says quickly.

"I think I prayed because I felt I had lost everything. I was begging, trying to bargain, just trying anything to get him back." I briefly look at Michael. "I was hurt. I was desperate. I was out of my mind. I never suddenly believed. I think I was just trying any and everything possible."

He grunts unpleasantly.

"Really, I'm not trying to be hurtful. Just truthful, Ethan. During that time period, I wasn't right. I wasn't normal."

"I'm not hurt or offended. I guess I'm just trying to wrap my mind around why you'd turn to prayer if you've never done it or believed in a higher being."

"I can't explain it any other way except extreme desperation and emotional instability. I was in pieces."

"Do you feel like someone heard your prayers? Do you feel like that's why Michael is still here?"

I shake my head. "No. I'd be lying if I said yes. I don't have any emotional feelings tied to a higher being the way Michael does, or the way you do. You can't explain your faith, or how or why you feel the way you do about the god you believe in. I can't explain why I don't feel anything."

Again, he grunts. "So what about your future children?"

"I don't want kids," I answer certainly.

"You don't?" Michael sits up suddenly.

"No, I don't."

"Why not?"

"Michael, look at me. Think about how I grew up. I didn't have anyone else like me around. Sure, my kid would have me, but would they have friends like them at school? Think about school trips. They'd never be able to go to the farm or the zoo. We could never buy them a dog or cat. We could never take them hiking in the woods. If they go to the beach, they can only walk along the shoreline because who knows how sea creatures feel about us. Why would I bring a child into that kind of life? Not to mention, no longer having my power. I've actually needed my strength to protect myself from animals. What if I need it a year after I have a child? What if I were confronted by another buck? What would I do?"

Silence.

"Adopt a child," Ethan throws out.

"Great idea, genius," I say. "They can go on school trips to the zoo, but we'll never be able to chaperone. When they ask for a dog, a cat, or even a damn turtle, we won't be able to give it to them. We'll never be able to have a normal life. I'm not doing that to a child."

Out of nowhere, my mind revisits prom night, Michael and me in the backseat. Talking about a child brings to mind something I'm just now realizing. We didn't have protected sex. We didn't have a red rubber on hand.

I lie back quietly with my heart now in my stomach.

"You okay?"

Michael lies back next to me and I nod.

"I get it. It wouldn't be all that fair to the kid. We're lucky to have found each other, but there are no guarantees that our son or daughter would have the same luck and find others of our kind to be friends with. I'm not mad," he says. "It's not a deal breaker that you won't have my babies."

I chuckle uncomfortably and then move closer to my boyfriend, my lips nearly touching his ear.

"We didn't use a condom on prom night," I whisper.

"What?" he asks, his volume matching mine.

"We. Didn't. Use. A. Condom. On. Prom. Night," I repeat, placing emphasis on each whispered word.

His eyes bulge. My stomach twists and turns in knots as I ask, "What the fuck were we thinking?"

"We weren't," he whispers back. "We got caught up in the moment, and then after leaving prom, everything else that happened distracted us from thinking about it."

He sits up, grabs a water from the bedside table and passes it to me. I gulp some down and then share the rest with him.

"You guys okay?" Ethan asks.

"Yeah, we're good," Michael answers as I lie back with my hand over my abdomen.

"Are you guys really leaving tomorrow?"

"You're welcome to come," I say, my jittery hand still covering my stomach.

"And be the third wheel when you guys really have the freedom to play house?"

"Shut up, fool. If you don't wanna stay here with our mothers," Michael says, "just drive up. It's not gonna be a third wheel situation. We were planning to visit Princeton, hang out with her old friends, and chill. It won't be like that."

"It really won't be," I confirm. "You're not crashing our honeymoon. I have shit to do, people to catch up with, and college to prepare for."

Ethan yawns. "I might just do that. It's summer break. There's no reason to stay here. I need to see a couple of friends tomorrow. I'll drive up afterward. I'll probably get there late."

"Sounds good," I say. "Plus you should have your car in case you want to leave or do something on your own."

"True," Ethan says.

"Damn, we're about to turn that house into the party spot."

I turn to Michael. "No we're not. You've lost your damn mind."

We all laugh.

I sit up, pull the pillow from beneath Michael's head, and throw it on the floor. "I'm sorry to kick you to the curb, but you can't sleep here. If your mom walks in, this is gonna look beyond inappropriate to her."

Michael exhales loudly and slowly rises into an upright position. With our eyes locked in on one another, he places his hand over my belly. An uncomfortable tightness is centered inside me, but I remain quiet as I look into his calm, reassuring eyes. I don't see worry, panic, or even sadness. I see a promise. A promise to be here for me no matter what it is we may be forced to face.

He moves in closer to my face, never closing his eyes as

he leans in, or even as our lips gently touch. Eyes still on mine, he eases back, finally pulling his hand from my belly. I lie back as he comfortably situates himself on the floor.

With my eyes on my boyfriend, I hold my belly. I grip it, making silent wishes for it to be empty and for it to remain that way. Giving life is a beautiful thing, but it's not an experience I want. I don't dream of having children, bringing them into a world they'll only feel lost and isolated in, where animals will be their enemies, and their own kind may become their foes simply because there's not enough of us, and the fear of loneliness drives people to insanity. I don't dream of making that a child's reality. I wish it weren't my own.

Chapter 6

ig Sean blasts through the speakers, vibrating the doors as we head for Hopewell. We attempted this yesterday. My fingers are crossed that nothing crazy takes place today that'll prevent me from making it home.

Michael lowers the volume, nearly silencing the song I was rapping along to. "You okay over there, Lil Sean?"

I chuckle. "Yeah. Just wanna get there."

"Are you anxious about being around all your mom's stuff, knowing your mom won't actually be there?"

"I'm sad about it. It sucks to wake up every day and not have her. I hate knowing she's gone, but seeing her stuff, touching her stuff…" I glance over at him. "I need that."

He reaches over, grabs my hand, and gently kisses my knuckles. "I love you, Miss Hayes."

"I love you, Mr. Reed."

"I'm excited," he says, his voice overflowing with enthusiasm. "I wanna see where you grew up, meet your old friends, chill once Ethan drives up. This shit is about to be fun."

I nod. "I think so, too."

"No parents." His volume is much lower, filled with naughtiness.

I side eye my boyfriend. "Don't look forward to some

freaky orgy, Michael. That's not happening."

"Orgy? I could care less what Ethan does. I need alone time with you."

"You mean you *couldn't* care less," I correct. "I *could* care less means you actually could care a little less than you currently do. And you'll have plenty of alone time with me, Michael."

"The kind of alone time that will allow me to do a few things to take your mind off Indigo?"

I laugh lightly as my friendly butterflies flutter around in my belly. "Maybe that kind of alone time."

"No pressure. I'm just starting to hate my hand."

I laugh. "Sounds like pressure to me."

He laughs too.

"Just stop using your hand, fool. That way you can't get tired of it."

"That's what I'd like to see happen. That's why I'm not pressuring you right now."

Laughs escape us simultaneously.

"I hear you, Michael. And to be clear, there's no pressure. I've been missing you, too."

"Other than last night, do you ever think about the times we were together?"

"I mostly think about the first time. Honestly, I didn't think you'd last that long. It wasn't the hour-long experience most fantasize about, but it wasn't the two-minute, high school experience I expected, either."

"That's because I rubbed one out in the shower."

My head snaps in his direction. I can feel my eyes expand. "You did?"

"That's why it took me so long to get out the shower, and that's why I lasted longer than 30 seconds. I wanted to get it in so bad. I knew it'd feel different with you, and I wanted you to have a nice first time. So, instead of a minute and a half, I made sure you got at least six or seven."

"Closer to eight," I say.

He chuckles and changes lanes. "Nice to know you think about it."

"Nice to have something worth thinking about."

We hold hands and I turn toward the passenger side window. As we drive down the highway passing exit signs and strangers going their own ways, I think about turning onto Elm Street, pulling up my driveway, and stepping inside my home. I'm doing all of that with my boyfriend and not with my mom. Though I can comfortably close my eyes with Michael, he can't ever give me what Andrea Hayes could. I've lost her warmth, her love, our bond forever. I'm torn at this moment. I'm looking forward to seeing our memories framed around the house, sitting on our porch where so many laughs were shared, but I'm not looking forward to opening that front door and not hearing her sweet voice call out to me. I'm not ready to step through the doorway and not smell her anywhere in that house.

I shut my eyes and exhale loudly as we take this bittersweet journey. I'm excited to go home, but pain is fully ignited inside me because I really fucking miss my mom.

* * *

As Michael makes a sudden turn, I jolt out of my sleep.

"Whoa! You okay?"

I nod, reach for the water, and gulp some down. "That sharp turn ripped me out of my sleep. Scared the hell out of me."

"Damn cat in the road."

I take a few more swallows of water as I look around at the very familiar houses. At houses I've been inside, had dinners in, attended parties at. This is my old neighborhood. *What the hell? Did I really just sleep for three hours?*

"Look familiar?" he asks, a half smile on his face.

"I slept the whole trip. Three hours," I say in disbelief.

"You always pass out around me. I stopped and got gas. You never moved, not even for water."

I finish off the bottle. "That's weird. I don't think kids even sleep that long in cars."

"You were tired."

"Not really."

"Your brain probably was. Your brain is a computer. It went into shut down mode."

"You're such a cornball," I say as we move down Elm Street.

I point at a house, its front door turquoise, the yard unmaintained. "Ms. Carol lives there. She's the sweetest person ever. Always gives out cookies and cupcakes to the neighborhood kids. Well, not me because I'm not much of an eater, but she always offered. She always tries to make people smile with her treats."

"Sounds like the neighborhood granny."

"Sounds that way, but she's not old. She was around my mom's age, and her son was my age. He died, though. A couple of years ago. Heroin overdose. The whole neighborhood was shocked because no one expected Spencer to mess with drugs. My mom and I were talking about how blind most people are. That shit is everywhere, not just in the hood. Suburbanites get high, too. Actually, I'm convinced that the kids who come from money use the hardest shit. Heroin, acid, shrooms, PCP."

"You ain't gotta tell me. There were kids doing coke at Trinity. Drugs are everywhere. Only ignorant people like to think it's a hood thing."

"It's three more houses up," I say before curiously asking, "Ever try anything?"

"Weed once with Warren. I thought I told you that already. Anyway, I didn't feel anything. You?"

"Once with my ex."

"What?" His tone hits a surprisingly high pitch. "You? You've smoked?"

"Don't get me wrong, drama king, I hate the idea of drugs, but my mom had just died and the media was harassing me because I was *The Miracle* that survived being ejected from a vehicle. Not only that, but they discovered that Andrea Hayes was my adoptive mother. They started writing those sympathy pieces about how I lost two moms, about how my biological mother disappeared without a trace, and about how my adoptive mother was tragically killed in a car wreck at the start of my senior year." I take a quick sip. "Anyway, my ex came over to offer his condolences. We took a drive, sparked one up, and we smoked. I felt absolutely nothing, and I'm glad I didn't. While I was curious, and also hoping it'd ease my pain, I'm glad it didn't have any effect on me. I don't want to be on drugs, don't want to be around that bullshit, and I sure as hell don't want to date anyone who messes around in that stuff."

"I hear you, babe. Ain't a damn thing cute about being dependent or strung out on anything. Even just recreational use is a problem for me. I don't want to sound like a hypocrite. I tried it because I was curious, but I couldn't be with someone who smokes even every once in a while. I don't try to control people. You're my girl, and I want you to be as happy as possible, doing the shit that makes you feel good. But I couldn't see myself as attracted to you if you were a smoker, one of those girls who makes their face up until they look like a completely different person, or a girl who calls herself a bitch. No judgement to girls like that, and I don't have a secret thing for my mother, but I love her natural beauty, the way she stands up for herself, and I admire her confidence and self-respect." He throws a smile my way. "I love the same things about you." He takes my hand. "Queen."

I smile as we pull up my driveway, stopping in front of the double door garage located on the side of the house.

"This place is huge."

I chuckle. "Your house isn't exactly a shed either."

"How many bedrooms?"

"Four," I answer quickly as I step out of the car. I close the door, let my head fall back, and gaze up at the vastness stretched above me. A sky free of clouds, planes, and even birds at the moment. Just endless blue. No horizon. A tropical sea above me.

I turn in a full circle, scanning my yard and home slowly. So many gardening attempts took place in our backyard. So many belly-aching laughs were shared on our deck and front porch. The walls that hold up this house hold all of our secrets as well.

Suddenly, I feel like a brick has been shoved down my throat. I swallow a painful heaviness that tears through my esophagus, slowly ripping my insides apart until it finally drops into my stomach, weighing me down to my knees. Before I can blink, Michael's at my side, kneeling down, stroking my hair gently.

"I'm okay," I utter.

"You're not. Get back in the car. Sit in the AC for a minute. Drink some water."

"No." I push his hand away. "I'm fine." I can hear the jagged breaths as my words escape me. "Just give me a minute."

He moves away from me in a hurry. I hear the passenger door open, but my eyes don't follow him. I focus on regaining control of my breathing.

"Here." His voice is a whisper.

He's back at my side holding a bottle of Deer Park at my lips. He tilts the bottle, and I take large swallows as it pours into my mouth. Maybe I should've been more open to grief counseling, more receptive to the suggestions that were offered to me. Perhaps I should've listened to what my body wanted to do, gave in, and released my feelings months ago. I wish what I'm feeling right now was a pain of my past. At this moment, this is just too much.

He smooths my hair back. "Better?"

I nod.

"It's okay to cry."

I shake my head, shake away the tears that so desperately want to fall. "No." I force myself to my feet. "I got slapped in the face with a lot of emotions all at once, but I'm okay."

"It's okay to not be, Jaylen."

"I'm not a piece of glass, Michael. I'm shatter-proof."

I move around him, avoiding eye contact as the concerned look he probably holds in his eyes will force me to acknowledge I'm not nearly as emotionally tough as I wish I were. I grab my purse from the car floor and head around the side of my house toward the front door.

Our curb appeal is on point as usual. Once we realized we didn't have green thumbs, we planted flower bushes and let Mother Nature take care of them. They sprout every spring and add brightness to our yard throughout the warmer months. A beautiful rainbow of brightness until fall hits, when the cold, crisp weather forces them into hibernation.

The lawn is freshly mowed. I'm sure my aunt sends my cousin Phillip over on occasion to keep things plush, presentable, and maintained. She's without a doubt the one behind the banner strung above the front door. It says, *Welcome Home*. I specifically asked her for my space, to let me do the first walkthrough on my own. Not only because I'm not ready to explain Michael being here, but because I also don't want her emotions to become so overwhelming that I have to focus on her instead of what I'm still trying to deal with internally.

I step up onto the porch and our wicker conversation set pulls my eyes in its direction. My eyelids lower. There's brief darkness, and then her. I see my mom sitting cross-legged, sipping caramel flavored coffee, with her hair tied up in a bun, looking 10 years younger than her actual age. Beautiful. She's the visual definition of perfection.

I return to reality as my eyes open at the sound of Michael's voice. Though I didn't hear his words, I repeat that

I'm okay before pulling out the note slid halfway beneath our welcome mat. I open it.

My Jaylen, please don't feel like you have to stay here alone. Me, your Uncle Phil, and your cousin Phillip would love to have you over. You can stay with us as long as you like, or we can come stay with you for a few days. It's up to you. I just want you to know we're here for you. I love you so much, baby doll. Please call if you need something. I'll be by tomorrow. Love, Auntie Cassie.

I shove the note inside my purse, push up on my tippy toes, and rip down my strung up welcome. The banner was adorable, and something my mom would've probably done, but I don't need the neighbors stopping by, offering their condolences once again, and making this process any harder for me.

I exhale loudly, and unlock the door to a place filled with memories I've been anxious to revisit but am suddenly nervous about seeing. Immediately, I turn to my left, to the dining room we only used for special occasions and holidays. There's no floral centerpiece, which is uncommon for our home, but there are several perfectly wrapped presents sitting on the table. Likely birthday and graduation gifts as my aunt wasn't able to visit me while I was in Virginia.

I look to my right. Our black console piano sits beneath framed pieces of my childhood artwork. The black shines as the sun's rays beam through the large window hitting the beautiful instrument. I think back on my mother's brief obsession with learning how to play. She learned the birthday song, found satisfaction, and moved down her list to the next thing she was interested in learning how to do.

Michael places his hand on my lower back. "Who plays?"

"My mom did. Well, sort of. She learned how to play 'Happy Birthday' and she was happy with that."

"You play?"

"No interest."

"Wanna open your presents?"

Immediately, I answer, "Later."

Without showing him the kitchen or living room, I head upstairs. My bedroom door is open, revealing my perfectly made bed. We step in. The white comforter is decorated with white, black, and blue circles. Perfectly positioned pillows sit at the head of the bed. My bookshelves are still packed with my favorite books. My walls still feature my artwork. Two throw pillows with my first initial printed on the front sit on my window seat. I took most of my clothes, shoes, and accessories with me, but I left everything else here, and my room is as I left it. I wasn't sure what would happen to this house since my mom is no longer here to take care of things, but I knew I'd return at some point, even if just temporarily, and this was how I wanted to see my room.

"Ms. Ward really worked hard to prepare that room for you at her house."

I nod. "Same colors. She added the window seat. She stocked a bookshelf. Though it was unnecessary, I appreciated it. She went above and beyond for me, and I appreciate her. She's a special woman with a big heart. And I need to call her. Don't let me forget."

"I got you."

I step back into the hallway. My mom's bedroom door is closed. A Post-it note is stuck to it. In all caps, it reads, *NOTHING HAS BEEN MOVED! I'VE ONLY DUSTED. LOVE YOU. AUNTIE CASSIE.*

I place my hand over the note and take a moment to really appreciate the people who are a part of my life. My Auntie Cassie is so caring, has respected every wish I've made regarding my mom's things, my belongings, and this house. She could've taken over and done whatever she wanted to. Many families lose relatives and those left behind fight over the deceased person's possessions, run through their money, and make selfish decisions without considering the others who are equally hurt by the loss. Not my Auntie Cassie. Her whole focus was on me, my mental stability, and my healing. She would've taken me in herself, but her marriage has been on the rocks for a while. The constant fighting with my uncle forced my cousin Phil to spend many nights with me and my mom. With all of the emotional troubles in my aunt's household and their financial burdens, taking me on wasn't ideal. She was still willing to try to make it work, but in comparison to what Ms. Ward could offer me, temporarily moving to Virginia seemed like the best choice for me.

Michael wraps his arms around me, hugs me tightly from behind, kisses my hair. "I'm right here. Cry if you need to. Scream if you want. Just let me hold your hand."

I place my hand over the door handle, and immediately, he covers my hand with his. He doesn't pressure me, doesn't force my hand to move. With his patient, needed support, I swallow and push down the door handle. The door opens, and as much as it hurts to not find my mom on the other side, there's something comforting about finding her things exactly as she'd always kept them.

Her bed looks showroom ready, perfectly made with her purple and gray floral bedding. One of her stone-gray nightstands holds a lamp, a framed photo of both of us, and a glass, retro-style rotary phone. The other nightstand holds another lamp, a glass clock, her television remote, and a book; *Poems* by Maya Angelou. Her 50-inch television is hung on the wall directly across from her bed, her window seat is lined with purple and gray pillows, and her dresser is still topped with framed photos, jewelry, and that awful blue frog ashtray that I bought her many years ago thinking it was a candy dish.

"Everything where and how you remember?"

I sit at the end of my mom's bed. "Exactly," I answer softly.

"Say it. Say whatever you're feeling."

"I miss her, Michael."

"I know." He lowers to sit beside me, but quickly pops

back up as if something bit his ass. Literally.

"What's wrong with you?"

"Can I sit? You made it clear you didn't want anyone to touch anything of hers without your say so."

I pull him down beside me. "That's very considerate of you."

"I just don't wanna cross any lines. I take this seriously, Jaylen. Your wants, your feelings, your grieving. It's all important to me."

"I know it is. I just didn't want her things moved, sold, or tossed out. She was mine." I point to myself. "My mom. If anyone is going to do anything with her possessions, it's going to be me."

"I get it."

We sit side by side and look around my mom's space. My eyes scan the framed pictures on her dresser. Some of the photos are of me, one is of her and my aunt, there's one of my mom standing in front of her dental practice, and there's one of the two of us sitting together on her custom painted Yamaha.

"Your mom was a biker?" he asks, shock filling his tone.

"I wouldn't say biker. She could ride. She had a motorcycle license. But she didn't belong to clubs. She didn't pop wheelies or do tricks."

"That's dope. Your mom was mad cool. Did you like riding with her?"

"Nothing to not like. She drove her bike responsibly. The open air feels good."

"It's still here?"

"Better be." I hop up. "Should be in the garage."

I hurry down the stairs, through the kitchen, and out into the garage. Parked inside is my mom's Lincoln, and beside it, her motorcycle.

Michael comes right up behind me. He places his hands on my shoulders and begins a slow massage. "It's still here," he whispers.

I take slow steps toward the bike. From the outside, it may look like my mom was a frivolous, loose cannon, but she never spent money she didn't earn. She never purchased wants without taking care of our needs. She was a hardworking woman, and she wanted to experience everything life had to offer. She worked hard, so she could play harder, and I admired that. I still admire her.

I run my fingers along the side of the purple and blue Yamaha. As I touch the cool metal, I begin to quiver. I wanted to see her stuff, touch her stuff, be around the things that made her happy, but to see her things and not see her is torture. I don't want to see this damn bike and not see her on it, bragging about how good she looks cruising down the highway in her gear. I don't want to see that damn piano and not hear her play the same damn song just to prove she can play it. I don't want to be in this damn house and not share it with her. Why did I come back here? Why did I convince myself that this would bring comfort?

I look down at the bike, at the blue she had added for me, and the purple she added because she adored the color. I take a few deep breaths, try to breathe through the pain, try not to let anger take over as I can't understand why she had to die. There are so many fucked up people still living and causing others pain, but my mom, sweet Andrea Hayes, had to die. I will never understand why.

"Babe?" he calls out to me.

I close my eyes and try to focus on my breathing. I try to remember that it hurts now, but time will heal these open wounds. The longer I'm here, the easier it'll get. I reopen my eyes. I look down at that purple and blue. Her smile comes to mind, our first ride together. I can't contain it. I can't keep it in. It fucking hurts.

With questions swirling, anger fueling me, grief sticking its jagged blade into my heart, I feel my soul split. Rage darts through my hands. I grip the handle bar, rip the bike from its parking space, and with a mighty grunt, I release it.

"No!" Michael yells.

My eyes shoot to his. His are wide, focused, disturbed. I follow them to the bike, caught in midair, just inches from the garage door. Slowly, it lowers until its back on the ground.

I don't turn back around to face him though I can hear him approaching me.

"I know it hurts. I don't know exactly what you're feeling, but I'm sure it burns like hell inside," he whispers. "I want you to express yourself, release your emotions. Just not like that. Don't destroy the things you needed to see, the things that meant so much to her. They mean something to you too, Jaylen."

I exhale quietly before briefly glancing back over at the bike. If it weren't for Michael's ability, it'd have crashed through the garage door, maybe even hit my car parked right on the other side. By no means do I want to destroy her things. I just want this pain to go away.

"Why don't you go in and relax a little?"

I slept for hours on the way here, but still I could go for another nap. A nap to shut off my brain and an immense amount of water.

"I'll get our stuff out the car."

As Michael leaves the garage, giving me my necessary space, I step back inside the kitchen. I pull a water from the fridge, and hurriedly guzzle it down. After the final swallow, I crumble the bottle, and silently scream at myself as I'm disgusted by my own actions.

Get a grip, Jaylen! All of this lashing out. All of this rage. Who the hell are you becoming?

Chapter 7

he flames light the room as cold air blasts through the vents to prevent the space from getting too warm. I've always enjoyed sitting by the fireplace. No matter what season, what occasion, the dancing of the blaze, the yellow, orange, and red glows always bring a necessary calm and relaxation to the room.

A short shower followed by a short nap has done nothing to help me find a happier place. Even with Michael here, I feel completely alone in my despair. Alone. Buried in a deep, dark coffin of unwanted grief, overwhelming worry, and immense frustration.

I sit on the sofa, my knees drawn up, and my sketch pad resting against them. As I slowly sketch a picture of a burning fire, and try to create the illusion of moving flames, I let my mom's words play in my head. *Don't just draw. Don't just use your talent to win school contests. Draw away your stress. Use this as a way to calm down.*

As I draw the fire, I imagine my pain going up in a blaze, and no longer existing. With each stroke of the pencil, my image heats up, comes more alive. I keep my eyes on my work in progress, though I hear movement upstairs. I'm not sure why it's taking Michael so long to take a shower and get down here. Females are typically the ones accused of taking forever in the bathroom. Not in this relationship. Either I'm strange or he is.

I sigh loudly as I flip my pencil around to scrub away too-carefully drawn lines. In the midst of fiercely rubbing away my mistakes, the sound of music grabs me. I freeze, can feel my eyes narrow as I try to determine what's playing. *Is that the piano instrumental of Celine Dion's "My Heart Will Go On"?*

Michael takes slow steps into the family room. With his phone in hand, music escaping it, he sways toward me.

I drop my pencil as confusion overtakes me, and an unexpected ball of laughter bursts out of me.

He's in my robe. His wet curls drip into the terrycloth. The sleeves stop midway up his forearm. The length stops well above his knees. He looks absolutely ridiculous.

He laughs too, as I struggle to regain composure.

"What the hell, Michael? You look all kinds of crazy. Didn't you pack clothes?"

He clears his throat. "Your ass better not make me look like a porcelain doll. I'm a paying customer. I expect to get what I want."

He tosses a dime at me. I miss it, and it lands on the cushion beside me.

With my eyes on this clown, I try hard to keep a straight face, especially since he's so committed to recreating this memorable movie scene.

"Michael," I call out to him.

He shushes me immediately.

Please don't be naked under there. Please don't be naked. There's no way in hell I could sit here and draw my boyfriend completely nude. Not with the possibility of his member changing shape in the middle of my attempt.

Slowly, he unties my blue bathrobe. I cover my face with both hands and cackle hysterically at what I've just seen.

"You're so unprofessional," he scolds.

"You cannot be serious, Michael."

As he fidgets and tries to readjust my underwear that he's wearing, his face scrunches. "How do you girls wear these tight ass drawers?"

"We don't need the space that your balls require, fool."

With the fire lighting the room, Michael lies across the loveseat on the other side of the coffee table. He shifts, trying to get comfortable in my bra and panties.

Hands down, this is one the weirdest moments of my life, but it's too funny to ruin. I reach down, grab my pencil, and return to my previous position, with my knees drawn, working as my easel. I flip to a clean page, look over the pad at my boyfriend, and immediately, crack up uncontrollably again.

I point. "Michael, umm, I can't do this," I explain as I try to catch my breath.

I throw the dime across the room. He attempts to catch it, but it hits him in his chest.

"I won't be seeking your artistic services again."

We both laugh as he pulls at my underwear.

"Michael." I point again. "One of your…your… one of your…" I trip over my words, still laughing like a mad woman. "It's hanging out, Michael. Fix your underwear. My underwear," I correct.

He looks down, see's what has me gripping my stomach as almost scary-sounding laughter barrels out of me.

"Shit." He tugs at my ill-fitting underwear. "It's because these damn things are made so weird."

"You've assaulted my eyes enough. Please, I beg of you. Don't make me draw you like this."

He smiles as he comes toward me. He pulls the pad from my leg-made easel and drops it on the coffee table before sitting next to me and wrapping his arm around me.

"I love seeing you laugh. I'd wear this every day if it meant I'd never see you down again."

"Really? Every day?"

"No. But clearly I'd go all out for you."

"Never doubted that. Actually, you've gone farther than I could've ever imagined. You've got one strange ass brain."

He chuckles. "You've got one beautiful ass smile."

The appreciation for his compliment forces my lips to arch upward, forces my stomach to do a cartwheel. It still stuns me that his words, which I've heard before, can still make me feel so damn special.

He leans in, kisses me gently. The fire is still going. We're all alone. I'm definitely in need of some stress relief, a passionate reiteration of our love. I want him. Here. Now. In my house. My home.

My hand moves from his face to his chest. Just brushing the side of the bra with my hand is enough to make me briefly detach.

"Take it off," I demand.

He grabs his chest, calls out my name in a sweet, high-pitched voice. "So aggressive."

"I will never forget this, and for sure, I needed that laugh, but in moments like these, I don't wanna see my boyfriend in my underwear. Take it off. Bring your sexy back."

He laughs at my corniness and turns so that his back faces me. "Unhook me."

"Unhook yourself. You've had enough practice."

He turns, tries to cut me with a sharp, serious stare, but slowly a smile arises. "Woman, would you please help me?"

"You put it on. Take it off. And just so you know, the longer you keep it on, the longer you keep your lips and hands off me, Mr. Reed."

He anxiously pushes the straps off his shoulders. I reach to grab the bottle of water from the coffee table, but the sound of the doorbell forces us both to jump up.

"You expecting someone? Did your aunt say she was stopping by?"

"No. I spoke with her a little earlier. Ms. Ward, too."

As we move toward the door, Michael wraps himself back in my robe. With each step, the presence grows stronger.

"Ethan," I say. "Remember? We told him to drive up."

He grabs my arm, stops me from moving forward. "Or psycho Indigo."

He was able to fully distract me from all of our worries, but just like that, they're flooding my thoughts."

"Let me get it," he insists.

"Firstly, I doubt it's her. Why would she ring the doorbell? Secondly, I'm stronger than you."

He immediately grimaces. This is a power-struggle we'll be facing for a while, maybe the rest of our lives. Males always want to protect and lead. He has the power to protect me in a lot of ways, but physically, in comparison to my capabilities, my strength will always put his to shame.

I don't want to emasculate him. Guys and their egos. My mom told me all about that.

"Get the door, Michael. I just wanna be close."

With a defeated look, he continues ahead of me the last few steps down the short hallway to the front door. Only a step behind him, I stand quietly as he peeks through the small peephole.

"Ethan," he says, twisting the lock and pulling the door open.

I move to his side. "Kennedy?"

She reveals an uneasy smile. "I hope it's okay that I came. Ethan invited me to take the drive with him. Thought it'd be fun to see Jersey and hang out with my new friends."

"I don't know how I sounded," I say, my tone softened, the astonishment removed from my voice. "I just didn't expect to see you. It's more than okay that you're here as long as you didn't share my address."

"I didn't."

A relieved smile replaces the uneasy one she's been trying

to hold, and I smile back. My eyes then move to Ethan. His wrinkled nose and raised upper lip force me to follow his squinted, disturbed eyes to Michael. Immediately, loud laughter flies out of me.

"What kind of crazy, freaky shit are you guys into?"

My loosely tied robe is showing the bra Michael has on underneath it.

Kennedy bites her bottom lip, trying her hardest to hold back the laughter.

Michael shakes his head. "Chill out. It's not what it looks like."

We all laugh at him, his discomfort, his attire.

"I was trying to make her laugh. I don't secretly cross-dress," he tries to explain.

"Please tell me you're not wearing her panties, bro."

Michael's head falls. Ethan will certainly never let him live this down.

"Come in guys," I say waving them in.

Michael closes the door as I exchange hugs with both of them. Not even a second after securing the locks, he rushes upstairs. To find something baggy, breathable, and manly to put on, I'm sure.

"Nice spot," Ethan compliments.

"Really nice," Kennedy says as she peeks over at the piano before she turns her attention to the dining room. "Welcome presents for us?" she asks, pointing to the gifts I haven't opened yet.

"Absolutely…" I say.

Thrilled, she asks, "Really?"

"Not," I add.

"You're so funny, Jaylen," she says sarcastically.

I chuckle. "I know. You guys want a tour?"

"Can we start with some water?" Ethan asks.

"Of course."

The three of us head for the kitchen. I pass them both

fresh bottles of water and pull one out for myself.

After a few sips, I ask, "How was the drive up?"

"It was nice. Lots of talking," Kennedy answers as she takes a seat at the island.

"Well, while you two talk about the drive, I'll grab the bags from the car."

"Don't grab too much," I tell Ethan. "Your ass ain't moving in."

He laughs and heads back toward the front door, leaving Kennedy and me to ourselves.

"How does it feel being here?"

Coolly, I say, "Not bad." My answer completely dishonest. I take another sip of water and then change the subject back to their drive. "Was the car ride with Ethan awkward?"

"No. We've spoken on the phone, so it was chill. Felt like I was with a friend."

"That's good. Nobody wants to have awkward conversations while stuck in the car with someone for hours."

"On the subject of awkward, Indigo called me."

I take another sip. "Why awkward? You feel stuck in the middle?"

She shrugs, pushes her brunette curls from her face. "Wrong is wrong, and in this situation, she's flat out wrong. I just don't want her to get hurt."

I nod. "That makes two of us."

"There's something wrong with her, but I don't want her to be killed."

"And I don't want to be a killer. Knowing I'm stronger than her doesn't make me eager to hurt her. I don't want to. She's making people want to."

"I wish I could save her," Kennedy says softly.

"You have an incredible ability, Kennedy, but the only person who can save Indigo is Indigo. She needs to save herself."

"I tried to tell her that."

"And?"

"She just kept going on about being alienated in addition to being an alien. Going on about an unhappy future. Crying about being abandoned by everyone."

"And what'd you say?"

She takes a large gulp of water. "I told her I still care." Her volume lowers dramatically. "I told her being alone doesn't have to be her future. And I said there are others for her to have, be friends with, and love. Verbatim, I said, Jaylen and Michael are not the end all be all."

"That's what I want her to understand and really believe. We all just ended up in the same high school. That's it. We're not her only possibilities."

Kennedy continues, "I actually offered her my friendship if she'd just let this whole thing go, leave you two alone, and promise to never make contact again."

"What'd she say?"

"She kind of went silent." Kennedy shrugs again. "Said she had to go and that'd she'd call me later."

I exhale, completely over this whole mess. "I just don't see how she could want this to go on."

Kennedy shrugs a third time and shakes her head. "Maybe not understanding her is a good thing. If you could, wouldn't that make you just as twisted?"

I grunt softly as I search for a hint of dishonesty in Kennedy's face. I search for slyness, a shift in her eye contact.

"What?" she asks. "Still questioning if you can trust me?"

"I know she's special to you. I don't know where you stand."

"I don't want to stand anywhere, Jaylen. I don't agree with her actions. I think she needs help. I think a lot of things, but I don't stand by anyone getting hurt. Not Michael, not you, not her, not anyone."

"Fair enough."

The room becomes quiet. I guess Ethan came with a

truckload of baggage. He's taking forever to come back in.

"So…" Kennedy says, dragging out the word with an inquisitive tone.

"So what?"

"What did we interrupt?"

I chuckle. "My boyfriend is not a crossdresser."

She releases a short laugh. "I believe that, but that's not an answer. I'm asking if you two were about to, you know?"

"Bone?"

She laughs embarrassedly. "Gosh. You're so blunt."

I laugh too. "I just threw that out to make you uncomfortable. Truthfully, we were getting there."

"So…" She lowers her voice to an almost inaudible volume. "What's it like?"

I smile as my mind recalls the beautiful nights I've spent with Michael. "The first time was so special," I say. "We've only been together like that on two separate occasions, though we've been alone many times. We've kissed more times than I can count, but we've only had sex three times. Twice the first night we were alone. Once on prom night. It didn't hurt, which shouldn't be surprising. We don't feel pain the way a human would, so I wasn't surprised that the sex was painless. The sensations were good. Really good, actually. I'm sure that wouldn't be the case with another guy," I say. "I feel comfortable with Michael. I'm in love with him. It feels right with him."

My mind shifts to the possible fetus forming inside of me and my stomach cramps in a sickening way. I'd like to know if I'm carrying. Though many don't conceive after one night, it is very possible. I need to be sure, to be able to check one thing off my list of worries. But would any type of human test work for me? Is there any human made product available that'll say for certain whether or not my alien body has a baby in it? Is waiting my only option? I don't know of any alien doctors who specialize in our species.

"Do you guys use protection?"

"Definitely," I say sternly, not wanting to hint at anything I'm not positive about.

"I've never gone all the way with a guy."

"Does that mean you have with a girl?" I ask, wondering how far she and Indigo actually took things.

"I'm not saying that either."

"You're not saying much of anything except that you've never been penetrated by a guy. I gave you a detailed response which is what I'd like to receive from you."

She covers her face with both hands and I can't help but laugh.

"Kennedy, you're the one who brought dirt into this conversation. I answered your question. Answer mine."

She nods, keeps her face hidden behind her hands. "Indigo and I did more than kiss, but we didn't do *everything*," she says. Her words sound muffled as she speaks into her palms.

I chuckle. "Move your hands. I'm just being nosy like you. I'm not over here passing judgment."

She pulls her hands from her flushed face.

The moment she makes eye contact, I strike her with a playful jab. "Slut."

We both crack up. She covers her face again and laughs into her hands.

Michael walks into the kitchen in sweats and a white tee. "What's so funny?"

"We're just talking," I answer.

He opens the fridge. "About what?"

"Girl stuff."

He closes the fridge and twists the cap off a water bottle. "So I can't know?" he asks before taking a few swallows.

"Go back upstairs and put my underwear back on and then we'll share our secrets with you, Rose."

The three of us laugh together. All of these laughs are so

necessary. When I first arrived here earlier today, my emotions were on the most complicatedly designed rollercoaster. Seeing my mom framed all over the house, her belongings where she loved them, but not seeing her destroyed me more and more with every step I took throughout the home we shared and loved. Surrounded by friends, love is present. Happiness is the mood. Their smiles, laughs, and efforts to support me bring a needed light, which is helping pull me out of the darkness of grief.

The front door opens. None of us move toward Ethan, though we've heard something hit the floor.

"Hey!" he hollers.

I yell back. "Just leave your bags out there! No point in bringing them to the kitchen! Lock up and come in here!"

Ethan walks in and immediately takes a few large swallows of water. "What did you pack?" he asks Kennedy.

"Just the bare necessities."

"Bricks? Because there's no way that clothes and hairbrushes weigh that much."

Balls of laughter fill the space.

"Maybe you just need to lift a few more weights. They didn't seem that heavy to me."

"Snap snap," I say, snapping my fingers twice. "She told you." I high-five Kennedy.

"She also rolled that luggage. I'm the one who lifted it to take it in and out of the trunk."

"Exactly," Michael says dragging out the word. "Stop your snapping. Kennedy, save your jabs. Pulling versus lifting. There's no comparison, sweetheart."

Kennedy rolls her eyes. "Either way, I appreciate you lifting my bags, Ethan. And Mike, I'm sorry if coming for your boy's pixie stick arms has upset you."

Laughter bursts from us all again.

"Kidding," Kennedy says.

We all drink a little water and I look around at the three

of them. Though the craziest situation brought Ethan and Kennedy into my life, I'm happy to know them. Trusting anyone too fast, no matter who they are is an example of poor judgement, but I feel I can trust them both. Ethan more than Kennedy because of her history with Indigo. Still, I do like her. She seems like an honest, decent person.

"So what's the move for tomorrow?" Ethan asks.

"Princeton," I say quickly. "I love my aunt, but I really don't want to see her just yet. She's just gonna take my emotions on another ride. I know my mom isn't here, but I don't want to be reminded five times in the same conversation. I'd rather avoid the visit and see where I'll be attending in a couple of months."

"Awesome. We should walk around and see as much as possible. You may even meet a few people."

I nod with my eyes on Kennedy. "That's what I'm hoping for. I'd like to meet some people who are a part of the Art and Archeology program, get some feedback on their experiences, and prepare as best as I can, you know?"

"You just want to take a bunch of art classes?" Ethan asks curiously. "Turn in paintings and pictures to receive grades?"

"I do want to paint, sketch, and whatnot, but I also want to study the history of art and take some finance courses. I like the idea of working in a gallery, learning how to sell art, stuff like that. I don't really want to be told how to be an artist. I'm not against improving or learning new techniques. I just don't wanna be forced to become a completely different artist, you know? I like my style and I'm sensitive about my shit. It's the business side of art that I'm really hoping to learn. And it won't hurt to have the name Princeton University boldly sitting at the top of my future degree."

"True. You're about to get any job you want."

I smile at Ethan. "Let's hope so."

"So what about tonight? What are the sleeping arrangements?" Kennedy asks.

"There's a guest room upstairs. My room. My mom's room and office space are off limits, of course, but the living room is big. We can all sleep down here. Throw on some movies. Talk until we pass out."

Kennedy beams. "That sounds fun. Old school sleepover."

"Where are the blankets?" Michael asks.

"Upstairs. Hall closet."

As Michael and Ethan head upstairs, I stay with Kennedy as she searches for pajamas in her overstuffed suitcase.

"I don't think I packed socks," she says as she moves clothes around in search of a pair.

"I have plenty. Whatever else you forgot to pack, I'm sure I have. You can change in my room and borrow anything you need."

We head up to my room and Kennedy closes the door behind us.

"I see where Ms. Ward got her inspiration."

"Yeah," I say as I look around my space. "She wanted Virginia to feel like home."

"Did it?"

"It did begin to feel homey for me. That was mostly because of her, though. The window seat and color choices were sweet, but Ms. Ward was…" I correct myself. "*Is*. She is what made Virginia feel like home. She's a very warm person."

Kennedy nods. "She seems that way."

With our eyes on one another, we smile simultaneously. I then quickly look away and search for socks in my dresser drawer.

"Color preference?"

"Nope. Anything'll do."

I toss Kennedy a pair of black Mickey Mouse socks. As she unrolls them, my mind goes back to my first behind-closed-doors encounter with Indigo. She borrowed my Mickey Mouse tee. Moments later, she attempted to kiss me. It threw me completely off.

"Need anything else?" I ask, hosting as best as I can.

"I'm good. I appreciate you not being weird about me showing up."

"It's kind of nice that you're here. It's nice to have girl talk with no ulterior motives."

"It is." She almost sounds relieved. "I wanna be cool with you, Jaylen. Not because I don't have other friends. My phone is loaded with people. Not because we're aliens and there aren't millions of us. Not because you're the first person to ever call me a slut."

I burst out laughing. She chuckles softly.

"Because of that," she says. "Because you're just you and I'm me. I think you're hella chill and honest. You're funny when you're not questioning my motives. I hope we can really be friends. There's nothing up my sleeve. There are no hidden agendas." She puts her right hand up. "I swear."

I smile. "Get dressed. Come down when you're ready."

I open the door and step out. Before closing it completely, I poke my head back in. "You know that I was completely joking, right? Not for a second have I ever thought that about you."

"That's why I laughed. Be out in a minute. Get out."

I laugh to myself and head back downstairs to help the boys set up our sleepover space. It's nice to talk to Kennedy. It's nice to laugh with her, be able to be alone with her, and know that no lines will be crossed. It's nice to have female friends. Like her, I have others I could text, but what makes Kennedy special is that we're the same species. We understand each other on a different level. I worked hard to have this with Indigo. I worked hard, but because of her feelings, we couldn't make it work. It's nice to just fall into this naturally and comfortably with Kennedy. Another girl. My friend.

Chapter 8

 $\mathcal{T}$ he four of us stroll along Princeton's historic, picturesque campus, each carrying a water in hand. For the first time ever, I'm excited to start school. I'm pumped to be a Princeton Tiger, to walk these grounds every day. There's such a mellow feel to this college town. There's so much history and architectural beauty to take in.

"I should've applied here," Kennedy says as she snaps another photo.

Together, Kennedy and I must've taken over 100 pictures. The boys don't seem as taken aback by the building designs and campus grounds. Ethan especially seems confused by the sights that are forcing *wows* out of Kennedy and me, sights forcing us to pack our phones with images, sights forcing us to constantly stop and gaze at our current surroundings.

I do a slow twirl in front of Nassau Hall. "This place is absolutely stunning. I'm ready for fall."

"You're ready to start school?" Ethan asks, disbelief and shock filling his voice.

"It's amazing here. Everywhere I turn, I just see art. Beauty."

"I get that art and design are your things, Jaylen, but this

95

is going to get old fast, especially when you have to see this every single day."

Kennedy and I both shoot Ethan disapproving stares.

"This can't get old," Kennedy states. "It doesn't even feel like we're in New Jersey anymore. It's like we're in another place, in another time."

I nudge Michael the second the idea strikes. "I want to draw these buildings. I want to draw each building on an individual sheet, and then once I'm done, put them together like one huge puzzle of the entire campus."

"That'd be dope." Michael wraps his arm around me. "You should make it look 3D like that house you've been drawing forever in your sketch pad."

I nod. "I plan to. It'll take a while. I'll sit on campus grounds in my free time and draw the buildings as I see them. If the finished pieces look anything like what I have in mind, they'll be some of my best work. I'd like to add color, too. Not just sketch them."

"Go for it, babe."

I wrap my arm around Michael. Though I know he's not the type to sit and stare at paintings leisurely or the type to enjoy an art class, his support isn't an act. That means something to me. It means a lot to know that while he can't always see what I see while staring at an oil painting, sculpture, or building, he appreciates it for what it is. Art. A creation. Someone's artistic vision. More than that, I appreciate him always wanting to see my latest pieces, always wanting to peek at my works in progress. His interest in what I love makes me love him more. I'm completely in love with my best friend. Though we don't agree on everything, and no two people ever do, I know I'm supported, cared for, and loved far beyond the surface by Michael. Knowing that, feeling that, being wrapped in those facts is enough to make me want to weather any storm with him no matter how catastrophic. Because when the happiness comes about, when the clouds move, when the darkness is driven out by beautiful sunlight, I don't want to dance in its rays with anyone else.

The four of us continue to tour the campus. Kennedy and I continue to load our phones with images, and we even stop to chat with a few Tigers who can't say anything negative about this prestigious Ivy League institution. With their help, we plan the rest of our day. After the mention of the art museum featuring travelling exhibits that will soon be rotated, I immediately bully Kennedy, Michael, and Ethan into a quick visit. Ethan isn't a fan of art, finds it boring, but reluctantly agrees after I threaten to lock him out of my house. Michael wants to take me to the National Gallery of Art in DC first, but quickly softens and agrees to a short visit as he doesn't want me to miss pieces that may not be showcased again. Kennedy has no problem with a visit to the art museum but has made it clear that we must stop by either the secret gardens or the campus chapel before heading back to my place.

I nod at Kennedy. "I'm down. Art museum for twenty minutes, the chapel because I know how badly you want to see it, and then we'll catch an Uber down to Lake Carnegie. I let a couple of old friends know I'm back in town. They plan to meet us there."

Out of the June mid-day heat, Michael and I walk hand in hand around the small museum viewing the various exhibits. In here, Kennedy and I both have our phones tucked away in our totes. The students we met explained that many of the special exhibits aren't to be photographed. Just to be safe, we decided not to take pictures of anything.

"One day your art will be in here."

My eyes meet my boyfriend's. "I hope."

"You hope, but I know."

I smile as I continue to admire the perfect pieces. Asian art, African, modern. The exhibits are small, but impressive. Greek pottery, oil paintings, sculptures. Art is everywhere, in so many different forms. I can't for the life of me understand how it can be so underappreciated.

Michael's cell sings. He pulls it from his pocket, silences the tune, and shows me the screen. A photo of Ms. Reed covers the screen, and the name 'Moms' is centered across her face.

"Answer her," I order.

"I'll call her back after we get out of here."

I pull my hand from Michael's and step closer to Kennedy. Her eyes are squinted, almost closed as she focuses in to read the description below the modern piece.

"What do you think?" I ask.

"It's pretty. And I don't say this to insult the artist, but it's simple. Why can't I draw that? You have no clue how bad I draw. I can barely draw a stick figure." She does a quick look behind us. "I'm serious. Even my happy faces are slightly off. They look high, like crack heads."

I cover my mouth, trying to muffle the laughter.

She whispers. "Shut up. People are going to think we're laughing at art when you're just being insensitive about how unartistic I am. It actually makes me feel bad that I draw crack faces instead of smiley faces."

My hand doesn't muffle my laughter enough. She shushes me while trying not to laugh too loud herself.

"What the hell is so funny? It's a bridge," Ethan points.

I cut my eyes at him. "We can see that, crack face."

The three of us laugh, forcing other visitors to take quick glances in our direction.

Michael immediately looks up from his phone. His brows knit together as he takes backward steps away from us. "I'm. Not. With. You. Guys," he mouths at me, exaggerating each word.

I chuckle quietly as I step toward him. "Why?" I ask softly.

"Cause you all are embarrassing. All that damn laughing. This is a prestigious art museum. You should know better, woman."

I laugh my way into his arms. "Shut up. You'd be laughing too if you weren't messing around on your phone."

He squeezes me. "Phone is away for now. We do need to call my mom when we leave here, though. She wants to talk to the three of us. She doesn't know Kennedy is here."

I nod. "We'll call her as soon as we leave here. I won't forget."

The four of us continue to view the displays. Though we're sharing laughs, momentarily acting like silly kids, the pieces surrounding us are inspiring me, flooding the creative side of my brain with all sorts of ideas. Looking at the variety, the different styles, the different messages, makes me want to try my hand at sculpting. Spread my artistic wings.

As I look over an Asian piece, I feel that oh-so-familiar feeling. My hand twitches as I turn. Kennedy, Michael, and Ethan turn as well. My eyes meet those of another young lady. She looks to be around my height, but she's thicker. More voluptuous. Bangs cover her forehead and brows, stopping right above her eyes. The rest of her hair is wrapped into a neat bun. Her dark chocolate complexion is brought out by her strapless, yellow dress. A thick, gold necklace, and thick gold bracelet match her strappy sandals. Strappy gladiator sandals that stop just above her ankle.

She struts our way. "I never would've expected to bump into Ques here," she says. Her thick accent sings of The Motherland.

Ques? I look over at my boyfriend, at his purple shirt, down at his purple and black Jordan Son of Mars sneakers. Based on his color choices for the day, I can only assume that she believes she just bumped into a Que Dawg. I don't know what else *Ques* could mean.

She briefly glances at Kennedy. "I get it." She nods. "Mixed company."

Kennedy and I make brief eye contact. Her face is scrunched as I'm sure mine is as well.

"I'm Kesia," she introduces herself, extending her hand.

I try to bury my confusion with a polite smile. "Jaylen," I say shaking her hand.

"Jaylen. Pleasure to meet you," she says, broadening her smile. Kesia repeats each of our names as she shakes our hands.

"Nice to meet you as well," Kennedy says sweetly, matching Kesia's smile.

"Are you all students or just visiting?"

"Just me," I answer, raising my hand. "We're touring the campus. I'm trying to get a feel for this place before fall."

"Congratulations."

"Thank you. You a student?" I ask.

"No. I actually live in Cameroon. I'm just here in the states visiting an ill family friend and taking in some sights. I flew in with my grandmother."

"Cameroon? Wow, long flight," Kennedy says. "Other than the sick family friend, and of course, I hope they get well, how are you enjoying your visit?"

"It's been wonderful. I like art. I'm happy to visit so many places at no cost. I also received a makeover. New hair style." She runs her hand over her bangs.

"Looks great. Hot bangs," I compliment.

"Thank you. So, what do you plan to study?"

"Art and finance."

"You're an artist?"

I nod. "I sketch. Some painting. No sculpting yet."

"Her work is dope. It'll be in here one day," Michael says unquestionably, forcing a wide smile out of me.

"I wish I could draw," Kesia says. "I'm much better at admiring."

We all release soft laughter.

"What about you all?" Kesia's eyes run across the three of them. "Do you plan to study at another university?"

Kennedy jumps right in. "I'm starting at Seton Hall this

fall. It's not too far from here." Her voice is full of excitement. "I plan to follow in my father's footsteps and become a doctor."

"It's hard work, but a field that needs more passionate professionals. Too many people become doctors for the money. I believe your heart needs to be in it. I can see that yours is. You're so proud to talk about your goals."

I look over at Kennedy. "She's right. Your passion does shine through when you talk about being a doctor. Your eyes light up. It's like you're dreaming while speaking about it. Shows where your heart is."

A wide, teeth-showing smile, spreads across Kennedy's face. "Thanks guys. There's just so much sickness, so much pain, and even with the internet, still so much ignorance when it comes to the body and good health. I want to teach people how to live better, help them live longer, and when people are suffering, help to end their pain."

"We need you overseas."

Kennedy nods at Kesia. "And I plan to do a lot of work overseas and here at home."

As we girls chat about future plans, Michael's phone beeps several times alerting him of several incoming texts. Then Kesia's phone sounds off. She presses the screen, silences the tune, and then grunts softly.

"I may have hung up on accident," she says, staring at the screen. She then lifts her head, looks at us and smiles. "I should run, but I'd love to keep in touch. It's always nice when you unexpectedly meet more Que…" she freezes mid-sentence. "I mean, such nice people, especially here in America. Most people don't speak highly of the younger generations. I guess they haven't bumped into people like you guys."

I pull out my phone and enter the number Kesia recites to me. Before parting ways, we all shake her hand again, and then we head for the exit, each donating on our way out the door.

Kennedy takes a quick look back at the museum. "Nice

girl."

I nod as I polish off my bottle of water. "Yeah, she was. I love her accent."

"What'd she call us? Ques?" Michael asks. "What the hell is a Que?"

"A fraternity," Kennedy and I answer together.

"They go back many years, too. You're wearing purple. Not the most common for boys. You're missing the gold, but she probably just made an assumption based on the color you're wearing. Plus, fraternity stuff is usually secret and Omega Psi Phi is predominantly black, so maybe that's why she tried to stay away from the Que thing. You know, trying not to make it awkward for Kennedy and Ethan."

Kennedy nods. "That makes sense. She definitely felt like she mentioned something personal. She said something about mixed company. She just may not know how to approach that kind of topic, especially being that we're different races and she's in a new country talking to strangers. Either way, it was a weird moment, but it passed, and I liked her. I'd like to keep in touch with her."

"Are you gonna hit her up?" Michael asks me.

"Yeah. She seemed hella cool, and I wanna keep in touch with as many of our kind as possible." I snap. "Speaking of calling people. Your mom," I remind him.

He immediately unlocks his cell.

Ethan pulls the empty bottle from my hand. "While you guys handle that, we're gonna to go buy fresh bottles of water."

Left to ourselves, Michael dials his mother. With the phone on speaker and held in between us, the ringing begins.

"Thank you for calling me back, Sweetie. Ethan and Jaylen with you?" Ms. Reed asks.

"Jaylen is. Ethan stepped away with Kennedy."

"Oh, the four of you are in Jersey together?" she asks, surprised. "I didn't realize she'd be driving up as well."

"Last minute decision," Michael says.

"Hello, Ms. Reed."

"Hey, honey. I texted you. How are you feeling today? How was it sleeping at your old house?"

"It was hard when I first got there, but with friends around, I didn't feel so sad. It was kind of fun, actually."

"And you guys are still at Princeton?"

"Yes," I answer. "We just left the art museum. Next, is the campus chapel, and then we're closing out the visit at Lake Carnegie."

"Take pictures for me. I know Mike isn't going to."

Ms. Reed and I share a laugh.

"Well, I don't want to keep you two for too long. I want you to enjoy the rest of your visit. What I called to tell you all is that we're going to Michigan. I know I can boss Mike around, no matter how old he is, being that I'm his mom, but I did jump the gun and buy you a ticket as well, Jaylen. I thought it'd be nice for us to get away from all of the Indigo mess. Really take a breather in a new place with others of our kind. I have a few friends in Michigan, and Ethan's mother has a friend there as well. I'd love for you to come."

"When?" Michael asks before I can respond.

"Next weekend. You guys still have time to enjoy New Jersey. Jaylen will still be able to visit with family."

I look at Michael. He tilts his head, slightly raises one brow, asks for my answer without moving his lips.

"Sounds like a great plan, Ms. Reed," I say. "I'd love to visit Michigan and meet others. Actually, we just met another of our kind today. Just a few minutes ago. Her name is Kesia. She's from Cameroon."

"How nice, Jaylen." Her voice hits a higher pitch. "Did you guys hit it off?"

"Yeah. She seemed cool. I have her number. I plan to keep in touch."

"I'm so happy to hear that." Her tone matches her statement. "Listen, I want to hear all about being home and

Kesia and Princeton, but let's get off here. I don't want to slow down your visit or for Kennedy and Ethan to return and she feel excluded."

"I understand," I say.

"We'll talk soon. I love you both."

I smile. "Love you, too."

"Love you too, Ma," Michael says before ending the call.

As Ethan and Kennedy head back our way, both carrying two bottles of water, I look over at Michael. His eyes are still on his phone.

"Another trip together," I say softly.

He looks up from his screen, smiles. "A family trip."

"We're not all family, though."

"Yes the hell we are. You're my future wife. Ethan's my brother from another mother." He lowers his voice significantly. "And Kennedy's a…" He stops, searches for a title.

"A close family friend, who I really like," I say. "And at this point, you have no reason to not like her."

Kennedy and Ethan hold out bottles of water for us as they approach. I pull mine from Kennedy's hand and Michael takes his from Ethan's. After we each take some down, we cap our bottles, and then start toward the campus chapel. A few minutes of walking brings us to the tall, stone building, offering a regal feel even before entering. The exterior looks like something one would see while studying the Middle Ages. It's too gorgeous to try to describe to Ms. Reed. I stand back to take a picture of the stunning design of this historical building.

As we start up the short flight on the West entrance, Kennedy turns. Her brows draw closer together and she bites down on her bottom lip.

"It's fine," I say quickly. "Let's go in. Take your time. Walk around. Take your pictures. I'll take some for Ms. Reed. I'm not religious, but I'm not a devil worshipper either. I'll admire the building. You guys can admire the building and also pray if you feel the need to. We've been through this. I respect all beliefs. Just don't try to force anything on me."

She nods. "I just don't want to put you in an uncomfortable position."

"I'm good, Kennedy. I promise. Now, let's go in."

Together we head inside. Immediately, I'm taken aback by the beauty. The stained glass windows, the high, arched ceilings, the low lighting. All one can do upon entering is pause, gasp, and look at the perfect artistry surrounding them.

"This is the most beautiful building I've ever been inside," Kennedy whispers, her head back as she stares up above. "I want to get married here."

I smile. "This is incredible. The detail, the design..." I exhale. "This whole campus is making me want to be every type of artist, designer, and creator there is. I would love to be able to see something I draw brought to life, and literally rob visitors of their words and breath."

I turn to Michael. Unsurprisingly, his phone is out and he's snapping photos. In any of the other campus locations, I'd be shocked, but this is the kind of beauty you want to be able to take a second look at and show to others. This is a sight you don't want to be able to forget, not even the smallest detail.

I hang back as Michael walks around taking photos. Kennedy sits on one of the polished, wooden pews with a lowered head, and Ethan walks slowly, turning from side to side, recording the visit. Standing alone, I look around at those filling the space, at how a place of prayer, a religious setting can immediately put an end to all playfulness. This environment has silenced all jokes. Both Ethan and Michael have their phones out and a sudden interest in our visit that they both lacked just minutes ago is visible.

While I don't share in my friends' beliefs and what they probably feel in this chapel, I fully respect it. Their response to being in this building reveals what their faith means to them. I'll view their photos later, but while they not only visit, but spiritually connect with the space, I stay where I am.

Following our visit to the chapel, we briefly wait in the heat for our Uber, and then take the quick, air conditioned drive down to Lake Carnegie to meet three of my hometown friends. The moment I spot them, Liana comes running my way. I walk quickly toward her. It's just too hot for me to run.

"Jaylen!" She hugs me tightly.

I squeeze her back. "I've missed you."

"I've missed you, too. I've missed my partner in crime."

I smile at my friend. Liana and I used to do everything together. Everything from girls' nights, to double dates, to skipping class. We always managed to keep great grades while making those high school memories we would someday look back on.

I touch her dyed hair. "Blue now. What's next?"

"I'm loving the blue too much to try anything else anytime soon."

We hug again. I hug the girl my mom told me I could trust, the girl my mom often complimented for staying away from the cattiness and for being and looking unapologetically different.

As I introduce Liana to Michael, Ethan, and Kennedy, Ricky and Junior, my other two hometown friends approach slowly. Immediately, I hug them both. Ricky and I became close throughout the course of my 11th grade English class. Junior and I became close after having several classes together, several of the same friends, and we briefly dated for a couple of weeks, not to mention, he came running to support me after the passing of my mom.

"It's so good to see you guys," I say.

I introduce everyone before we find shade beneath a tree. It's so crazy to sit amongst those who I connected with because we lived in the same area, attended the same school, and shared some commonalities, while also sitting with people who I instinctively connected with. We all look so much alike, but

Liana, Ricky, and Junior will never know just how different they are from the rest of us.

Liana says, "You guys make a cute couple."

Ricky sucks his teeth. "You say that every time she's dating someone."

"You say that like I'm always dating different guys. I've only dated two that she knows and she's just meeting Michael. Don't make it seem like she says that every other week," I say.

We all release short laughs.

"Is this awkward?" Ricky asks me.

"Not at all," I answer. "Michael knows Junior and I briefly dated, and Junior knew I was bringing my boyfriend. And you should know I'd never date a crazy dude who expects me to cut off all of my old friends, male friends, or anything like that. Girls who find guys like that sexy are…" I tap my chin. "How do I put this nicely? Stupid!" I say quickly. "They're stupid girls. So, stop trying to make this weird, Ricky. The only thing awkward here is you."

Again, we all laugh.

I ask, "So what are you guys' plans? Liana, I know you're going away to college. Ricky? Junior? College?"

"You know I have to go. I'm Haitian. I can still get beat," Junior says, eyes widened, a chuckle following his statement. "Eighteen or not, my mother will beat the hell out of me if I tell her I'm not going to college."

"You staying close?" I ask.

He shakes his head. "Howard University. I'll be studying biochemistry and molecular biology."

"I know your mother is pressed to tell people that."

"Everybody. Even strangers."

We all laugh.

Michael jumps in. "That's what's up. Moms wants me to go somewhere, but I don't know what I wanna do."

"I feel you," Junior tells him. "Really, I wish I could have a little more time to figure things out. At least intern or work in a hospital or lab for a year."

Michael nods. "That's what I'm trying to do. Spend a year figuring things out before I put myself and Moms in debt."

"I asked for time off. My mother said hell no, slapped me with the application, and that was that. Haitians don't play. I texted her about attending part-time. I thought texting would keep me safe."

We all laugh.

Junior continues. "She called me screaming. I went home and she was still screaming. Shit, I'm going to college to take a break from my mother."

I chuckle. "You better stop talking about her before I tell on you. She's tough, but she wants the best for her only son. Her only son, who she does any and everything for. Mister I want griot and fried plantain several times a week. Mister don't miss any of my games. She just wants to see you make it and make it big."

"What's griot?" Kennedy asks.

"This fried pork dish he's obsessed with. She marinates it overnight and fries it for her baby every time he asks for it. Once she gets in from work, she makes him his favorite meal no matter how long it takes her," I say with my eyes on Junior.

"I get it, Jaylen. I know she loves me. I know what she wants from me. I want that, too. I just want to love what I do. How do I know I love it if I haven't done it? She's looking at the money. I'm thinking about days, weeks, years of doing something I just kind of like and will probably get bored with."

I listen quietly.

"So take a year off if you can," Junior tells Michael. "Just use that time to really work and intern. We all like to do a lot. We gotta figure out what we love and can't imagine having to stop doing."

My boyfriend and my ex dap each other up. I sit, looking around at those I'm closest to. This is what our lives are supposed to be like right now. Full of possibilities. Full of uncertainties. Full of planning. They shouldn't be full of fear. The fear of an ex-best friend figuring out where you are and destroying your life by attempting to take away someone you love.

Chapter 9

*A*fter such a nonstop busy week, I am more than happy to be sitting where I am right now. Following our visit to Princeton, Liana invited us to a party, which ran over into the early hours of the next morning. After a night of fun with friends, Michael got to meet my Auntie Cassie and cousin Phillip. Both gave me the thumbs up on my boyfriend, which surprised me because I never thought Phillip would give any guy his approval. The next few days were the busiest for Michael, especially after Kennedy and Ethan left. He borrowed my car daily, vague in exactly where he was going, and he's been spending hours a day in his phone endlessly searching and applying for jobs and internships to begin when we return from Michigan. Though the rest of my year is set and planned, getting through the past week was overwhelming and at times felt impossible. No matter who I bumped into or who I just wanted to play casual catch-up with, condolences were offered and questions were asked about how I was dealing with an unimaginable loss. I'm not ungrateful, and I do appreciate the love and support, but it would be nice if people could wrap their minds around the idea that not constantly having to talk about it makes it easier to go on. Since it seems to be a subject no one can stay away from, it feels amazing to sit here on a plane heading to a place I've never visited to meet others who can understand me as well as those who I met at Trinity do.

I sit in the window seat beside Ms. Housley, my sketchpad in my lap, water in my cup holder, and a pencil in hand. Sitting in her lap are two crossword puzzle books. With the help of my brain overflowing with endless information, I'm sure we can get through both within the first hour of this flight.

"Are you nervous?"

I briefly glance at her kind, freckled face. "No. I'm actually excited to get away. It was nice seeing my hometown friends and my mom's old friends, but everyone brought up the accident. Everywhere I turned, everyone I bumped into, reminded me that she's gone—as if I don't have to face that horrible reality every second of every day. And I couldn't stop thinking about Indigo. I like that I'm heading to a place she doesn't know anything about. I'm happy to be somewhere she can't get to. I'm happy to be separated from everything except..." I look over at her again. "Except you guys."

She smiles and touches my hand gently. "Separation is good. Being surrounded by love and safety is even better. This trip will give us all what we need. Mike needs this opportunity to really calm himself down and see clearly. You need distance, but also a break before college begins. Princeton is about to kick your tail."

I chuckle.

"Ethan needs a nice getaway before his classes begin again in the fall. And Michelle and I could both use some time away from work and the regular day to day."

"I've been wanting to ask something, but I don't know if it's appropriate," I say.

"No, I will not accept payment for the deck," she responds.

I laugh. "I'll just mail it to you."

Ms. Housley laughs too. "And I'll send it back. You owe

me nothing except the promise to control your anger and to not damage any more of my property."

"I promise."

We shake hands and exchange smiles.

"But, that actually wasn't the question I wanted to ask. I was curious to know why you and Ms. Reed stayed out of touch for so long. You two seem so close."

"We went to school together. Became great friends. We kept in touch for quite some time, and then life just got in the way, especially after having children. She found a great hospital she didn't want to leave in Virginia. Ethan's father and I found great positions we couldn't turn down in Philly. The distance made it hard to remain as close. We were saving money, raising kids, trying to grow within our careers, buying homes. Days become years so fast after college. I only moved to West Virginia a couple of years ago after Ethan's father passed. I sold our condo back in Philly and was able to buy something a lot more spacious in West Virginia. Though we're not next door neighbors, I hope Michelle and I can remain this way. I've missed my friend."

"I'm so sorry about your loss, Ms. Housley. I didn't realize he passed just a couple of years ago." I lower my voice significantly. "Michael told me it was in a plane explosion. Ethan hasn't said anything at all. He hasn't mentioned his father once."

She whispers too. "He doesn't like to face the reality of it. It was a small plane, and all the other victims were identified. Mr. Housley wasn't. I explained to my son that since our kind dries up in death, he likely burned completely away in that fire. He wouldn't have been pieces of flesh stuck to bones like the others. Ethan doesn't want to hear it. He likes to believe that maybe his dad will walk through the door one day and say, *just kidding*." She shakes her head, looks at the seat in front of her. "He never will."

I reach over and grab her hand.

"I'll be okay, darling. Tell me about Kesia. Michelle told me you met a new friend at Princeton."

"We've texted a little. She seems dope. I love her personality. She's super close with her grandmother. They're visiting friends in Jersey. I wish we could meet up again before she heads home, but she'll be back in Africa before we leave Michigan. She's bummed about it, too. She really wanted to chill. I wanted to see her while I was still home, but they've been busy spending time with their sick family friend. It was hard to meet up."

"If it wasn't so far, I'd suggest you invite her. I have a friend coming to Michelle's friend's house. We're all pretty excited to be around each other. There's more of us in Michigan, but life makes it hard for a lot of us to end up in the same place, at the same time, for the same reason. Especially to relax. Too bad she can't be there."

I lean in closer, whisper, "Sounds like this is going to be an alien retreat."

She chuckles. "Something like that."

She opens one of her crossword puzzle books. As her eyes read across the first clue, I do the same. My brain provides me with an instant answer.

"A French silk. Four letters across. The answer is soie," I tell her.

She throws me a quick look and then pencils in the answer. "Thanks, show off."

Before she can read another clue, I say, "Charged bit. Three letters across. The answer is ion."

She places her hand over the puzzle, blocks me from being able to read any more clues. "Draw your picture, Jaylen."

Together, we laugh. As she pencils in the answer, I turn toward the window. We soar high above the clouds, above our problems, to a place I can't wait to get to. I don't know who I'm about to meet or what they're going to be like, but I do know that in a very important way, we'll be the same. I close my eyes as we head for Holland, Michigan, the place I plan to relax, meet more of my kind, and hopefully learn more about myself after questioning so many things for so long.

* * *

Nearly four hours later, after a quick layover in Chicago, we arrive in Michigan. In a rental, we make the 35-minute drive. With my eyes on my phone screen, I text Ms. Ward, *We're officially in Michigan. I'll call you later.* I shoot Kennedy a message as well. *In Michigan. I hope you'll be able to fly up. I know ticket prices are no joke. Need a little help? I can put in on the ticket. And I know Indigo may reach out to you. It's not up to me to tell you who you can and can't talk to. Just be careful about meeting up. Platinum Blondie reads minds, so no matter what you say, she'll know if you're lying. TTYL.*

"Did you text Ms. Ward?" Ms. Reed asks.

"Just did," I say.

I scroll to Kesia's name and begin typing. *I'm in Michigan. Feel free to text me anytime you'd like. Sucks that we won't be able to really hang out and get to know each other before you go back home, but I'd still love to keep in touch. You can never have too many friends, especially those who are "like you".*

After sending the message, I watch through the windshield as we turn onto the private property and pull slowly up the curved driveway.

"They live on the water?" Michael asks, leaning forward.

"I told you that," Ms. Reed says. "They live right on Lake Michigan."

"I thought you said they lived *by* Lake Michigan." He removes his seat belt. "They're rich. Like really rich!"

Ms. Reed chuckles. "They've done well for themselves. Benjamin is a cosmetic surgeon. Has been for some time. Everly is a bestselling author. Jackson, their boy, is a jokester. He's still in high school, a little younger than you guys, but a nice kid. You guys should all get along."

"Why didn't you ever bring me up here with you?"

As Ms. Reed parks in front of the three-car garage, she turns and looks back at her son. "You never wanted to come. You asked if they had any kids around your age. At the time, Jackson was in a special program studying abroad, and you said you didn't want to come and spend a weekend listening to us old folks talk. You wanted to stay at Warren's instead. You turned this down to play basketball with friends you saw every day. Us old folks ain't so boring, huh?"

I laugh as I look at Michael, at his face as he admires the luxurious property in front of us.

"This is what my future needs to look like," Michael says.

Ms. Reed opens her door. "Get a degree, son."

We all step out of our temporary vehicle. As Ms. Reed makes a call, I admire the huge, soft-yellow, modern Victorian home before me. My eyes run across the roof, stopping at the turret, then move down across the many windows, the fiberglass double doors, and the gray stonework covering the base of the lovely property. I stand looking at what could be my future. This is something two people worked for and enjoy on a daily basis. I don't want to experience this kind of luxury every once in a while on a vacation. I want my talent, my love for art, to bring about this lifestyle. I don't want celebrity status. I want comfort, to be surrounded by beautiful moving water and to own a property that's comfortably isolated and gated, allowing me to enjoy the land it sits on without being confronted by dangerous wildlife.

"Michelle!"

I turn toward the loud, delighted voice. A petite woman hurries toward Ms. Reed, squeezes her tightly, and smiles so big it makes me smile.

"It's great to see you." She runs her hand across Ms. Reed's hair. "And you just never age. You look amazing. Please, introduce me."

Ms. Reed first introduces her friend to Ms. Housley, then

me, and then the boys. The smile never leaves her friend's face. Her kind, brown, deep-set eyes immediately put you at ease, let you know right away you're meeting a good-hearted person. I feel welcome and I haven't even walked inside her home. I haven't even had a conversation with her.

"It's wonderful to meet all of you. I'm really excited to actually sit down, talk, and get to know everyone. And please kids, feel free to call me Mrs. Everly. We don't need to do formal last names here. Well, I guess you all aren't kids, but you get my point." She turns to Ms. Housley. "And you can feel free to call me Ev or Everly, whichever you prefer. Have you heard from your friend? When should we be expecting them?"

I notice someone, who must be Jackson, step out the front door as Ms. Housley answers, "Later this evening."

I look down at my hands, at how they're not shaking the way they were when I first met Indigo and Michael. I notice my breathing is even. It was even when I met Kesia as well. I guess because I'm always around our kind now, the feeling that used to force me to visibly shake and breathe uncomfortably, just forces a few twitches out of me to let me know the presence is stronger. The feeling of comfort here is like no other. I walked the halls of Trinity with some of my kind every day for months and never fully felt this inner peace. For the first time ever, I'm standing in a place where our kind is the majority, the only ones present.

Jackson waves us in from the front stairs. "Come on in everyone. I'll give you the tour."

Ethan, Michael, and I start toward the door when Michael freezes abruptly.

"What?" I ask.

He doesn't respond, remains standing, eyes open, one leg in front of the other in mid-step, with his lips slightly parted.

A chill runs down by spine, forcing a shudder out of me. "Michael, what's the matter with you?" I ask, panicked as he remains paused.

Ripples form in Ethan's forehead as he calls out to him. Michael remains motionless and silent.

My eyes dart to Ms. Reed. Her cheeks are inflated, her lips held tightly together in what looks like a smile she's fighting back, laughter she's trying to contain. My eyes run to Ms. Housley and then shoot over to Mrs. Everly. Both are smiling, looking our way. Neither look as worried as Ethan and me. I look back at my statue of a boyfriend. I touch him, ask again, *what's wrong,* before my eyes slowly move to Jackson. His focused, unblinking eyes are on Michael.

Ms. Reed loses control. The laughter comes out. "All right, Jackson. Let him go."

Jackson lets loose a guffaw and breaks his gaze, allowing Michael to finish the step he was in the middle of, allowing the statue to come back to life.

"Told you guys he was a jokester," Ms. Reed says.

Jackson hugs Ms. Reed, introduces himself to Ms. Housley, and then comes our way. "Not the typical way to meet, but unforgettable for sure, right?"

Michael's green eyes are unusually wide. "That was the creepiest, coolest thing I've ever experienced."

"Cool?" I ask. "I thought we walked into The Twilight Zone."

"Well, that's where we belong anyway, right?" Jackson asks, smoothing back his wet neck-length hair."

"Good point," I say softly.

"It is weird that you would find that cool, though," Ethan says to Michael.

"It was creepy because I didn't know what was happening and why I was telling my body to move, but it wouldn't. Cool because, hey, I've never experienced that before and it was just temporary."

We all formally introduce ourselves to Jackson as the group of moms heads inside.

Jackson asks, "Want the tour first or do you just want to skip it and head down to the lake?"

"Water?" Ethan and I say in unison.

"Of course," Jackson says. "I forgot I was hanging with a bunch of aliens." He chuckles and we follow him inside and into the kitchen.

One behind the other, bottles of water line the top three shelves of his double door, stainless-steel refrigerator. The bottom shelf is neatly stocked with a variety of Gatorade. Leafy green vegetables and colorful berries can be seen through the deli drawers. There are no condiments lining the doors, just all-natural fruit and vegetable juices.

Guests must find this strange. Shelves and shelves and shelves of water. Very little food. No milk. I ask, "What do your friends think when they go in your fridge?"

Jackson passes us cold bottles. "They see the water and just assume my parents are health nuts. But typically we prepare for visitors. If we know humans are coming by, we buy snacks and meat. You know, real people food."

"No real people here now," I point out. "Why all the Gatorade? Why the juice?"

He closes his fridge. "My mom thinks it has an effect on our bodies, especially when we're being active."

"Do you feel like it does?" Michael asks.

"I eat and drink what my mom asks me to, but the truth is, I never feel any different. The only thing I need for sure is water. I can do without, and have gone for some time without Gatorade, juice, or a substantial amount of food. I think my mom is just trying to find other things that work for us. She's experimenting, trying to be what none of us are or could ever be. Normal and human."

But she is normal. She's normal for wanting to find answers about herself, for not just accepting the little that she knows and pretending to be content. She hasn't learned enough from those of our kind that she already knows, so she's doing her own research. Sounds normal and sensible to me.

With bottles in hand, we follow Jackson around his home. We walk through the great room, view the lake through the 2.5 stories of glass wall. We walk up to the third floor, into Jackson's mess of a bedroom where clothes are thrown everywhere, a guitar rests on top of his unmade bed, and a trashcan filled with empty water bottles sits in the corner. We peek into his parent's master suite, but choose not to walk through their personal space. We then enter his mother's office where her best sellers are neatly shelved and likely written.

The large pieces of artwork hung along her walls grab my eye before I'm able to read over her titles. I step closer and look over an oil painting of a colorful galaxy. The stars are brightly painted. Some so teeny, some larger, all scattered, giving the painting such a glow. I move over to the next piece of artwork, lean in even further, and closely examine the sketch of an odd evolution. The first of the five creatures isn't of a smaller, hunched over primate, but of a giant. One that instantaneously makes me think of Sasquatch. The creature is very tall, is painted to be quite hairy, has a protruding spine that can be clearly seen, and a head that stands out too much to be proportional. In front of it stands a similar creature, but a bit shorter, with a head that's less eye-catching, a spine less noticeable, and shorter hair covering its body. Each creature loses hair, shows a decrease in the size of its skull, has a spine that shows less and less, and loses inches from its height. These changes stop with the fifth and last drawn creature who in every way looks like a typical human being. Hair is in all the normal places, but not long enough to look beastly. The head fits the body, isn't large enough to look strange. The spine isn't noticeable, doesn't show any abnormalities or deformations. The entire sketch is black and white, except for small, blue circles colored into the side of each skull. Small circles that look more like little blue lights. Little lights that I'm now just noticing get slightly larger as the skull size decreases throughout the strange evolution.

"What the hell is this?" Ethan asks as I open my mouth to ask the same thing.

"My mom had that drawn. It's the only copy. One of a kind. Her idea of our evolution," Jackson explains.

"She thinks we started out looking like big foot?" Michael asks.

He shrugs. "My mom's a writer. Her imagination is a wild and scary thing."

I point at the first creature in her evolution. "But that looks like a scary, mythical animal. Like a beast with a strange light in his head. Not an alien."

"My mom doesn't believe in big-headed, black-eyed, slimy green aliens. She believes those are simply creations of another person's imagination. Just like that." He points to the picture. "That's just a creation of hers. Who the hell knows what anything looked like a million years ago? I'll tell you one thing, though. It makes more sense to think we started like that than some green freak."

"And the circles of light on their heads?" Ethan points.

"She doesn't know what to make of our minds and how they're capable of these special abilities, so she had a focal point added that looked more like a solar light. It gets bigger because she believes we've advanced over time, our abilities have strengthened, and our minds have become capable of doing more."

"That's a different and interesting thought," Ethan says, trying not to sound offensive.

I say nothing, turn from the picture, look over another hung painting. A painting of a planet created mostly of water, painted mostly in different shades of blue. Beside it is another planet, painted in various shades of brown and orange, textured to look as though the unknown celestial body is dry and cracking. I spin around, scan the entire space Mrs. Everly writes in and has decorated freely to show her true personality.

While human guests will likely believe this art ties into her fiction stories, we know these pieces were created because of what she is and doesn't know. They're questions and possible answers made into room décor.

We exit her writing space, continue the tour, and walk down into the basement where we make bets on games of pool and table tennis we plan to play later. We then walk back upstairs to the main floor and enter the sunroom. The moms chat at the round table as we pass by a wooden sectional decorated with coffee-colored throw pillows and head out back. We walk along the short stone path that leads to the forty-step staircase. Taking careful steps, we head down to the shoreline of Lake Michigan. Jackson's backyard. His large, private beach.

"Your house is amazing," I compliment.

"Yeah, it's pretty cool, but I'm used to it."

I shrug. "I'm sure you are, but you can't deny the beauty. You have a beach behind your house. Like a real beach. This is big. A lot of land."

"I'm lucky," he says dryly.

"So, where's your father?" Ethan asks.

"At his house. And by his house, I mean his office. He's always working."

I nod, fully understanding his lack of enthusiasm. He's got this huge home, probably everything he wants, but seems to be starving for some time with his dad. I guess that's the dilemma all parents are faced with. Parents work long and hard to give their kids the best, but working long hours takes away from the most priceless thing a parent can give their kid. Quality time and attention. What a struggle. You can't win for losing. Just one more reason I hope my body isn't carrying another.

I sip some water and look out at the lake.

"So, who's going to share first?" Jackson asks, finger combing his hair back.

"Share what?" Michael asks before gulping down some

water.

"You guys know I can keep anybody where I want them. What can you do? We're not on the schoolyard. Share," he encourages.

The water bottle in Jackson's hand leaves his grip, levitates with no strings, and slowly floats toward Michael. With no hands on the bottle, the cap twists off. The bottle tilts pouring the remainder of the water out onto the sand. With no physical assistance, no hands reaching out, only eyes on the bottle, the cap twists back on tightly, and the bottle floats back over to Jackson. In front of his face it dangles for seconds, until he finally reaches out to grab it.

A half grin forms on Michael's face. "Don't litter."

Jackson beams like an amazed child. "Dude, that was fucking incredible! Do you know I'd never get up to get anything if I could do that? I'd clean up while lying on my bed. I'd bring the refrigerator to the couch. When my mom tells me to 'come here', I'd just float her to me instead."

We all laugh.

"Seriously, telekinesis is a sick gift to have. I'd switch with you any day," Jackson tells Michael.

"I told him he has a bomb ass ability," I say.

Michael shrugs. "All of us do. I'm not the only gifted one here. I'm sure we'd all like to swap and borrow each other's abilities."

Jackson's eyes move quickly between Ethan and me. "Don't stop the show now."

"Well," I say, dragging out the word. "I'd love to entertain you, but I'd rather not damage your property or you just to give you a show."

His eyes narrow, brows lower in puzzlement, and then his lightbulb turns on and his eyes bulge in an almost scary way. "You have super-strength, don't you? Show me. Break something."

"Jackson, I'm not your circus freak," I say, sipping down

more water. "And breaking things wouldn't be how I'd want to show off. How do you think your mom would feel about me breaking something?"

"The same way my mom did when you broke her deck," Ethan says, reminding me of my irresponsible mistake.

"Yeah, best you don't get on my mom's bad side. She's the nicest person ever until you give her a reason not to be. This house is her other baby. You damage anything in it, and she might damage you. That was a stupid thing to ask you to do. Glad you were smart enough to not listen."

"Smart." I nod. "Now that's my other gift. Not listening to you was just common sense, but when it comes to historical information, facts, dates, whatever, my brain is just another Google."

Jackson looks at Michael, "You can keep your telekinesis. I'd take super-intelligence over anything."

"Me too," Michael says, wrapping his arm around me. "My girl is literally a know-it-all and she never has to study. I wish I didn't have to study a bunch of subjects I have no interest in. I wish I didn't have to spend ten minutes at a time on long ass math problems I'll never have to solve in my real life."

"Your ability is my dream," Jackson tells me. "What's polydipsia mean?" he asks quickly, almost before finishing his last statement.

"Polydipsia," I repeat. "Extreme thirst, usually due to some kind of medical condition," I answer. "That was pretty random. What kind of question is that?"

"My father picks random words and medical terms for me to define and…" He uses air quotes. "…commit to memory."

"That's a good way to build the vocabulary."

"It's a bullshit way for him to pretend he's involved."

I don't respond to that. I want to tell Jackson that his father is working as hard and as much as he does so he can live in such a beautiful home and be privileged enough to travel abroad for special programs. I want to tell him that this lifestyle costs and his father is working to provide that. But who am I to butt in? I don't know a thing about their relationship. I don't know if Jackson just wishes to spend more time with his dad or if there's some deeper issue that's standing between father and son.

"So what about you, Ethan?" Jackson asks.

Ethan passes me his water. "The best has been saved for last."

Michael chuckles, as Ethan distances himself from us.

"Is he about to fly?" Jackson asks.

I smile. "Not quite."

In a flash, Ethan zooms past us, creating a breeze that blows my hair across my face. Sand flies up behind him as if racecar tires just sped across it. Trying to get a clear view of him is impossible. He has the cheetah beat and looks almost like a cloud of fog when he's in full motion.

I have no idea when he stopped and turned around, or if he stopped at all, but in seconds, he zips by us again, blowing the hair I just pushed back across my face again.

"Holy shit, that was fast," Michael says.

Jackson shakes his head. "Everybody's ability is better than mine."

Michael and I laugh, pulling a smile out of Jackson.

"Stop whining," I say. "You can pause people. That's pretty awesome. I'd aggravate the hell out Michael if I could do that. I'd ask him to grab me a water right before a good play is about to happen and then pause him before he can make it back to the TV."

Jackson cracks up and I can't help but laugh at the thought of Michael stuck inches away from the TV screen right before a shot is made or a touchdown is run. Michael throws me a killer side-eye.

I smile at my boyfriend. "You don't think that'd be funny?"

"You're mean, woman. I'm glad your brain can't control me. You'd torture me."

I giggle as Ethan heads our way at human speed with his hand held out. I uncap his water for him and hand it to him to chug down. As he gulps loudly, Jackson and Michael hold out their fists for him to pound.

"So do you guys have any other friends you wanna invite up?"

"I don't know that many of our kind," I answer quickly. "Kennedy wants to come, but I'm not sure if she'll be able to. It's not a cheap trip."

"My mom will take care of it," Jackson says surely. "Tell your friend to book a flight."

I immediately shake my head and decline. "We can't ask that of your mom. We just met her, and you expect us to ask her to fly our friend up and then back home? That's crazy, Jackson."

"I'll ask her," he says. "She'll want to do it, too. Look at all this. We can afford it. Invite this Kennedy and whoever else. We can have a lake-front football game we'll never forget. All of our powers used to try to win for our team. Come on, how crazy would that be?"

"Jaylen, you're on my team," Ethan says sternly. "I'll be damned if I take a tackle from you."

We all laugh, then sit together behind Jackson's house along the shoreline of Lake Michigan. I'd love it if we could find a way for Kennedy to come up. In addition to that, I'd love to find a way to meet up with Kesia. I'm dying to learn as much as I can from her about our kind, as I'm sure her grandmother has shared some insightful details with her about our species and shared legends of where we originated from. It's just so hard for her to talk on the phone being that she's a guest in the location she's currently staying. Casually talking on the phone while sitting with an ill friend is ill-mannered and heartless. I'd love for her to extend her trip as there's no guarantee we'll be able to keep in contact once she goes back home. The problem is, I don't know her well. Though my mom left me her life insurance and I could afford to get Kesia and her grandmother back to Africa should they decide to hang in the U.S. a little longer, I'm not sure if they'd take offense to the offer, and I don't feel comfortable asking Mrs. Everly, a woman I just met, to buy their tickets. If I made the offer, would they view it as odd or charity? Would they see it as friendly generosity? Not having a clue as to what their reaction would be makes me not even want to bring it up.

I'm happy to be around more of my kind, but I doubt Mrs. Everly knows any more than I've already learned. She would've shared it with Ms. Reed which would've trickled down to Michael. Maybe what I know about our kind is all I'm meant to know until I meet other aliens by chance or my strange life experiences teach me something odd and new.

Chapter 10

our days into our trip, Michael and I finally have a minute to ourselves. Hand in hand, me in my monokini, him in his trunks, we stroll along the shoreline of Lake Michigan behind Jackson's house.

He squeezes my hand. "Nice to finally have you all to myself again."

I smile. "It is. It's been interesting hanging out with Jackson and all of his prankster friends. It was nice to meet Ms. Housley's friend. It's been fun seeing Michigan and not really having the time to worry about Indigo. It's all been distracting and great, but I miss you. I want to cuddle. I want you to hold me and for us to be able to talk without interruption."

"When we get back to Jersey, we'll get back to us."

"I can't wait. Being around so many of our kind has been amazing, but Jackson is annoying the hell out me. Every time I try to move, he pauses me. It's a miracle I haven't kicked his ass through a wall."

Michael chuckles softly. "The last two times, I told him to do it just to piss you off."

I pull my hand from his. "You're an asshole, and I will get you back."

"I'm sure you'll try."

"I will. Count on it."

He reaches out, grabs my hand again. "Talk to Kennedy? Kesia?"

I look down at the water rushing against our feet. "Yup. Kennedy will be flying in this evening. Jackson's over-eager ass jumped on the phone and practically forced that ticket on her. She wanted to come anyway, but I think she was going to ask her dad to pay. It feels weird having someone buy you such an expensive ticket when you don't even know them. Kesia and her grandmother are on the bus right now. They get in this evening too. I lied to get them here."

"Lied? About what? I thought you said she was excited."

"They both are. I lied about the tickets, though. I bought the tickets just for her and her grandmother but lied and told her a few friends I invited couldn't make it. She didn't want my money to go to waste and said it'd be nice for her grandmother to see Michigan and enjoy being on the waterfront. I told them I'd help change their flight information when they get here."

"It's not the worst lie you could tell."

"I just hate lying."

"I love that about you. I love knowing that I'm getting the truth, even if it's something I don't want to hear."

"I love knowing that I might get some answers tonight. I'm so pumped about this bonfire. I want her grandmother to share all she knows about our kind, to pass along stories that have been passed down to her, to educate us with all she's learned over the years through her own personal experiences."

He nods excitedly. "Tonight should be one for the books. All of us together sharing what we know, comparing what we think we know, and being honest about what we don't."

I stop, turn to Michael, and look him the eye.

Concern flashes across his face. "What?"

"There's something I don't know. Something I don't like."

"What's that?"

"The secrecy. You're up to something." I shake my head and let go of his hand. "And I don't like it. I can feel it, Michael. Something's up. In Jersey, you were taking my car every day, but you wouldn't share where you'd been. You just kept saying you were busy. In Jersey, you were in your phone for hours at a time. I didn't think much of it, but since we've been here, I can't help but feel uncomfortable. You hide your phone screen when I walk by. You never used to do that. You don't want me to see what you're doing on the computer." I sigh. "I understand the need for privacy, and I believe everyone's entitled to some space, but if you're only looking for jobs and applying for internships, what's there to hide? I just don't get the sudden…"

"Jaylen," he cuts me off. "Listen."

"You listen, because I wasn't done talking."

He folds his arms across his chest, stands silently, and nods for me to continue.

"I don't need to see your phone or to go through your search history. You're entitled to your privacy. I just don't like how you jump when I'm coming by or how you shut your phone off and give me some awkward smile when I come sit by you. This is new. I don't want to sound crazy or like a psycho girlfriend, but I'll be damned if I sit around silent when there's something weird as hell going on. I like our openness. I don't want to lose it, especially now that we're supposed to be living together."

He laughs. Arms still folded. "What do you think I'm doing, psycho?"

I don't laugh, don't match the smile on his face because the concern I feel isn't a joke to me. "I don't feel like you're doing anything dirty. I'm not worried about other girls. I just don't know where the hell you were driving around to every day. I don't know what you're doing on your phone. What I do know is you deeply hate Indigo and you haven't said a damn thing to me about her since we've been here. It's been nice being so far from her, but I don't like that you're hiding everything all of a sudden and not bringing her up at all. Makes me think you're plotting. What? I have no clue."

"Please let me talk." His expression is no longer playful.

"Talk."

He holds both of my hands in his. "I'm sorry for making you think I've been scheming without bringing you in the loop. I am working on a few things, but they have nothing to do with Indigo. That's a promise." His face moves in closer to mine and those forest-green eyes stare intently into my chocolate eyes. "That's my promise to you, Jaylen."

I nod, my eyes still on his.

"I'm just working on my life, like you're working on yours. You're getting prepared for the fall because you'll be starting a new chapter in your life. You'll be a college student. I'm preparing for a life of not being a student, but a man. I'm not going to be in your house sitting around all day hoping I eventually figure out what I want to do. I want to be out every day like my lady, and then in the evenings, I want us to talk about our days and then spend every night showing each other how much we love and miss each other."

I smile at the idea, at the thought of it being just us two under one roof. I love the idea of us being enough for each other, enough to keep our smiles alive and our love constantly growing.

"I also can't forget about our backseat action on prom night."

Instantly, my smile fades. My belly twists into a tight knot. Twists and does a dizzying, nauseating flip. I want to throw up every drop of water I drank before coming out to take this stroll.

He touches my belly, and immediately my eyes move down. I watch as the water softly sweeps over our feet, at how it slowly inches us and the sand beneath us into its cool depths. Into a lake of never-ending, soft waves.

Children are beautiful. They make the world go round. For many, they make life worth living. They're just not what I want for my life. This life. I want love. A forever love with Michael, someone I don't have to raise or constantly worry about because they live in a world where every animal is a possible threat. I'm not burdened with worry when it comes to Michael because he already understands how to survive and has a gift that'll serve as his lifelong protection. I don't have to put a career on hold for him. Today, I can begin taking the steps toward a successful art career that'll allow me to smile every day as I make money. Money that'll come easy to me because my hours will be spent doing my hobby. There's no space in my life plan for a child. I couldn't want more strongly for my insides to remain a home to nothing but the copious amounts of water I pour into it throughout the day.

"What's wrong?"

I put my hand over top of the hand he has resting over my stomach. "I don't want a child, Michael."

"I know, but if there's a bun in there, I want to take care of you and it. Simple as that."

"It's not simple."

"It isn't, but we did what we did without thinking long enough to strap up."

I release a loud, fear-filled breath. "Fuck!"

"Yup. That pretty much sums up what we did and why you're losing it."

My eyes quickly find his, and I let out a short laugh.

"I'm going to say the one thing that never works when a person is mid-panic, worried, and pissed all at the same."

I stand silently, my eyes still locked in on his.

"Calm down, woman."

Together we laugh.

"You know what we haven't considered? Talking to Jackson's dad. He's one of us, in the medical field, and could help us find out for certain."

I nod. "Yes! That's it! That's how we find out. We don't have to worry about human products giving us false answers, don't have to go through the stressful experience of visiting a human doctor, and even though we aren't patients of his, I'm sure he'll protect our privacy." I exhale, feeling mildly relieved. I need an answer, and Jackson's father may be how I receive one.

"See what happens when you calm down? You think clearly. We'll find out and we'll be okay, Jaylen. Either way."

I grab a hold of my boyfriend's hand and we take a few steps into Lake Michigan. I look out at the wide, endlessness of the lake. I look out at a future unknown.

"Think we'll ever get bored with one another?" I ask.

His eyes carefully look me over from bottom to top. A smile forms slowly, showing those beautiful white teeth of his. "Bored with you?" He looks me over again, raises one brow. "Hell no."

I giggle and briefly look away from a smile and a pair of eyes that make me tingle all over.

"You've already asked me something like that before," he reminds me. "Are you feeling something you're afraid to say? Getting bored with me? Feeling like you might at some point? Don't hold anything back, Jaylen."

"I'm not." I shake my head. "Just asking questions. I'm definitely not bored with you. You're too funny, too sweet, and just too *you* to get bored with. And," I say, stepping closer so our bodies press against one another. "I'm completely in love with your heart. Your temper could use a little work and you're stubborn as all hell, but your heart is in the right place. I know that. I feel that. All I want is for you to be happy. Not just with me, but with you. I want you to live life doing what you love. Whatever that turns out to be. I love that we mesh so well. I love that being in your company is so comforting. I just want us to be two happy ass adults, who love their work, can travel to crazy islands because we make so much damn money, and who just love life and each other. I know if we're both happy with ourselves and in our individual lives, what we bring home will be beautiful. That's all I want. I don't give a damn about how young we are, how long we've known each other, none of that. I am certain that you are the only person I want that with. You're the person I'm supposed to be with."

Michael wraps his arms around me, stares into my eyes, doesn't smile, doesn't bring his humor, his clownery into this moment. "We're going to be that couple. We're going to be that happy. I'm going to be that man for you. Do you trust me?"

I don't need to think, to even blink. "Yes."

We kiss tenderly as the water dances around our feet. His hand moves up to my hair. He finger-combs it into his grip. He kisses me more intensely as his body comes more alive, reacts to mine.

This summer heat, his body heat, this setting, our lack of clothing, force me to release a moan into his mouth. Again, these urges are an inconvenience. I can't get wrapped up in how much I want Michael right now. I can't trick myself into believing that it'd be even slightly okay to give into these feelings. We're on someone else's property, guests in someone else's home. As much as I want him, miss the feel of him, and want to be alone with him, we have to respect Mrs. Everly, her family, and her home.

I pull back slowly. "We need to stop," I whisper.

"We should go for a drive somewhere."

I shake my head. "We should sit down and enjoy this time together without being inappropriate. We're already making out. Anyone could step out here and see us."

"We're grown, Jaylen. We're allowed to kiss."

"Kiss, maybe. Full on making out is a totally different thing and you know that."

He holds my face between his hands, brings his face in closer, rests his forehead against mine. "I'm dying right now."

"Me too."

"I want you," he tells me, his voice low, pure seduction to my ears.

"I want you, too."

Our lips meet again. I grip his hair this time as his hands slide down to my waist, squeeze me, hold me firmly against him. More than anything, I want to take that drive he suggested, park somewhere, anywhere, and finish this. Finish this the way my body is telling me we need to. But we can't.

I step back, shake my head, hold my hand out. "We have to stop. Really, Michael. This is getting too heavy."

He licks his lips, nods.

"You should sit down. Let the coolness of the water help get your blood circulating again and shock you back into less naked thoughts."

He nods again, walks into Lake Michigan and completely submerges himself. Once his head is back above the surface, I take a seat at the shoreline to watch him as he strolls back my way. As he moves through the water, I look over his wet physique. I exhale at the beautiful sight of him, at his slim, but defined body. *Damn, my boyfriend is hot.* I fan myself, try to take my own advice and focus on other things as the water cools me down.

He takes a seat beside me.

"Feel better?" I ask.

"Not really, but I'm good for now. I'll handle some necessary business in the shower later so I can get through the bonfire without offending anyone."

I laugh. "A date with yourself. How romantic."

"Speaking of dates, I wanna take you on another one. Not out here. Not at a location where someone we know can just walk up on us. I wanna take you somewhere nice."

"I'd love that."

"I have something up my sleeve. I looked up beaches around here, and this place called Oval Beach is supposed to be one of the best in the country. You're not an eater, so there's no point in buying you a plate to stare at. I thought you'd like a beach date instead. A real one, though. Not like this. Off Mrs. Everly's property. Away from Moms. Away from Jackson, Ethan, Ms. Housley, everyone."

"I'd love to go, but Kesia, her grandmother, and Kennedy get in this evening. It'd be rude to invite them here, just to leave them, even if just for a few hours."

"Let me handle things. If everyone is comfortable, can I have you for a few hours tomorrow evening?"

I grab his hand. "Absolutely."

He beams, his excitement uncontainable.

"Damn, you broke out with the Kool-Aid smile."

"You'll be wearing this Kool-Aid smile tomorrow evening."

"I look forward to it."

He pecks my lips before standing. With his hand held out, he asks, "You ready to go in, or you wanna hang here a little longer?"

"I'm in no rush."

"I don't wanna leave you sitting here alone, but I have to get an email sent and a paper faxed."

I ask, "To who?"

"Just stuff I didn't get finished with in Jersey."

Not really an answer. I nod, never reaching out to grab his hand. "You go ahead and handle what you need to. I'm just going to sit here for a little while longer. I'll be in shortly to shower so I can go pick up the ladies."

He bends to take my hand in his. He gently kisses the back of it before throwing me a wink and heading in.

Alone, I sit with my eyes on my legs. I watch as the water rushes up them, bringing sand with it, and then pulling the grainy particles back out into the greatness of the lake. I close my eyes and listen to the rhythm of the water lapping against the shore. I enjoy the sound of nature's lullaby. I enjoy a peace

I've been seeking since leaving Virginia. A peace I couldn't find anywhere until here.

Chapter 11

$\mathcal{B}$ ehind closed doors, both holding fresh bottles of water, Kennedy and I sit on the guest bed we'll be sharing. Immediately upon arriving, before stepping inside Mrs. Everly's home, Jackson welcomed Kennedy with his now-annoying greeting. The reaction of those he freezes can be amusing, but no one wants to be turned into a figurine when their hand is held out, and they're mid-greeting, trying to introduce their self to a group of new people. Jackson clearly doesn't understand the concept of time and place.

"Did you check in with your dad?" I ask.

"Before I even got out of the airport. When he says touch base immediately, he means it."

I smile. "He loves his baby."

"That he does," she says proudly. "But he doesn't really know how to feel about me being up here. I just took a trip to Jersey to visit you and I told him that last minute. If I wasn't 18 and didn't just graduate from high school with honors, he wouldn't have this."

"Did he want to come?" I ask.

"No. He's got plenty of work to keep him busy. Him and me."

"You?"

"Yeah, that's why I didn't stay the full week in Jersey with you guys. My father will occasionally ask me to stop by, and while a patient is under anesthesia or in a coma, he'll ask me to use my gift. Usually to save children."

My heart swells and I cover it with my hand. "That's amazing, Kennedy. You're amazing," I tell her, reaching out to touch her hand. "I really hate seeing commercials featuring sick kids or seeing a Facebook post about a dying child. All kids should be able to get through their entire childhood without worrying about sickness. Really, I wish no one ever got sick, but especially kids. Seriously, Kennedy, you're the closest thing to an angel that I could ever believe in."

She plunges forward, wraps me in an unexpected hug. "That means a lot to me. I'm not innocent, but I do try to be a good person."

"You *are* a good person," I say firmly as she releases me. "Not just because of what your gift is and how you use it, but also because of what you stand for. You stand for what's right. I know how much you care about Indigo. I know you want that friendship. Still, you're not willing to stand by her knowing that she may bring harm to others. That says a ton about you."

"Your actions speak volumes, too, Jaylen."

"And what do they say?"

"That you're a good person as well. I was worried about you meeting up with Indigo and her aunt, but I liked that you wanted to talk it out and move past it with as little drama as possible. More than that, I can appreciate that you didn't still want to hurt her once you realized Michael was okay. I knew your violent actions all stemmed from anger and devastation. The person I saw once you were more clear-minded was a good, rational person. Not a vengeful one."

"Is that what you think about Michael? That he's vengeful?"

"I did feel that way until I really talked to Ethan about the situation. Now, I feel differently. Michael is never going to feel totally safe because of what Indigo tried to do to him. She tried to take his life. Can you imagine how differently he must view the world and life itself now?"

I shake my head. "I can't."

"Not just a random person either, but someone who was once his friend. When you really look at the situation as a whole, it really sucks."

"It more than sucks, Kennedy."

"She really snuck around his house?" she asks incredulously.

I nod slowly. "He didn't know she could vanish, but he could feel her presence. We still don't even know how many times or how many ways she got in." My body shifts at the thought of what Indigo may have seen between Michael and me. I groan before continuing. "Michael was so uncomfortable and Ms. Reed could feel her too from time to time. They felt the negative energy. Michael told me he felt threatened by it, but just couldn't see anyone. Only noticed little things out of place. When he was home, he felt the discomfort and creepiness of knowing he wasn't alone. He just didn't know who his uninvited guest was."

Kennedy cringes. "That's sick."

Again, I nod. "Indeed it is."

"Makes me feel bad for Michael. I mean, Indigo harassed him for God knows how long before she pulled that mess on prom night. I get why he's torn and doesn't know what to do. Look at her track record. It says crazy."

I take a few sips of water, never responding to her statement.

"You know what's worse?"

I shrug.

"I still care about her."

"I know. And that's just another thing that makes you a good person."

"But am I?" Kennedy asks. "Am I a good person for caring about someone who would kill another?"

"I think so. You're not supporting her. You're not defending her. You just care about her because of your history. You two had a friendship and a relationship and I'm sure it was special to you. Those feelings don't die just because Indigo did something awful."

Kennedy takes a few large swallows from her bottle and then lowers her head. "I saw her," she says in a low voice. She lifts her head, makes eye contact. "I met up with Indigo while I was in Virginia."

I nod, completely unsurprised. "I figured."

"You mad?"

"As I've said before, it's not up to me to tell you who you can and can't talk to."

She sits silently and stares at me as though she's waiting for me to scold her.

"Do you want me to be mad, Kennedy?"

She shakes her head quickly. "Of course not. I just feel like I'm betraying her by sitting here with you, and I felt like I was betraying you, Michael, Ethan, and their moms by talking to her."

"I'm sorry you feel so stuck in the middle. I don't want you to feel that way. You can talk to who you want to as long as you don't share anything that could hurt anybody."

"I didn't. I didn't share anything except that I was going out of town and wouldn't be around much this summer."

"Did she ask where you were going?"

Kennedy nods. "I lied and told her I was going to Canada."

"What'd she say?"

"She was sad about me leaving, but more interested in what you guys have up your sleeves." Kennedy takes another sip of water. "I can't lie, Jaylen, it was hard. It was hard to talk to her because deep down I know you guys are secretly plotting to hurt her. With that in my mind, just looking at her was challenging. She's so wrong for everything she did, but I don't want her to die. I know I've said that to you many times before, but it's because it's something I can't stop thinking about. The truth is, I don't think I could interact with any of you guys anymore if something like that were to happen. I can't be buddies with killers."

I look away from Kennedy and out at Lake Michigan through the large window. "I understand and take all of your feelings seriously. I don't wanna be a killer," I say, turning my head to look at her. "And like you, I don't wanna be friends with killers either. But I'll stand by my friends and become one if she attacks another person I love. I really wanted to make peace. She wouldn't let me. I don't know what to do with Indigo." I shrug. "I really don't. Just know that I haven't been sitting in Michigan for days trying to figure out what my role is going to be in killing her. Michael isn't talking about it either. We came here to relax. Her name and this whole mess may come up tonight because Michael may ask if you've seen her. But there's no plan, Kennedy. I promise. We've been on vacation."

She turns and stares out the window. "That's relieving."

"Was the mind reader there when you met up with her?"

"The platinum blonde lady from the graduation?"

I nod as her head turns back my way.

"No. Just Indigo, her aunt, and some redhead chick who didn't talk much."

"Redhead was our kind?"

"Definitely."

Perfect. Another of our kind on Indigo's side. Who knows what she can do and how much damage she may be able to cause us should Indigo force us into battle. The unknown is the absolute worst.

"I didn't mean to put a damper on the mood."

"You didn't," I say quickly. "You're being honest. I

appreciate that. Never apologize for your truth."

She smiles and I throw one right back her way.

"So tell me about this bonfire."

I climb off the bed. "Just a bunch of aliens, sitting around a fire on a beach, drinking unmeasurable amounts of water, and talking about life. Should be nice," I say as I change out of my tank into a Michigan T-shirt Mrs. Everly was kind enough to buy me.

Kennedy chuckles softly. "And Kesia's close?"

"Yeah. They should be here…" I glance at my phone screen. "Any minute."

I had every intention of picking Kesia and her grandmother up from the bus stop, but Ms. Housley was already out in the rental picking up another guest and insisted that she bring them back with her to prevent them from waiting.

"I hope it isn't too awkward for them. You know, riding back with Ms. Housley when they've never met her," I say.

"Ms. Housley's super nice. Why would it be awkward?"

I shrug. "They're strangers."

Kennedy chuckles, shakes her head. "That can't be something they're worried about. They did agree to come here, so obviously, like us, they're seeking friendships with more of our kind. Maybe looking to not feel so alone in a world of humans."

"Maybe."

Together, we head downstairs and out the front door. Though the bonfire is being set up out back on the shore, I want to be the first to greet Kesia upon her arrival to the house. I want her to see a familiar face. Sure, I'm still a stranger in many ways, but she's met Kennedy and me face to face. That should offer some immediate comfort.

Kennedy and I step out onto the curved driveway as the black rental pulls up. I smile. *Impeccable timing.*

All four doors open. Ms. Housley steps out from behind

the wheel. Ms. Ava, Ms. Housley's friend who arrived the same evening we did, exits from the driver-side rear door. While we met days ago, she's less talkative than Ms. Reed, Ms. Housley, and Mrs. Everly so I don't know much about her except that she has a daughter. Kesia steps out from the rear passenger door. Immediately, she waves as we head her way. Stepping out behind Kesia is another young woman, her chestnut-brown hair tied high into a messy bun. Her toned frame and shirt that reads, "Keep Calm and Dive On," let me know that she must be Lark, Ms. Ava's daughter, the competitive swimmer and diver. Still seated in the passenger seat is Kesia's grandmother. Large sunglasses cover her eyes. The Kaba dress she's wearing is detailed in earthy colors; dark orange, deep-brown, tree-green. Her short, black natural hair is separated into twists that almost look like curls. On her feet are brown strappy sandals.

As Kesia helps her grandmother step out of the truck, I smile and say, "I'm glad you guys made it safely. How was the ride?"

"I don't remember," her grandmother answers, her accent even stronger than Kesia's. "I slept through most of it."

We all release short laughs.

"I'm Jaylen," I say, my hand extended.

"We're not doing business. We can hug. It's fair to say that, in many ways, we're family, right?"

My eyes move to Kesia as she taps her cheek letting me know that my welcome doesn't need to be formal, but warm.

I smile at her grandmother. We kiss each other's cheeks and as we hug, I thank her for coming.

"Thank you for the invitation. I'm happy to extend my trip in such a beautiful place." Her accent is so strong, I have to really focus to fully make out what she's saying.

Kennedy moves in to greet Kesia's grandmother as Kesia and I hug.

"Thanks for the invitation, Jaylen. This place is amazing," Kesia says jovially.

"You'll have to thank Mrs. Everly. This is her home and she's the one who allowed us all to invite guests."

"Please point her out to me. I want her to know I appreciate her kindness even though we weren't the friends you originally invited."

That's right. I did lie to get them to come. I told her my other friends couldn't make it and she didn't want me to waste the tickets or my money.

"Regardless, we wanted you here. We're all happy you both could come," I tell her before leaning in to whisper, "What should we call your grandmother?"

"Eden," she answers in her talking voice.

"Yes," her grandmother says. "Call me Eden."

"Ms. Eden," I say, as my mom would never allow me to call an elder by their first name in such a way.

Kesia and Kennedy greet one another like old friends, hugging and expressing how great it is to see one another again though they've only met once before. I look over at Lark, instantly realizing it seems as though we're only happy to see Kesia and Ms. Eden.

I hold my hand out for hers. "Hi. You must be Lark."

She nods while shaking my hand. "Nice to meet you, Jaylen"

Ms. Housley walks over to me, wraps an arm around me. "Where are the others?"

"Setting up, I think. They're all out by the water."

"We should head back there, too, then. Leave the bags," Ms. Housley says. "The boys can come unload the truck later." She reaches out and grabs Ms. Eden's hands. "There are a lot of steps that lead down to the shore. I don't know if…"

"I'll be fine," Ms. Eden interrupts. "Might take me a while to get back up them, but I can walk without a problem or assistance. I'm well-rested and my legs work just fine. No special accommodations please, dear. Don't follow Kesia's lead. She always wants to do something for me. I always say, old and handicapped are two different things. I'm old, but I'm not handicapped."

"Do you want to change? Do you need anything before we head down?"

Ms. Eden smiles at Ms. Housley. "You're not listening to me. You're following Kesia's lead. I don't need anything at all. Please, don't worry about me."

We all smile. I hope I have the same spirit and life in me at that age. I also hope Ms. Eden can share more about our kind, fill in some of the blanks for me that no one else has been able to.

We walk through Ms. Everly's home, through her family room, through the sunroom, and then out back. Ms. Eden, Kesia, and Lark take in the view the rest of us have already been stunned by.

"This is paradise," Ms. Eden says. "This is what we all work our hardest for and only a small percentage of us actually get." She touches Kesia's cheek. "You can have this. You're a smart girl, you're determined, and you're hardworking. This is what I want for you."

"I'll make sure to have a room added just for you. If I can afford something like this one day, you are ..."

"When," Ms. Eden states firmly, cutting Kesia off mid-sentence. "When. You have to speak it into existence. No doubts. This will be your life."

"When," Kesia repeats. "When I can afford something like this, you are going to be living with me and enjoying the luxuries as well. You've done everything for me. I cannot wait to repay you."

They share a kiss and my mind goes to my mom. This is a conversation I would've had with her. I could see myself planning my mom's future out for her, placing her in a guest room in my house so that we'd always be close, never losing touch. Just as Kesia feels about her grandmother, if my mom were still alive, I'd want to repay her, too. Great parenting, whether from a human or not, should never go unappreciated. While my mom never made me feel as though I owed her, I'd still want to do any and everything to show my love and gratitude if she were still here, especially since she didn't birth me. She chose me.

We all start down the forty-stair flight toward Ms. Reed and Mrs. Everly who are already seated, and the boys who are having way too much fun getting the fire started. While Kennedy and I were talking and changing, the boys were out here setting up the wood for the fire, placing water bottles in the coolers, and setting up chairs and blankets. *Damn, we were no help.*

Ms. Reed and Mrs. Everly stand as we all head down toward them. Kennedy and I reach the sand first.

"Remind me of their names again, sweetie," Mrs. Everly says.

"Kesia. And her grandmother's name is Eden. Ms. Ava's daughter's name is Lark," I tell her.

"Got it," she says softly.

Mrs. Everly waits at the bottom of the stairs, a smile covering her face as she watches them step down carefully.

Ms. Reed steps closer to the boys and snaps her fingers once. "Hey! Leave the fire alone before one of you gets burned. It's lit. Let it be. And Jackson," she points. "Respect your elders. Don't use your ability on Kesia's grandmother."

Jackson nods.

Michael walks over to stand in between Kennedy and me, puts one arm around each of us, and pulls us close to him. In a whisper he says, "Your lazy asses didn't help us with anything."

I smile. One, because we did unintentionally get out of having to help set up. Two, because he's not treating Kennedy like an outsider. He's still on the fence about how he feels about her, but I'm glad he's not allowing her to sense his distrust. No one would want to travel this far to be made to feel like the odd ball out.

"We'll help clean up," Kennedy offers.

"What?" I ask, looking over at her. "Speak for yourself."

The three of us laugh. Michael keeps his arms around both of us as we patiently wait for everyone to get down to the sand.

I stand on my tippy toes and lean in closer to Michael. "Watch your mouth. No cursing."

"Yes, mom."

I nudge him. "I'm serious."

Kennedy clears her throat. "You need to watch your mouth, too, missy. I've heard you drop quite a few bombs."

"Yup." Michael nods. "Let her know, Kennedy. She ain't innocent. Her mouth is worse than mine."

I chuckle and shake my head at their attempt to double team me. I know I have a potty mouth, but unlike Michael, I can easily filter what I say in front of people. Michael's mouth runs several speeds ahead of his brain, which leads to him saying all sorts of things around the wrong people, which later require him to apologize.

The moment Kesia and Ms. Eden's feet hit the sand, Mrs. Everly and Ms. Reed greet them warmly. Hugs and names are exchanged, and then the boys walk over to welcome the last of the guests to arrive.

Michael interlocks his arm around Ms. Eden's and escorts her to one of the striped chairs. Ms. Reed, Ms. Housley, Mrs. Everly, and Ms. Ava all take seats on the colorful, striped chairs as well. Kennedy, Kesia, Lark, Jackson, Ethan, Michael, and me all sit on the blankets. The fire burns as we sit surrounding it. Ethan, the closest to the cooler, passes bottles of water around the circle, and immediately, we all take some down.

"I just want to thank all of you for flying in, or riding all this way to be here. Regardless of how we all met or how long we've all known each other, we're connected in a way humans will never understand. I'm glad so many of us could come together. You are all welcome to anything in my home," Mrs.

Everly says. "I hope this vacation is one we'll all enjoy and forever remember."

Smiles come alive on all our faces.

"Unfortunately, my husband is overwhelmed with work and likely won't be in until later tonight, but hopefully you'll all get to meet him tomorrow morning. Well, Kesia, Eden, and Lark. The rest of you have gotten to meet him and see glimpses of him on his way in or out. He's a busy man."

"What does he do, if you don't mind my asking?" Ms. Eden asks, her strong accent forcing me to listen for key words to understand her quickly asked question.

"Cosmetic surgery. He has his own practice, but is in the process of renovating and expanding to keep up with his clients. The expansion is what's keeping him away. He's recently seen an increase in out-of-state clients as his rates are better so he's trying to keep up."

Ms. Eden nods, her large sunglasses still covering her eyes. "This is a great example of how hard work pays off. I'm glad my granddaughter gets to see this."

"I'm glad all of you get to see this," Ms. Reed says, her eyes scanning all of us sitting on the blankets. The younger generation.

"It's inspiring. That's for sure," I say. "I was telling Michael that I hope my art leads to this kind of lifestyle."

"It will," Ms. Eden says confidently. "You all must say *it will*. I always say to Kesia that she must speak her dreams into existence. Say that it will happen and it will."

I nod. "I'll practice saying *it will* and *I will* as opposed to just making wishes or saying *I want*."

"Do you plan to attend art school here or travel abroad to study?" Ms. Eden asks.

"I got into Princeton University," I answer.

"That's where we met. Remember? I told you I bumped into Ques unexpectedly at the art museum," Kesia says, her eyes on her grandmother.

That word again. Okay, I'm done guessing. What the hell is a Que? Nobody here is wearing purple. There's no way she's referencing the fraternity as me and Kennedy initially assumed.

"Kesia, I have to ask. You keep calling us Ques and we're just not sure what that means," I say.

Kesia immediately throws her grandmother a glance filled with astonishment, and then turns back to me. My eyes move to Ms. Eden, but there's no reading her eyes behind those glasses, so I look back over at Kesia.

"What do you mean you don't know what I mean? We're called Ques. Well, Quisis, but we call ourselves Ques for short."

"Key-sees," I repeat.

"Yes. Q-U-I-S-I-S," Kesia spells out. "You've never heard that name before?"

I shake my head. Perplexity is written on the faces of the others. As I had hoped for, we're receiving somewhat of an education.

"What do you call yourselves?" Ms. Eden asks.

"Aliens," Jackson answers. "Or we'll just group ourselves together by saying things like *our kind*."

"Well that explains the confusion. At the art museum, I thought you all were being discrete because of Kennedy."

"Kennedy is one of us," I say.

"I realize that now. There's no way a bunch of Ques would risk being exposed to humankind by talking so openly about themselves with a human present. Not even in a setting as private as this."

"You're the lucky one, dear," Ms. Eden tells Kennedy. "The rest of us have to watch out for animals, even the common ones. We never know if an animal is going to run from us or for us. You have quite the gift."

I nod as I know firsthand how difficult it can be to live on a planet with wildlife that either fears you or hates you. I know how scary it can be to do something as simple as walk to the mailbox, only to have the friendly neighborhood dog pick up on your presence, and nearly break its chain in an attempt to rip your neck out. Ms. Eden put it lightly. Kennedy is more than lucky to not have a presence that can be felt. I wouldn't need my strength if I had that beautiful gift.

"Are there a lot of Ques in Cameroon?" Lark asks.

Kesia shakes her head. "Not tons. We do have our family there. We sometimes meet students who are studying abroad. I have met a couple that way. We don't outnumber the humans if that's what you're asking."

"Have you ever dealt with a human suspecting that you're different, or maybe even seeing you use whatever abilities you may have?" Lark questions, her head cocked to the side in curiosity.

"Most of the weird looks are given to my grandmother," Kesia answers. "She gets stared at quite a bit, unless she's around people who are familiar with her."

We all remain silent. I'm sure everyone wants to ask why, but no one wants to be offensive.

Kesia turns to her grandmother. Silently, Ms. Eden slowly pulls her glasses from her face. She hands her fashionable shades to her granddaughter before looking around the circle at all of us, finally revealing her eyes to the group.

No wonder she gets stared at. Her gray, almost silver, wide-set eyes are naturally very thin. While spaced far apart, the inner corners look pinched together, and slant downward. They're shaped very much like what alien eyes are thought to look like, only they aren't wide with missing pupils.

I speak first. "Your eyes are definitely attention-grabbing. I can see why someone would take a second look. Not just because of the color, but the shape as well. They're very beautiful. Beautifully unique."

"Thank you, my dear, but even I must admit, I look a bit..." She searches for a word. "Odd," she says.

"Odd is a good thing," Kesia tells her. "She reminds me

of a special kind of feline," Kesia says, her eyes briefly looking at each of us surrounding the small fire.

"I agree," Mrs. Everly states. "Odd is a good thing. I think they look beautiful."

Ms. Eden smiles. I try not to stare, but she owns quite the captivating pair of eyes. I look around the circle at the struggle we're all sharing. They make you want to look just a little longer, but staring causes discomfort, is considered rude, and none of us want Ms. Eden to feel that way.

"So, Ms. Eden, is there anything you can share with us about Quisis overall?" Jackson asks. "Jaylen couldn't wait for you to get here so she could learn more about our kind."

My head snaps in Jackson's direction. *Damn, dude. Let me speak for myself.* I wish I had a pause button for his damn mouth.

"You can ask me anything, Jaylen. If I know the answer, I will share it," Ms. Eden says kindly.

I roll my eyes at Jackson before making eye contact with Ms. Eden. "There's a lot I'm curious about. I haven't even known what I am for that long. Though my friends have helped me to learn more about myself than I knew before, I don't know where we're from and how we got here."

Ms. Eden chuckles. "How we got here? Humans still don't know if they began with Adam and Eve, came from apes, or if lightening played a part in their creation. I wasn't the first Quisi so I can't tell you if we flew over on a space shuttle or started at the bottom of the ocean. I can tell you for certain that I came from my mother and father just as you did."

I nod as her answer isn't just a reasonable one, but makes perfect sense. Who really can say for sure where things originated unless they were there, the first? I say *Quisis* to myself, ask my brain to tell me something since I've been relying on Kesia and her grandmother throughout this conversation. Nothing comes to mind. My brain has fallen short when I've asked about future events or about a person's next move, but when I question anything historical or documented, my brain has always been able to tell me more about it. I guess we really are an unknown species, completely undocumented and unrevealed.

"If it makes you feel better, it's been passed down that we're from Quisaldan, a planet that ran out of the water we needed to sustain us."

"I got that story," Ms. Reed says. "Never heard of Quisis or Ques or Quisaldan until just now, but it was told to me that we are on Earth because it was the only planet with enough water to keep us alive."

Ms. Eden nods. "I'm sure another Que will have a story with small differences. We're all passing along what was passed down to us. Who can really disprove any of it? Humans don't even believe in our existence, the internet has nothing about us anywhere on it, so what we don't know is left for us to fill in."

With my eyes on Ms. Eden, I say, "I would just think that something about where we come from would have to be documented somewhere, even if under a different name. I mean, we supposedly made it to Earth. That would mean Quisaldan was a pretty advanced planet, centuries ahead of Earth. Tools and technology would've been needed to learn where Earth was located and that it could sustain our kind. A lot of resources would've been required to build a craft that was big enough and reliable enough to carry our entire species over such a great distance."

"Good point," Ms. Ava says.

Ms. Eden nods. "Very good indeed, but dear, when I was born, it was here on Earth. I'm just passing on our legend the way it was passed down to me."

"I understand. I'm just sharing my thoughts. Some things keep picking at me, and naturally, I want answers."

"But, Jaylen," Ms. Eden says sweetly. "What would change if you knew exactly where our kind originated from? Would you suddenly become different? You have to keep in mind that this is a topic humans can't even agree on."

I shrug. "I probably wouldn't be any different, and I get everything you're saying, but I'm still struggling with a lot of these unanswered questions. I don't even understand why we're so sure we're aliens. We have all of these unexplainable abilities, there's no proof of an original planet that our kind originated on, and we have no science to lean on."

"But we do, dear," Ms. Eden tells me. "We may not be able to open a biology book and find something that describes our kind perfectly. We may not be able to find articles or medical journals specific to us, but that can't be where your focus lies. We don't survive on fairy dust, blood, or magic powder. We require water like any other living thing. We require rest. Those are two core things all living beings need. Reference any science journal and you'll see that. If you need a document to prove that you're an extraterrestrial, you may remain dissatisfied for the rest of your life, Jaylen. We may never be found out. You can't count on scientists to tell you every single thing that exists. Believe me, there are unknown species that have yet to be discovered. Will they be?" She throws up both hands. "Who knows? It doesn't make them any less real. Just because humans can't read about them online and haven't seen them yet, doesn't mean they aren't real. Tell me, Jaylen, are you breathing?"

"Yes," I answer.

"I don't want you to get hung up on type. We know we have a rare, undiscovered blood type and our type isn't the only rare one in the world. Kesia read up on new blood type discoveries a few years back. I'm sure ours is being studied in a lab somewhere right now. Regardless of what they find, blood indicates that we're alive. For certain, there is blood in me. Is there blood in you?"

"Yes."

"Do you require water, air, and rest?"

I nod.

"If you decide to birth a child one day, will you be capable of that natural act?"

My stomach drops causing my entire body to jerk suddenly. I answer, "Yes."

"You sound alive to me, so get rid of any ideas you may have about being a fantastical or magical creature. Now tell me, are you capable of things humans aren't?"

"Yes."

"Humans can go for hours and hours without water while they're awake. Can you?"

I shake my head. "No."

"Why?"

"I don't know, but it causes an unbearable pain."

"Exactly. According to what we've been taught, humans need water, but too much can be harmful. Have you ever suffered from water intoxication?"

"Never."

"Do you know what happens to us when we die?"

"I've learned that we dry out and shrivel up into this small, cocoon type of thing."

"Ever hear of that happening to human remains?"

"No."

"Think you're human?"

"No."

"Think you're a fairy tale, magical creature who breathes, who has blood in you, who needs water to live?"

"Not likely," I say softly.

"What's left, dear?"

My eyes look down at the sand and then find Ms. Eden's again. "Us. Aliens."

She smiles compassionately.

"But, Ms. Eden, something is still missing. I know I'm real. I know I'm alive. I know I exist. I know I'm going to forever have questions, but something has to fuel us. Though we need more, water is keeping us alive the way it does every other living thing, but something has to give us energy. I barely eat, but I grow and I move around without feeling weak. Where's that energy coming from? What keeps me so strong?"

"The sun." Kesia answers.

Great. Now we're alien plants.

"Drinking water all day isn't enough to give us full use of our abilities. We'll still be able to use them, but we require sun exposure for strength and energy. I know firsthand how important the sun is to the use of my ability. I can use it longer and it feels more effortless. Understand, I'm not speaking about extreme heat. We live in Cameroon." Kesia fans herself with her hand. "Those 105 degree days feel exhausting and draining, but comfortable warm days allow me to use my ability for quite a while, without exhausting too fast, and without requiring immediate rest."

"We're plants," Kennedy says playfully.

I remain quiet as the others laugh at Kennedy's comment.

"Still not satisfied?" Ms. Eden asks, her distinctive eyes on me.

"I've learned something new and I'm really happy about that. You're right. No one who wasn't there, the first, will be able to give exact details about our beginning. Still, I'm thankful to know more about myself. About us. That's satisfying." I smile sincerely. "Thank you, Ms. Eden. And thank you, Kesia."

I turn to Michael, smile at the hot Quisi sitting next to me, then to Kennedy. I smile at her too, at someone I feel close to and whose company I really enjoy. I then look around at the others. The other Quisis. I like having a name. It gives our kind more of an identity, makes me feel a part of something. Something solid. A group. Not a bunch of scattered, confused individuals. We're Ques. We're not a fraternity. We're not a club. We're a species, an alien race. Animals may be a great threat to us, but one thing we have over humans is our abilities. We have gifts humans wish for, dream about, and have to enjoy on TV. But those gifts are our realities. We can use them whenever we choose.

"Jaylen," Ms. Ava calls out. "You mentioned you haven't known what you are for very long. Who told you?"

"When I transferred to Trinity high after the passing of my adoptive mom, I met Indigo and Michael. Michael was the one to really give me information. Indigo was very secretive, though she dropped hints. And then I met Kennedy. She gave me more information. Between the three of them, I learned a lot."

"Sorry to hear about your mom."

"Thank you, Ms. Ava."

"Are you still in touch with Indigo? Does she have others of our kind that she's friends with, or is she pretty much on her own?"

"Indigo is the problem," Ms. Housley explains to her friend. "She's the one Michelle was talking about. The one who caused all of the prom night drama."

"Right," Ms. Ava says dragging out the word slowly, clearly remembering a conversation they had.

"To answer your question, I'm not in contact with her at all anymore," I say.

"Is it okay to ask what happened on prom night?" Kesia asks.

Kennedy, Michael, and I all exchange brief glances. Neither of them seems eager to speak up. Likely because the topic is such an uncomfortable, angering one. Kennedy feels stuck in the middle and still has emotions tied to her ex. Michael is hurt, scared, and can easily begin boiling when the topic is being discussed.

"I guess I'll give you guys a quick rundown," I say before clearing my throat and taking two large gulps of water. "I transferred to Trinity High back in January. Right away in homeroom, I met Indigo. Skip ahead a few hours, Indigo is at my house for a study date. We were talking and out of nowhere, she tried to kiss me."

"Tried?" Ethan asks.

"Tried," I repeat, throwing him a quick side-eye. "I backed away." *From that kiss at least.*

Ethan chuckles. "Just trying to get all the facts. Please proceed."

Another side-eye. "Moving on," I say.

The group listens attentively as I talk about my friendship with Indigo, as I detail the buck attack Indigo didn't help me survive, as I share how Indigo purposely excluded Michael from my birthday guest list. I talk about how Michael could feel an unknown presence in his house, but neither of us were aware of Indigo's ability at the time. I give factual details that show how controlling Indigo can be. I talk about prom night, about how she wrote down my vehicle identification number so she could report my car stolen.

"She also ripped your tag off," Kennedy adds.

"Right," I say. "Which is why an officer pulled up behind my car while we were pulled over."

"Pulled over doing what?" Jackson asks.

Michael turns to him. "Waiting for her foster mother to call her back." His tone is serious, far from the playful voice Jackson asked the question with.

"Anyway," I continue. "We found out the car was reported stolen, dealt with the cops for a while, and then Ms. Ward, my foster mother, came to the scene to prove ownership and legal guardianship. After we left the scene, Michael was irate. I stupidly pulled over again, hoping to calm him down, and long story short, we got attacked by a bear. Everything that happened left Michael weak, so I left him to go get water from the car. I guess I didn't realize how exhausted my body was because I ended up falling and unable walk. Who shows up? Indigo."

"And me," Kennedy says, slightly raising her hand. "I didn't have anything to do with the tag or the call, but I was with Indigo most of that night, essentially following them because she said she was so worried about Jaylen."

I rub Kennedy's back. "No one's blaming you," I say softly. Louder, I continue telling the story to the rest of the group. "Indigo gave me water. I sent her down to Michael to give him the rest of the water. She walked down to where I had left him and poured it out."

"Poured it out?" Kesia asks in complete shock, her face scrunched in disgust.

"Poured it out," Michael repeats for her. "I had used my abilities that night and I took a hit from the bear, so I was weak. My body was done. If Moms hadn't gotten to me, I wouldn't be here."

The others shake their heads in disbelief. It's hard to believe someone could be so callus, could let their anger lead them to make such a despicable decision.

"She's unstable. Emotionally unstable," Ms. Eden states.

"Sounds like fatal attraction to me," Lark says.

"Indigo is a lot of things," I tell them. "She's controlling. Definitely has an obsessive personality. She's selfish, but in all fairness, we all can be. We all make stupid mistakes. Maybe ones that aren't as big as the one she made, but Michael is still here. I thought she'd want forgiveness and to move on, but she wants to drag this out. It's almost like she wants us to hurt her. I tried to make peace with her, even asked her people to join us in putting this behind us. Instead of non-violence and forward movement, she attacked Ethan out of nowhere."

Ms. Eden holds her hand out, leans forward in her seat. "Listen to me."

Nobody speaks.

"She's not well. From the beginning, it sounds as though she's been unpredictable and in a rush. Who would attempt to kiss a person they've only known for a few hours? And we're talking about another girl. How did she know Jaylen would even be open to exploring another female? Listen," she says again. "If you all were speaking about a man, you would call him aggressive, a stalker, and instead of controlling, you all would be calling him abusive. I don't give passes because of gender. She's dangerous. That's it."

I look at Kennedy. Her eyes are on her hands.

"I feel terrible for you," Ms. Eden says to Michael. "You can't prove that she was in your home. Pouring water out isn't a crime according to humans. So what do you do? What can you do?"

All of us sit with that question nagging at us. None of us are experts in plotting. None of us have killed before. None of us know what to do.

"I'll tell you," Ms. Eden continues. "I'm no advocate for violence. I would never want to see an innocent person harmed, but this person isn't innocent. She can't be trusted. Unfortunately, you have no one you can run to except those who are here. What do you do? You protect yourself. You have every right to protect your home and your life."

We all sit quietly. I look across at Ms. Reed. Her eyes are on her son. His are on Ms. Eden. I turn to Kennedy. Her eyes are still on her hands.

"Just my thoughts. I don't want to give you poor advice." She looks over at Ms. Reed. "I don't want to advise another woman's son to do something she's against."

"I'm against my son getting hurt." Ms. Reed says. "I don't want to hurt Indigo. She's a child, for goodness sake, but I would hurt her without a thought before I stand by and let her hurt anyone here."

"I am so sorry to hear you all are dealing with something so horrible. I'm sure the constant worry and the thought of having to hurt someone when that's not something you stand for has to be hard," Kesia says, holding out her trembling hand. "Look at me. I've been shaking since you told me she poured your water out. That means she saw you in pain and didn't care. I can't begin to understand a person like that. That's heartless. I'm with my grandmother. Protect yourself, your life, and your home. That includes family. She's dangerous."

We all become silent again and my eyes can't leave Kennedy. I know that a piece of her heart still lies with Indigo, and in the end, she doesn't want her touched. Kennedy wants a safe, happy ending to be on the last page of this frustrating, complicated chapter. That's what we all want. Well, all of us except Indigo. For whatever reason, and I'm still not sure who Indigo wants to hurt more, she wants to fight this out. A killer, I'm not, but I'm not a fool either. I'm not going to foolishly fail to protect myself or my loved ones just because Indigo was once a friend. I don't want to live the rest of my life knowing I had to cut someone else's short, but I may have no choice but to do just that. Not wanting to kill her doesn't mean I won't have to. Kennedy knows Indigo is the one forcing our hands, but that doesn't make this conversation an easy one for her to listen to. For Kennedy's sake, as I can tell by looking at her that this discussion is eating her alive, I think a subject change is needed. I once complained about this conversation being constantly put off, but right now isn't the time for it to be had.

I reach over and grab Kennedy's hand. I hold on to it. "Maybe we should talk about something else. We're in Michigan, far away from Indigo. We will need to revisit this topic, but for now, let's enjoy this. We've all made new friends. We've all got stories. Let's do the whole campfire thing, even though we won't be camping out here. Let's get to know each other on a more positive note. Just the thought of what may have to be done sucks the happiness right out of me. All of us, actually. The smiles go. The laughter dies," I say. "I want to laugh. I want to know about Cameroon, Lark's diving, everything. I'm sorry if I'm out of line. I'm not trying to shut everyone up. I just want the sad faces to become smiling ones again," I say, squeezing Kennedy's hand.

"I like that idea. Let's talk about good times," Ms. Eden says. "Sounds like you all have been through enough. An evening off is necessary."

"Tell us about your diving, Lark," Kesia says.

Lark beams before speaking. "I'm a total water girl. I love to swim. I love to dive. I love giving lessons to children. If I could spend all of my time in the water, I would."

"Feels like you do," her mother says.

She giggles. "My mom thinks I use swim as an excuse to get out of spending time with her. I don't. It went from being my hobby, to my sport of choice, to my job."

"You compete?" Kennedy asks her.

She nods. "Definitely. Throughout high school, I was on the swim team. I also competed in diving competitions in different cities. I've won almost every competition I've entered. I've won scholarships."

Kennedy's eyes light up. "You must be really good. Did you get a full ride?"

"She is," Ms. Ava states. "She's amazing."

"Thanks, mom. And to answer your question, Kennedy, college is completely covered."

"Congratulations!" Ms. Eden says, clapping a few times. "I'm happy to hear that."

Lark reveals a winning, pageant-like smile revealing her beautiful teeth. "Thank you. It feels amazing to know that once I graduate, I won't have a ton of student loan debt weighing me down. But since I'm around other gifted aliens—I mean Quisis," she corrects quickly. "I guess I can share my special little secret with you all."

All eyes are on Lark. All of us wait to learn something else new.

"I can breathe under water," she reveals. "My competitors have breathing to consider and must learn deep-breath holds, but those aren't concerns of mine."

My mouth falls open.

"This sucks. This really sucks," Jackson says, forcing laughs out of nearly everybody. "I'm grateful for my ability, but it's lame next to everybody else's."

"What can you do?" Larks asks.

"I can hold people wherever I want them as long as I can lay my eyes on them. It's kind of like hitting the pause button. I can freeze a person in place."

"You're crazy," Lark tells him. "There's nothing lame about that."

"Feels lame next to a person who has telekinesis, one who's a speed racer, one who's a genius with hulk-like strength, and another whose presence can't be felt. Oh yeah, I can't forget about you. You're a mermaid."

We all laugh at Jackson's whining.

"You have a special ability, Jackson," I say. "There's no need to compare. There are so many ways to use what you have. For example, if an animal comes at you, just pause it and back away to safety. Most of us have to make contact. Well, not Ethan and Michael. Ethan can run and Michael could mentally toss it or something. My point is, you have something useful, brat."

He chuckles. "I know. I'm just a little jealous. Let me deal with my emotions, Jaylen."

I touch Kennedy's back, softly ask her, "Feeling okay?"

She nods with a smile and then says, "I'm good."

"What about you, Kesia?" Jackson asks. "Anything you want to share? Any special talents?"

"I can fly," she says without hesitation.

"No way," Kennedy says, completely floored.

Jackson shakes his head, his mouth wide open in awe.

"Kesia, are you serious?" I ask.

She shakes her head. "No. I wish."

We all release short laughs. The present energy is so positive. The sharing, the smiles, the laughs kind of make me wish this day wouldn't end.

"I have a mental ability as well," Kesia says. "Not joking this time."

"What kind?" Jackson asks.

"Tell me, Jackson. What's something you absolutely wouldn't do right now? Something random. It doesn't have to be serious."

Jackson tilts his head, looks up, tries to think of something random he'd refuse to do at this moment.

"Anything," Kesia tells him.

"I don't know. There's a lot I wouldn't do right now. I wouldn't curse in front of my mom. I wouldn't jump into the lake. I wouldn't break out in a random dance." He points. "I wouldn't sit on that fire."

"Okay," Kesia says.

She keeps her eyes on Jackson. He remains quiet but slowly rises to his feet. We all watch him intently. With happiness covering his face, he stands tall, turns his feet out in a perfect first position.

"Record this," I whisper to Michael.

With his phone out and on Jackson, Michael records him doing a series of plies. We laugh hysterically as he moves into fifth position and completes several, sloppy pique turns. His toes are pointed, his hands are far from graceful, and his many attempts are pure comedy to the rest of us. His smile, which hasn't left his face since he originally stood up, makes him look like even more of a goofy, uncoordinated buffoon.

Four sloppy turns later, he bows. We all continue to laugh. Finally, Kesia cracks up as well, breaking her gaze, forcing Jackson's smile to instantly fade.

"What?" Jackson questions. "Why all the laughing?"

"What do you mean, what?" his mother asks. "You gave us a little show."

"Show?"

Michael turns the phone around, showing Jackson the video he just took. A video of him performing an unexpected ballet routine for us.

As he watches himself, he finger-combs his hair back, shakes his head, softly questions when he did this, and then laughs. He can't help but to give in to how ridiculous he looks.

"That just happened," Kesia tells him. "I didn't hurt you, though I could've made you hurt yourself. I just took control of your mind for a minute. You said you wouldn't do a random dance. Looks like you did."

"Now that's an ability," Ms. Reed says. "I wish I had that for the past four years. I would've made my son love doing homework."

We all laugh. With one huge thing in common amongst all of us, we enjoy our closeness and continue to share about ourselves. Never have I been so eager to talk about myself and my personal business with strangers, but amongst so many of my own, so many who consider me either family or a friend, I share about my strength, my intelligence, my past animal attacks, and oddly enough for me, share the mystery surrounding the death of my biological mother with people I just met. I listen to their stories, laugh at their jokes, ask questions. I open up and watch those around me do the same. We sit for hours, never revisiting the subject of Indigo, never going back to the unpleasant subject of self-protection and murder.

Chapter 12

I do a slow twirl, giving the girls an all-around view of my royal-blue, strapless, maxi dress.

"You look so nice," Lark compliments. "The curls are perfect with that dress. So summery. Perfect for a beach date."

"Thank you," I say, looking myself over in the mirror. "I owe you for helping me curl my hair."

"That's what your girls are for. I hate curling the back of my own hair, too. Just return the favor whenever I get asked on a date."

"Consider it curled," I say as I spray my wrists with perfume.

Kesia pats an empty space on the bed. "Come. Sit for a second before you go."

I put my perfume back in my suitcase before climbing onto the bed. "What's up?"

Kennedy scoots over, making room for Lark to sit as well, and just like last night after the bonfire, the four of us sit together, on this bed, ready for girl talk.

"Talk to me," I say.

Kesia's lowered head immediately brings concern to all of our faces.

Kennedy reaches over and touches Kesia's shoulder. "What's wrong?"

"Last night was so much fun, so different from my typical evenings. I don't mean the bonfire. I mean the four of us sitting for hours, talking through the night about life, love, feelings, fears, everything. I love my family, but once I go back home, I won't have you guys. I feel as though we became instant friends and I really like the way that feels. I never expected to meet so many Ques. Now I don't like the idea of having to leave you guys."

"Aww, Kesia." I lean in and give her a hug.

"Really, I feel so close to you. Not just because of instincts, but because you are all such kind souls." She looks me in the eye. "I know you mentioned last night that you're not a believer, but I feel so blessed to have met you. All of you. I want us to stay in touch and make plans to come together at least once a year. I know it'll be harder for me because I live on another continent, but it's something I'd like us to do. I'd like to see these friendships grow."

"I'd like that, too. Wish we could see each other more than that, but none of us are neighbors," Lark says.

"We'll make it happen," I say surely. "And when we can't travel to see one another, we'll video chat, call, even write if we have to, but we're not losing touch. I've had friends, but I've never had friends like you guys. Girls who I can be completely naked with. And by naked, I mean, I can expose everything about myself. My abilities, my non-human qualities, my fears. Last night when we talked, I didn't worry about how things would be taken by you guys. I just spoke freely, knowing I'd be understood."

"Geez, now you guys are making me sad about the fact that we'll be going our separate ways soon. I haven't been thinking about it since I've only been here a day," Kennedy says. "But now that it's been brought up, it does suck. We haven't all known each other that long, but it does feel like last night we began building a sisterhood."

"Sisterhood." I nod. "I like that."

"I do, too. Sisters," Kesia says. "I would like us to be able to support each other, confide in each other, and love one another. Let's not be the stereotypical girls of our generation. We're Quisis, but we're a lot like humans emotionally. Let's not get jealous of one another, put each other down, or backstab."

"I'm with that," I say, my mind suddenly thinking of Indigo, of how I thought we could bond in this way. Sadly, we couldn't. At least, not for an extended period of time. Her feelings often got in the way, which affected our friendship in the worst way.

"So, we all promise to keep in touch?" Lark asks.

"Promise," I say.

Kesia smiles. "Promise."

Kennedy nods. "I promise," she says, her smile stretched wide.

"Me too," Lark promises last.

We chat for a few more minutes before I double check my dress and hair in the mirror, give myself a final spritz of perfume, and head out in the vehicle Mrs. Everly is letting me borrow to meet Michael twenty minutes away at Oval Beach. I drive carefully, closely following the GPS's directions. I'm so pumped to spend alone time with Michael, away from everyone we know, in a place neither of us has been. There's something so romantic about the beach. Something so dreamy and movie-like about being with your significant other in that setting. I can't wait to write our names in the sand, to walk the shoreline hand in hand with him, to share kisses.

Twenty-two minutes later, I arrive and park in what looks to be the last available space on this side of the parking lot. I search for the rental Michael drove in as I step out of Mrs. Everly's vehicle. I spot it, parked several cars away from me. Because the silver sun shade is covering the windshield, I know he's not in it. Must already be on the beach laying out a blanket or something. I knew when he asked me to give him a head start that he was hoping to make this special for me. I can tell he wants me to walk into whatever he has planned as opposed to me helping him set up. This afternoon is for me and knowing that tickles me, makes me feel like I have the sweetest boyfriend ever. Makes me feel like the luckiest girl ever.

My feet sink into the warmth of the sand as I slowly step, occasionally on my dress, toward the shoreline. My curls blow freely in the summer breeze. My instincts come alive as I feel Michael's presence, though I haven't spotted where he is just yet. Families pass me on their way to the parking lot and I smile pleasantly and greet them as their faces reveal nothing but the joy they experienced at Oval Beach. Still, I haven't laid eyes on Michael, but with my every step, his presence grows stronger. For sure, I don't have to walk too far down the beach. He feels close by.

The sound of children's laughter fills the air, blankets cover the sand, and families and friends are gathered closely together enjoying each other's company, digging in the sand, munching on snacks, and sharing earfuls with each other.

I stand for a brief moment taking in the sight. So many strangers gathered. No one person here knows where we're all from, what we do for a living, if we're generally happy or not. Whatever is happening in all of our lives doesn't matter at this moment. For some reason, on this particular day, we all ended up in the same place at the same time, and after a quick scan, it doesn't appear as though anyone is having a lousy time. We're all sharing Oval Beach, and its atmosphere and natural surroundings have allowed everyone here to find happiness and an escape.

I grab my dress to avoid stepping on it anymore, and before taking my next step, I look around for my boyfriend. He's definitely right around here. I can feel him, and undoubtedly, he feels me too. Under a blue umbrella, I spot him sitting shirtless, next to a red cooler and a two-handle picnic basket, his legs stretched out in front of him. His eyes are on me and I return the smile he's sending my way.

I head over, apologizing to a family I have to step around to get to the blanket Michael is lounging on.

He stands. "You look beautiful."

I thank him after he pecks my lips.

"You didn't get lost did you?"

I shake my head as we both sit on the blanket. "No. Just got caught up in conversation with the girls before leaving."

"Everything okay?"

"Yeah. Kesia just needed to talk. She was feeling a little down."

"Because you were coming here?"

"No, because she has to leave for Cameroon soon. She's sad that she's leaving us. We've all bonded already. Last night, the four of us girls sat up for hours talking about our lives. We got to learn so much about each other. It was nice. I really like all of them. I feel just like Kesia does. Like I've met girls I want to grow deeper friendships with, but we're all about to go our separate ways."

"You guys just have to keep in touch."

"We all promised to."

"Good. I'm happy for you."

"Happy for me?"

He nods. "Yeah. You went for years not having others of our kind around you. Now, you know plenty. You've met some cool girls you can keep in touch with who will be able to understand you in a way your other friends can't. I'm happy you have that. We all need friends, but when it comes to us, we need more than that. We need friends we can really be ourselves with. Other Quisis."

"It's kind of nice to finally have something to call ourselves, huh?"

"Hell yeah. It changes things a little bit. It makes me feel like..." He shakes his head. "I don't know. It just feels different to have a species name."

"I know what you're trying to say. We have a name now. It makes you feel like we're a part of something real. A real group. A real species. A species with an identity."

With a slow nod, he agrees. "Exactly."

"How do you like Ms. Eden?" I ask.

"I feel bad because I find myself staring at her a lot, but I like her. She's cool as hell. She's real with it. She speaks the truth."

"How do you feel about what she said to you last night? You know, about Indigo?"

"I agree with her," he answers right away. "No doubt, I have the right to protect myself. She was coming into my house, stalking me. If she wasn't playing ghost games and I had seen her, I could've hurt her and no cop would've arrested me for protecting my home and life from an intruder."

I don't respond. I sit silently with my eyes out on Lake Michigan.

"But last night I stayed up for a while thinking."

I ask, "About what?"

"About being here. About life. About Indigo."

"And?"

"I don't want to have anything else to do with her. I don't want to make this situation worse. I just want it to end."

I make eye contact with my boyfriend. I read the sincerity in his forest-green eyes.

"I love being here. Not because it's Michigan and Jackson's house is so luxurious. I love it here because of the distance it puts between us and Indigo. She could be sneaking around my house right now, but we're here. I'm not worried about Moms, you, or myself. Here I can think about whatever I feel like. I can relax. I'm free of her bullshit."

"You didn't feel that way in Jersey with me?"

"I loved being with you, but I was uncomfortable. Not because of you or your house. I was worried that maybe you had mentioned to her that you lived on Elm Street or she had researched the accident and found out what area you grew up in. Indigo is crazy. I can't let myself get too comfortable when I don't know what she's planning. I already know what she's capable of."

I continue to watch him as he speaks. Every word, every worry, every feeling of his, I can relate to.

"I don't wanna hurt her, though. I did before, but I can't get into that with her now. I've got things in the works. I wanna focus on moving forward. Not on Indigo. I'm planning my future. Our future."

I nod. "Me too."

"I needed this separation, this time away from Virginia."

"We all needed this. Your mom knew what she was doing when she planned this."

"Moms always knows what to do for me."

I chuckle. "Such a mama's boy."

I shrug. "I'm not even gonna deny it. I am. I love my mama."

We both laugh.

"Water?" he asks.

"Please."

He lifts the top on the cooler and pulls out a cold bottle for me.

"This is such a cute little setup you have here," I say, taking the bottle. "Where'd you find a picnic basket?"

"Mrs. Everly had one. I told her I wanted to spend the day at the beach with you. She told me that girls love picnics and that it would really add to the romance."

Maybe for a girl who eats. Seeing that cooler was enough for me. Michael, the beach, cold water. That's all I need. Still a cute idea, though. It's touching to know that our relationship is supported.

"It's very cute. Very storybook," I say.

"I know you don't care about the basket. You don't care

171

about food. I only brought it because she was so happy to add feminine touches to this date."

"It's cute," I repeat. "What's in it?"

"Beef jerky, my sunflower seeds, a plastic cup for me to spit the shells into."

"So in other words, the basket is for you."

He chuckles. "You don't eat, woman."

I chuckle as well before taking a few large swallows of water.

"How's Kennedy doing?" he asks, his voice suddenly filled with concern. "Last night, Ms. Eden was speaking the truth, but I know it was getting to her."

"It was. I could tell, too. That's why I changed the subject. But, she's okay. She laughed throughout the night while we were having girl talk. She didn't slip into a funk and just stay there. She's fine."

"Do you think she's talking to Indigo?"

"She saw her," I reveal. "She told me that she met up with Indigo when she left my house and went back home."

"What if the mind reader was there?"

"Her name is Scarlett and she wasn't. There was another Que there, though. A redhead. I'm so glad Scarlett didn't show. Kennedy says she can't stop thinking about the situation. She thought we were here plotting to kill Indigo. If Scarlett had been there to pull that from Kennedy's mind, they may have taken the address from Kennedy's brain as well and came up here."

"That's what I don't like. That's what I want to put an end to. I wanna get rid of the *maybes*, the *may haves*, and the *I don't knows*. I want Indigo to hear from me that I'm done. I want her aunt to look me in the eye and believe I am not going to come for her psychotic niece. Being here and not having to think about it every second of the day reminded me of what normal feels like. Our lives and daily thoughts shouldn't include murder plots, even if it is in self-defense."

"I agree and I am so happy to hear you say this, Michael. I knew you'd come around. I knew you just needed time." I smile at him. An honest, relieved smile. "You just made my day."

He leans over and pecks me again on the lips. "Always happy to make your day."

"I just want to live a long, peaceful life with you. I want to have more summer vacations like this, but the unnecessary drama can go. I'm not about that life."

"That makes two of us."

We both chug down a little water with our eyes on one another.

He stops drinking before I do. "Talk about me during girl talk last night?"

I take another swallow before answering. "Definitely. They wanted to hear about us, how we met, what we've done, what you're like."

"What'd you tell them?"

"I told them how hot I thought you were when I first saw you walking into Mr. Bower's sociology class. I told them about you coming over right away after you heard about the buck attack. I told them about our first kiss by the fountain. I told them about the night of my birthday. I told them about prom."

"The night of your birthday?"

"Yup. Girls talk about the same things guys do. We just don't talk about it nonstop. They asked about my first time. I told them. I told them how you held me all night and how close I felt to you."

"Did they ask how I performed?"

I laugh. "Not like that. They asked how it felt. I told them that it felt great, but only because it was with you. Never in a million years would it have felt so perfect with someone else. I know that for sure. Even if it were another Que, it wouldn't have been like that. It needed to be you."

He reaches over and takes my hand, doesn't speak, just holds it tightly in his.

"Then I told them about prom night. About how I went with Josh because we were broken up. I told them you requested that song for me and how we danced. Kesia and Lark couldn't stop saying *Aww*. Kennedy was there so she chimed in and gave her witness statements."

"You tell them about the parking garage?"

"Absolutely," I say. "They wanted the dirt so I gave them what they asked for."

"It's not weird talking about it?" he asks.

"Nope. I wouldn't publicly broadcast it or anything, but I'm not ashamed to say that we've had sex. I haven't done it with fifty different guys. I'm not in middle school. I'm 18 and I had sex with one guy. My boyfriend, who I love. The only guy I've ever loved. There's nothing to feel weird about."

He brings my hand up to his lips and kisses the back of it. "I love so much about you, Miss Hayes."

"Like what, Mr. Reed?"

"Well, to state the obvious, I think you're beautiful. You've got a banging body for someone who lives off water. It goes to all the right places. That's for sure."

"I think water does Kesia's body better."

"I don't want to piss you off by talking about another girl, but I can't even lie. That girl is thick."

I nod, unable to pretend she isn't naturally stacked. "I'm not pissed at all. Kesia is a thickum. No need for me to hate or act blind."

"Jackson can't stop looking at her."

"I don't think she's looking back, but I'm all for team swirl."

He laughs. "Jackson is cool. A little annoying, but I like him."

"Me, too. He's like the little brother I never wanted, but maybe kind of need. He frustrates the hell out of me by using

174

his gift, but he keeps things light and fun. He's a nice guy. I don't think he has a mean bone in his body."

Michael shakes his head. "He doesn't. He's a good dude. I told him he could come down and visit us whenever."

"Fine by me. Any and all of them are welcome."

"Even Lark?" he asks uncertainly.

"Yes. Even Lark. Why did you ask that way? Hear something that I didn't?"

"No. You just haven't mentioned her."

"Nothing we've been talking about has made me want to point her out individually. She's hella cool. She kind of lays back in the cut, listens for a while, and then surprises you. She's funny. And she helped me curl my hair."

He runs his hand over my curls. "Looks good. You know I love your hair curled."

I smile. His compliments always touch my heart in a special way, always make me feel so special, so beautiful. While I could never see myself chopping my hair off or even changing its color to please a guy, I love doing little things like changing the style to make Michael's eyes light up when he sees me. All girls want to look good for their boyfriends. Mine makes it easy. He loves me the way I am, just happens to prefer seeing this long hair curled as opposed to straightened.

"Thank you," I say.

"Really, you look gorgeous. Seeing you walk toward me in this dress, seeing your hair blow in the breeze, made me realize how blessed I am to have you. You make me want to be a better person. Don't get me wrong, I want to be a good man. Successful. Inspiring. But you make me always want to go one step farther. I want to impress you as much as I want to impress myself.

"You don't realize it, but you do impress me. I'm taking the safe, traditional route. I'm going to college, getting the degree, and going from there. You're actually doing something very brave. You're not falling in with the majority and going to college with a bunch of uncertainties. You're taking your time to make sure you pursue what's right for you. Time is the one thing we can never get back. You're taking a different path to ensure you don't waste your life working a job you don't love. How can I not admire that?"

Michael grabs a hold of the picnic basket, places it directly in between the both of us. With his hand resting on top, he looks at me. "I really wanted today to be special. I've been up to a lot and I have so much to say to you."

My stomach sinks as my eyes move down to the basket. *What the hell does he have in there?*

"Some guys say things because they sound nice. I want to prove to you that everything I've said, I've meant. I want to prove to you that I'm committed to you and this relationship."

No, no, no. Please don't propose. Please don't propose. Do I love my boyfriend? Hell yes. Are we ready to be engaged, to soon be married? Hell no. We haven't lived together long enough, we don't have careers, and we're only eighteen. I hope there's something else in that basket. I might pass out if there's a ring sitting in there.

He pushes both of the basket handles down. My eyes are fixated on the wicker. My mind is frozen in fear. My heart hammers, almost painfully against my chest.

He lifts the top with a trebling hand. Out he pulls two bags. One of beef jerky and one of ranch flavored sunflower seeds. I stare at Michael's face. I don't watch what he reaches for next. I'm too afraid to, too afraid to give him an answer that may devastate him.

"So like I was saying, I want to prove to you that we're solid, that you're in this relationship with someone who sees and wants a future with you. I want you to know without a doubt that you're with a man. Young, but still a man. Your mom made sure you were set. You have a house and her life insurance check. I don't want you to think you're with someone who plans on taking advantage of you in any way.

Saying it is one thing, but proving it, actually showing you that I'm making moves, is another thing."

From the basket, he pulls out a small, seashell shaped trinket box. Gems and glitter cover the entire shell, giving it a beautiful shine, a colorful sparkle.

The trinket box sits in the middle of his palm. I don't move to touch it, though my eyes are glued on it.

"Open it," he says softly.

I shake my head. "I'm scared to."

"Scared?"

"Yes." I nod. "Scared. What is that, Michael?"

"Open it and see."

I reach out for the seashell. Now it's my hand that's trembling. My heart is erratic. It feels like there's a cyclone spinning at its highest speed inside my belly.

With shaky hands, I open the shell. Immediately, my mouth drops open and out comes a loud gasp. My eyes shoot from the box, to Michael, and back again. *No, no, no, Michael. I can't accept this yet. We're not ready for this yet. Wait, how the hell could you afford this?*

"It's not what you think," he tells me.

I drink a little water before pulling the ring from the shell. Small diamonds surround the large, emerald-cut sapphire. Diamonds also accent the white gold band. The stunning piece shimmers even in the shade provided by the large umbrella.

"It's absolutely beautiful," I mutter.

My eyes can't leave the gorgeous piece. It's what any woman would want their love to slide on their left ring finger after being asked that heart-stopping, four-word question. It's just not the kind of thing you want to see right after graduating from high school and living with your boyfriend for only a week.

Michael takes my shaking hand in between both of his. "It's not what you think. This is a promise ring."

"This is one hell of a promise."

"Let me explain."

"How could you possibly afford this?" I ask before he can explain a thing.

He shushes me.

With his hands still holding my shaky one, he smiles. "I'm not proposing to you. I plan to one day, but I can tell by your reaction that we're on the same page with that. It's too soon."

"Way too soon," I say. "I know we're going to be living together and people will see that as us playing house, but we need to live together much longer, be in our careers, both be making money, both be…"

"I know all that," he interrupts, stopping me from going on. "That's why this is just a promise ring."

My eyes finally leave the mouth-dropping piece of jewelry and find my boyfriend's.

"I promise what I feel for you is real. I promise you won't ever feel unloved or unappreciated while we're together. I promise as you get your education and grow within your art career, I'll be working and stepping up the career ladder myself."

I remain silent, my eyes still on his.

He reaches back into the basket. "I have some stuff to show you," he says, pulling out a manila folder. "I want to show you what I've been up to."

The shakiness of my hand calms a little, but my heart refuses to slow down. I drink a little more water, repeat the words *promise ring* to myself several times in an attempt to regain full composure and find calmness again. It doesn't work. Promise ring or not, how could an eighteen-year-old possibly afford this?

"I'm going to college."

I can feel my eyes bulge. "College? What?"

His words are like a bomb. They drop and blow my mind completely. Completely away from this promise ring and its cost. Completely away from everything except what he just said. *College? The guy who hates school, who was so in need of a year off is going to college?* I don't know whether to be happy or scared. Happy because he's pursuing his education or scared because maybe he feels forced to enroll which could lead to him dropping out.

"You heard me right. I'm going to college. I've already started the enrollment process. Actually, I'm almost done with my part. I'm just handling financial aid stuff right now. Those were the papers I needed to get faxed yesterday afternoon."

"What school?"

"I'm going to Drexel University. I'm enrolling as an online student, but there is a brick-and-mortar campus."

Where? I ask myself, quickly learning that the school is located in Philadelphia, Pennsylvania.

He continues. "I'm starting out as an online student. If I decide that I want to transfer and become a campus student, the drive is only an hour away from your house."

"Why online?" I ask.

"Because I want to work. I'll be living with you and I want to contribute. I also want to pay for books and for my education as much as possible. Moms shouldn't have to do it all."

I smile as he speaks. Everything he's saying is just making him that much more attractive to me. Every word is making me fall even deeper for him, making me love him even more.

"I'm actually pretty excited about it."

Still smiling, I ask, "What are you planning to study?"

"In a few years, your man will have a Bachelors in Communications. I like that I can do so many different things with that degree. I could work in public relations, mass media, broadcasting. I could do a lot of different things and I'd get to be myself, interact with people, be funny, show my personality, be creative." He places the manila folder on my legs. "My degree information is in there. Read it whenever you want."

My smile has grown to the point that my cheeks hurt. I

shake my head in shock, in disbelief. "Michael, you have no idea how happy you've just made me. Not because you're going to college, but because you really are taking your life and future so seriously."

"I just needed to be more open-minded and really see how much I could actually do and actually enjoy doing all while making money. I also need change, you know? I can't do the exact same thing every day. I think this is the field for me."

"I think so, too," I say. "You definitely have the personality for it. You're so outgoing when you're interested in something and want it badly."

"I want this," he says, doubt nowhere in his voice.

"I believe you."

"And I want you."

My stomach does a few happy flips. "I believe that, too."

I inch closer to him, never setting down the ring, and hug him tightly. "I'm so proud of you."

"I'm not done," he whispers.

"There's more?" I ask, letting him go.

"I got a job," he says, again blowing my mind. "I've been so secretive and busy because I wanted to tell you everything all at once. I wanted to give you a promise ring and actually have something to show you. Anyone can make a promise. It takes a man to actually make moves."

"Where do you work?"

"Ford," he tells me, his voice full of enthusiasm. "I had interviews back to back with a couple of different dealerships, but I didn't get the first two. Got hired by Ford on the spot. He said he could tell I loved cars, knew my personality would win people over, that I would make sales, and when he asked me questions, he could tell I knew my shit. One of their current employees is leaving, so I'm replacing him. I start the week after we get back to Jersey. I'll be part-time, but I could later become a full-time employee."

I shake my head again, totally surprised and so overjoyed.

I would never have guessed this was what Michael had been up to. He's right. Anyone can make an empty promise, say something because it's pleasing to another's ears, but it takes action to make it count. Actions will always speak louder than words.

"Michael, Michael, Michael. I am so proud to call you my boyfriend. Not that you were immature or anything, but you were really unmotivated about school not too long ago. Graduation must've set a fire under your ass."

"A lot of things set a fire under my ass. I don't wanna be a loser who lives off his mother or girlfriend. I don't wanna disappoint myself by not doing the most with this one life I have to live. I don't wanna disappoint Moms. She's worked her ass off to give me a good life. And you know I don't wanna disappoint you. We're out of high school. I wanna be a man for you and that's how I want you to see me."

"There's no way I could see you in any other way, especially after all you've just told me."

Satisfaction is revealed in his smile.

"You've upgraded. You're no longer my boyfriend. You're my manfriend."

His laugh forces me to laugh as well.

"That makes me sound like a dog."

"Just a joke. Seriously though, Michael, you've made me so damn happy. I knew we had an amazing future ahead of us. You're such an incredible person, son, friend, partner, man," I say. "I'm so glad you're mine."

"I'm glad I am too."

We both lean in for a short, soft kiss. One that neither of us closes our eyes for.

"So will you accept it?" he asks, touching my hand.

I look down at what I briefly forgot I was holding. I admire the beautiful, blue sapphire. I smile down at what I plan on wearing every day from here on out.

"I accept your promise, I believe your every word, and I

am so looking forward to going back to New Jersey with you. I'm excited to make it our home. I'm excited to build a life with you."

He pulls the ring from my hand and I hold out my right hand.

"Not that one. I want your left."

I quickly switch hands, completely unsure as to what hand and finger a promise ring is worn on.

He holds my left ring finger in his hand and as I watch him, he slowly slides the sapphire on. "I want it here until I'm down on one knee sliding on its replacement," he says softly.

With my hand held out in front of me, I stare at the precious, blue stone. Happiness overfills my heart as I look at what will constantly remind me of this day and his promise to me. A promise I have no doubt he'll make good on.

"And to answer the question you asked me earlier, I spent a little of my graduation money to buy this for you."

"You what?" I ask, letting my hand fall onto my leg. "That money was for college."

"I know. I only spent a little. The band is real. You don't have to worry about your little alien finger turning green. The stones," he says, briefly looking away. "Well, they're not exactly…"

"Real?" I ask.

"I couldn't afford the sapphire I wanted to get you."

I place my hand over my chest and exhale in relief. "I'm glad it isn't. If this ring were real, that'd have cost a few thousand or more, I'm sure."

"I was considering just buying the band, but it looked too much like a wedding ring."

"Michael, I'd be happy with a rubber band. It's what it stands for that's most touching and meaningful to me."

He gives me a half smile.

"Seriously," I tell him, as I stroke his cheek gently. "This date was incredibly thoughtful, this ring is stunning, but your promise outshines the hell out of this beach and this ring."

A smile revealing his beautiful teeth slowly appears.

"I love it, Michael. That's a promise. And I don't want it to be real. Buy the real one for our engagement, when you can actually afford it."

"Years from now, when I'm down on one knee, I'll definitely be giving you a real rock. Probably bigger, too."

"Bigger? I won't be able to lift my damn hand."

He chuckles as he reaches inside the picnic basket again. Out he pulls an empty, long-neck, glass bottle. Michael removes the cork and passes the bottle to me. I hold it and question him with my eyes.

"It might sound corny, but I thought you'd like to take something with you. Some water. Some sand, maybe. Something to remind you of this day."

"I couldn't forget this day if I tried. And that is not corny at all. Like the ring, it's just thoughtful." I look out at Lake Michigan and then run my hand across the soft, warm sand. "I'll pass on the water," I say. "I'll take some sand."

Before filling the bottle, I grab Michael's hand. I slide my fingers in between his and look into those green eyes. "I really appreciate this. What a date," I say, smiling at a face I adore. "I really love you and I really want to kiss you again."

He puckers up. "Kiss me."

I look away from his eyes, his lips, and around us at the families sharing this space with us. We've shared a short kiss, but we can't full-on make out with small children around. That's not only inappropriate, but gross.

"Another quick kiss," he whispers. "Just one. Really quick so we don't traumatize the kiddies."

I look around, notice that no one is watching us. I look back out at the beautiful lake, at where I'm sitting. I look at my finger, at the symbol of his promise. I then look at him, his green eyes, his lips. I have to kiss him again. Not because he put a ring on it, but because I just need to. After such an amazing surprise, after all the forethought, I have to kiss him. I need to pause this moment, for time to stand still, even if just for a few seconds.

He leans in, licks his lips, whispers, "Just one more."

I lick my lips too, tilt my head slightly, and bring my lips to his. As the small waves kiss the shore, I kiss my love.

Chapter 13

n separate vehicles, Michael and I head back toward Mrs. Everly's home. I push my hair back, running my fingers through hair Michael was just gripping. Gripping in the moment of heated passion we fell into after our romantic date on the beach. I still can't believe it. Michael went from unmotivated, unenthusiastic, high school student, to part-time, money-making, car salesman, who is excited about enrolling in college. Proud doesn't begin to explain how I really feel. I don't feel like we're two teenagers in young love who just graduated from high school and are planning an unrealistic future together. I feel like he's become a man and he's working to ensure our future is successful. I feel like a grown woman who is putting in hard work now so the future can be full of play.

With my eyes on the road, my thoughts stay on Michael, on what we just did in the backseat of the truck his mother rented for us to get around Michigan in and lent to him for this date. I was only supposed to be helping him put the cooler and picnic basket in the car, but after hearing his promise, looking down at the ring on my finger, and just brimming with love for him, I couldn't keep my hands off his body. I couldn't keep my lips away from his. I couldn't control the urges burning inside me.

As I change lanes, I softly bite down on my bottom lip. I can still feel the softness of Michael's lips pressed against mine. I can still feel our tongues tangoing in a steamy dance.

I run my nails along the side of my neck. I touch where the warmth of Michael's breath tickled me as I straddled him. I touch where he left a trail of soft kisses. Kisses that awakened so many senses.

My stomach drops and my body becomes an intense blaze at the thought of being on top of Michael for the first time. So eagerly climbing on top of his lap surprised him and myself. Even as he put on protection, and I covered the back windows with the blanket we sat on and a beach towel we never used, I didn't take any time to think about how I'd never done that. I didn't consider how little sexual experience I have and how I may not be that good. All I could do was feel. Feel the happiness pulsating, my attraction for him heightening, and my desire for him becoming uncontrollable.

I pull a bottle of water from the cup holder and gulp some down. I try to cool myself off, but the water isn't cutting it. There's no way I could've even imagined sex feeling that way. I'm convinced that things only get better with Michael because we're supposed to be together. We're instinctively, intimately, and whole-heartedly connected to one another. He's my soul mate and this growing love we share is unbreakable.

Twenty something minutes later, Michael and I pull up the curved driveway. Before heading inside to fill the girls in on the details of my date, I look at my reflection in the car door. I turn to the side, make sure my dress looks good from all angles, looks the way it did when I left. I push my curls back again, take a quick look at both sides of my head, check to make sure my curls still look presentable. Though I wasn't lying on my hair, it was being pulled. I'd hate for my appearance to tell a story I don't want shared with everyone.

Michael and I make our way inside. I take Mrs. Everly her keys, thank her for the use of her vehicle, and then dart up the stairs in search of my girls. I can usually hold on to my personal information. I typically don't rush to share it. But I'm pressed to show off my new ring, to share with the girls what Michael promised me, and to reveal what he's secretly been up to. Right where I left them, they're all gathered in the guest room we've been occupying.

"You guys aren't in prison, you know? You can leave this room," I say.

Short laughs escape each of them.

"We challenged the boys to a game of pool. It didn't take us long to throw in the towel. Jackson is obsessed with using his ability on us," Larks tells me. "He gets on my damn nerves."

I chuckle. "I know the feeling.

"So, how was it?" Kesia asks.

I hold out my hand and wiggle my fingers in front of the girls. They each gasp. Their eyes pop open in shock. Kennedy grabs my hand, moves in for a closer look. Kesia pops up from the bed and wraps her arms around me in a congratulatory hug.

Lark covers her mouth, her eyes unable to look away from my ring. "I can't believe it, Jaylen. He popped the question. You're engaged!"

"No," I say, forcing Kesia to release me immediately.

"What do you mean, no?" Kesia asks, her accent even stronger now that she's confused.

"It's a promise ring," I explain.

They all become silent. Uncertainty covers their faces and I know exactly why. I told them during girl talk last night that Michael and I would be living together. Kesia casually brought up an engagement ring coming soon and I laughed it off. I know that for many a promise ring looks like an easy way for a guy to get out of actually marrying his partner. That's not what's going on between Michael and me. They just need an explanation.

"I don't get it. What's the promise? You already live together. You're already monogamous. Why not an engagement ring? Why not do it the right way?" Kesia asks, incapable of looking happy for me.

"Let me break it down," I say, hoping to erase the judgement from their faces. "I understand that the whole idea behind a promise ring is confusing, but for now, it's all that I'm comfortable accepting. Michael is promising to work toward his goals, to pursue his education, to grow alongside me, and to continue loving me. Already, he's making good on those promises. Remember, I told you guys that he's been busy and I don't know why? Well, he was going on interviews and enrolling in school. He got a job and he's about to begin pursuing his Bachelors in Communications."

"That's great," Kennedy says. "Glad he's not all talk."

"The truth is, we're still young. We haven't lived together for very long. I just told him maybe a week ago that I don't want children. He may realize after graduating from college that he wants kids. I'm a realist, you guys. I don't believe it will happen, that we will break up, but anything is possible. We may realize after living together for a year that we're not capable of staying under the same roof, seeing each other every day, and keeping each other happy. People change as their lives do. Wants change as people grow. He's promising to work as hard as I do, to love me, and to try to make this work. That's enough for me for now. When he gets down on one knee, we both have to know without a doubt that it will work. Living together has to be comfortable, degrees have to be hanging on the wall, and incomes need to be coming in. When we're planning our wedding, I don't want to be testing anything out the way we sort of are doing right now. I mean, I am completely in love with Michael." I touch my heart. "I love him to pieces, but that doesn't mean that things won't go left when it's just us, living together, dealing with each other's shit on the daily. I want to live with him and grow with him for a few years before I even consider taking his last name. If what we have shatters, and again, I don't think it will, but if it happens, I don't want to have to run to court to go separate ways."

The girls remain silent.

"Listen," I say, glancing down at my ring. "He wanted to show me how serious he is about us and our relationship. What he did for me today means the world to me."

"I understand and I'm not trying to steal your joy," Kesia says, her tone much sweeter. "I just don't want to see you hurt. A promise and a marriage certificate are totally different things. If he's going at your pace and you're getting what you need from him, then I am happy for you. Sincerely."

"I'm more than happy. He's giving me more than I need."

"Until you explained it, I didn't understand what a promise ring was," Lark says, "But seriously, I think it's the cutest gesture. He's already got a job. He's enrolling in school. He's serious, Jaylen. I really think you've got a good guy. And you don't have to force him to grow up. My mom always tells me to pray for a guy whose parents did their job. She says there's nothing worse than raising the man you're dating."

I look over at Kennedy. I give her a chance to say whatever's on her mind. I give her the opportunity to chime in with her friendly feedback. She doesn't say anything. Her lips form a one-sided smile, but they never part.

"So, what's the plan for this evening?" I ask, trying to force everyone in the room to focus on something else.

Kesia shakes her head. The corners of her lips pull downward. "Please don't change the subject—share your details. I didn't intend to ruin your happy mood. I just needed clarity. In my country, we don't have promise rings and such."

I nod. "I get it."

"Believe me when I say I believe you two share a real love. In the short time I've known you all, I've been able to see it. I just want to make sure you're not being blinded by that love.

It doesn't seem as though you are and he isn't getting comfortable. He's handling his responsibilities and that says a lot to me. I try not to judge the unfamiliar. I just needed a better understanding. I have one now, and I am truly happy for you both. Your ring is beautiful and so is your relationship. Please share the details."

I exhale softly before my smile returns. I share the details of my date, quote Michael's words, tell them about the sand we bottled, share the details of our steamy backseat action. I tell them everything. My stomach flips and jumps several times as I speak. A smile remains on my face as I describe one of the most special days of my life. I place my hand over my heartbeat as I share my afternoon. I feel so loved. So full.

Detail after detail, smile after smile, I keep going until I realize I'm repeating myself. Though they're listening attentively, I don't want to dominate this time we have together. I don't want to own the entire conversation. There's more to talk about than just my relationship.

"Kesia, how's Ms. Eden been today? Still enjoying herself or is she ready to go home?"

"She's having a great time. She's been sharing all of her stories with Ms. Reed, Ms. Ava, Ms. Housley, and Mrs. Everly. She's fascinated by the view. She's not ready to leave. She's thankful to be here, that we were invited. I'm so happy we bumped into each other at Princeton," Kesia says.

"Me too. Feels like... like..." I struggle to say the word. "Family. Everyone's presences are mixing, creating this feeling of comfort and home. I've never slept so well, felt so cozy, felt so safe."

They all nod. It's a feeling only our kind can understand. It's a feeling of togetherness we don't get to feel regularly because our lives, schools, and jobs have us scattered. Though most of us are said to reside in Michigan and Canada, I doubt they all live on the same block. Here we are, all together, away from animals, on a private property with no humans around, living as the majority. This is a first for me. A first that can't be a last.

"I think we're having another bonfire tonight," Kennedy says, looking out the window. "I know Jackson is hell bent on having a lakefront football game."

"Not happening," I say quickly. "If Kesia doesn't end up on my team, she's gonna have me out there miming or doing something else random. No thanks."

We all laugh.

"Did you check in with your dad?" I ask Kennedy.

"Definitely. He knows I'm going to New Jersey before heading home."

"Why?" I ask, as we never discussed her coming back to my house.

"I want to heal Kesia's ill family friend before I go back to Virginia."

We all look at Kennedy, all smile at the kind healer in the room. Kesia covers her mouth. Her face scrunches as tears form in her eyes. "That is so kind of you."

"This is what I'm supposed to do," Kennedy tells her. "I was given this gift because it was intended to be shared. I love helping people, saving them from their suffering. I want to help your friend."

Kesia wraps Kennedy in a tight hug. While they embrace, I can't help but to think about Indigo. If she had that gift and knew someone was suffering, would she offer to help without being asked? Or would she only help those she liked, those she wanted something from? Is Indigo a good person who is suffering from an emotional imbalance caused by heartbreak and disappointment, or is she merely the self-centered, unstable, dangerous individual I saw at the breaking of our friendship? My heart wants me to believe there's kindness and goodness in her, though it may be buried deep. Deep beneath her pain. My head is telling me to look at her most recent history, her irrational choices, her psychotic behavior. My head is telling me to erase all memories of the Indigo I thought I knew and to let sink in that I've seen her true character.

"How would you help her?" Kesia asks. "You can't just walk into the house and heal her in front of everyone. Though her family would be grateful, I wouldn't want your true identity to be revealed and shared."

"I was hoping you could help me with that," Kennedy says.

"I'm heading back to Cameroon from here. I don't know how I could make it so you'd be alone with her. You're a stranger to the family."

"We'll have to figure something out. Maybe I could deliver a present for you. I just need a few minutes alone with her."

I remind her, "You only need a few minutes, but she also needs to be asleep. You have to touch her, and your touch causes a physical reaction while the healing is taking place. If she's awake when you do this, she's gonna freak the hell out. Trust me, I know. It feels weird and scary."

We all try to figure out how Kennedy could help a sick stranger. A stranger always surrounded by family and friends. Sure, she likely rests often, but I doubt her relatives will be eager to leave Kennedy alone with their sick, sleeping loved one.

"I'll come up with something," Kennedy says. "Even if I have to ask my dad to drive up. Kesia's gift could be a home visit and second opinion from a recognized, medical professional. They'd leave my dad alone with her, right? He is a legitimate doctor. He could put her to sleep. I could do my thing, and boom." She snaps once. "Job is done."

Lark nods. "Not a bad idea."

"We'll have to work out the details, but I'm sure we could make it work. My dad would do anything to help save someone, especially if they're tied to one of my friends. Scratch that," she says, waving her hand in a swift motion. "We're past friends. This is family. By helping her, I'm helping you, too,

Kesia. You and Ms. Eden. You guys are my family now. He'll make it happen. He'll work his ass off to make it happen for you guys because you guys love her and we love you."

Tears fall from Kesia's eyes and I can't help but smile. Standing in this room with these three very special young women warms my heart completely. Talking to them for hours last night was so easy. Being around them is so comfortable. So natural. This is true bonding, true love, true sisterhood. I'd do anything I could to help any of the three of them, and deep down, though we haven't known each other for long, I know they'd be there and do whatever they could for me. This location is breathtakingly beautiful. This house is spectacular, featuring every upscale, luxurious amenity a guest could hope for. But more than our surroundings, more than this house's features, the company, the amazing individuals I've been spending my time with are the best part of this unforgettable trip.

"I'm feeling a lot like you were feeling earlier, Kesia," I say.

"How's that?"

"Just a little sad that we're together now but won't be once we all part ways and head back to our homes."

"The thought sucks," Lark says.

"It'd suck even more if we stayed in this room being a group of emotional girls. Let's go out to the lake. Let's have another night like last night where we hang out with everyone for hours, and then end the night having the most amazing girl talk until we just can't help but pass out."

I smile at Kennedy as her idea is exactly what I had in mind. I'm so ready to repeat last night, to spend time with my girls talking about any and everything.

After a quick shower, I slip into shorts and a tank, then smooth my hair up into a messy ponytail, half still curled, half frizzy. With joy covering our four faces, we head down the stairs. Lark and Kesia stop in the sunroom, decide to sit with the others and join in on the controversial debate they're having about gun control and gun rights in America. Ms. Housley speaks heatedly about her position on the topic. Standing, her cheeks red with burning anger, her arms flailing around, her light, hazel-brown eyes narrowed into slits, she speaks strongly about mass shootings, innocent children losing their lives, and her disgust for the violence taking place in this country. Jackson and Ethan talk over each other, trying to get a word in to speak on school shootings, but Ms. Housley refuses to stop sharing her points.

Kennedy and I excuse ourselves, head out the back door, down the forty stairs, to the lakefront to join Michael.

"Lonelyyy… He's Mr. Lonelyyy," I sing to Michael who's alone at the lakefront starting the fire.

He chuckles.

"Why aren't you in the sunroom with everyone else?" Kennedy asks.

"I'm trying to get everyone to come out here. I wish they'd stop talking about guns, shootings, and violence. We're on vacation."

"How'd that even come up?" I ask. "Ms. Housley is furious."

"She was checking something online and saw a news article about a mall shooting. A couple of kids got hit. Reading that hurt her," he says, unfolding the chairs.

Kennedy grabs a folded blanket and lays it out. "I think it hurts all of us to keep reading about or seeing videos about violence and innocent lives being taken."

Michael agrees, then tell us, "It started as a sad but calm conversation about the downfall of this country, the increase in mass murders, and how she would rewrite some of the laws if she could. Jackson and Ethan feel differently about some of the changes she believes should be made and the debate started from there."

I spread out a blanket. "That's not a fun discussion to be

having."

"It's not. That's why I got the hell out of there and came out here to finish setting up. Nobody's here on this beautiful property wanting to focus on the fucked up world outside of those gates. Once we leave here, all of us are gonna be refocused on Indigo and that whole mess. While I'm here, all I wanna do is laugh. It's horrible that kids lost their lives in a random shooting." He points to the sky. "I have to believe that they're with God now and I hope that psychopath is either in jail or in hell. But today, in this moment, here with my family, I don't wanna focus on anything negative."

"Me neither," I say, smoothing the corner of the last blanket.

"Well…" Kennedy says, moving carefully around the laid out blankets and stepping closer to Michael. "Before we begin talking about flowers and rainbows, I'd like to ask you a question."

"Anything," he replies immediately.

"Do you want to kill her?"

I step closer to Michael, stand directly in between them.

He scratches his thick, curly hair. His eyes don't run from Kennedy's, don't reveal rage, don't reveal dishonesty. He shrugs. "I can't lie to you, Kennedy. I wanted to. I really did. Not just because I was angry, but because I don't know how to feel safe. I thought about her being able to vanish anytime she wants to, possibly popping up on me or Jaylen at any point, maybe even breaking into my house again and Moms being there alone. Those thoughts made me want to put an end to her existence."

I reach out to grab Kennedy's shaking hand. I believe her when she says she doesn't agree with Indigo's choices, but her feelings for her, her love for her, goes beyond words. Just hearing what Michael wanted to do to Indigo forces trembles out of her, forces mixed emotions to shoot through her veins.

"But now," he continues. "After being here, after getting

the ball rolling with college, I don't wanna have that burden. I want Indigo to stay as far away from me as possible. If she keeps the hell away from me, I'm good. That's my word." He holds his right hand up. "I wanna tell her that so she can move on knowing that I'm not plotting."

"You really feel that way?"

"Kennedy, I promise you that I don't wanna kill Indigo. What I felt before changed when I was able to fully get away from everything. Anger does strange things to your mind, but things are clear now. As bad as what she tried to do to me was, I'm not that guy. I can't stand here and say honestly that I would create some Hollywood plan, track her down, and take her out. I'm not a murderer."

Kennedy exhales, though I can still feel her hand jittering inside of mine.

"I really hope you believe me," he says.

She nods. "I do. And I'm relieved." She exhales again. "I know something is very wrong with Indigo, but I want her to live and get help. She's wrong, but I can't support murder."

"I get it," Michael says. "Trust me, I get it. And I also know that no one on planet earth will ever understand how the three of us feel. She used to my best friend." He grabs my free hand. "She used to be your best friend. And Kennedy, she used to be your girlfriend, your love. Our connections and histories with her weren't built on negativity and pain. We all loved her. No one else who knows what happened will understand how we feel in this situation."

"So, we have to be there for each other," I say, squeezing both of their hands. "We have to listen to each other, even if it's just to hear the same thing over and over again. This has been hard as hell on the three of us."

"I agree, and though it felt awkward before, I'm here for the both of you," Kennedy says. "At this point, it feels less like I'm betraying her and more like I'm just living my life and enjoying these friendships."

"Hug it out," Michael says, pulling his hand from mine. He steps past me and eagerly wraps his arms around Kennedy. "You can still care about Indigo. You've got a heart and you're a good person. I would never make you feel bad about that."

My heartbeats are exceptionally merry as I witness what looks to be the start of a closer friendship. My bond with Kennedy has strengthened. I don't question her sincerity anymore, don't worry about whose side she's on. She's been honest, and like anyone else would be, she feels torn because she cares for all of those involved in this messiness. Her honesty is all I need and I'm grateful for this sisterhood. As much I want to stay in touch with Kesia and Lark, and I'm sure I will, undoubtedly, I'll actually see and spend more time with Kennedy. Though our schools aren't next door to each other, they aren't separated by oceans either. Our sisterly bond isn't likely to become undone due to distance or lack of contact. Really, I could see us texting every day, even if just to say *hello*.

Standing in between Michael and Kennedy, in front of the lit fire, only feet away from the wide-spread lake, I smile at our new beginning. This new chapter in our lives is starting with genuine friendships, no malicious intentions, and hope. We are so hopeful we'll have successful college years, followed by high-paying careers that we wake up anxious to get to. We're so hopeful our friendships will remain true, strong, and full of the laughs and support humans and aliens need throughout life. We're so hopeful love will offer the warmth we all need when the world becomes unbelievably cold and cruel. We're so hopeful, so excited, so determined, so ready. Just so ready to begin our lives as adults who have grown close to other Quisis we can call at any time who will offer understanding that no human on this earth ever could.

"What are you guys thinking?" I ask.

"About life," Michael says with his eyes on the lake before us. "Your whole outlook changes when you graduate from high school. All that kiddie shit dies."

"Not for everyone. Some people never grown up. Some people act like high school kids in their thirties. You can see that just by logging into Facebook."

Michael looks at me. "That's why we have to continue to grow and make real shit happen in our lives that we can own and take credit for. I wanna be able to say, *I did it.* Not, *thank you, Mommy, for paying my rent and buying me new drawers.*"

I laugh at what's so not funny. My mom used to warn me about going to college and getting involved with guys who drag their feet, show no interest in actually learning, and don't care about making something of their lives. She told me to steer clear of guys who only attend because their parents make them, and whose greatest interest is the next party or next new girl to smash. She told me to watch actions and to not get caught up in smooth lines. That's why I'm so proud of and love the guy at my side. His actions are louder than any and all of his words.

"What about you, Kennedy?" Michael asks.

She stands silently, stares blankly ahead.

I nudge her. "Hey. We're talking to you. What are you thinking about?"

She looks our way, laughs, forcing a curious smile out of me.

"What?" Michael asks. "Thinking about something dirty?"

"No, just random. Really random."

"Spill it." I nudge her again.

"I don't know why, but for some reason I just started thinking about The Walking Dead. Do you think zombies would want to eat us the way they want to eat humans?"

Zombies? Really, Kennedy? You're standing feet away from Lake Michigan with funky, flesh eating, dead people on your mind? What the hell? I can feel my entire face twist.

"And, if they did want to bite us, would we become alien zombies?"

"Damn, that's a good ass question," Michael says, scratching his head at the thought.

I turn, notice the others coming down the stairs, everyone empty-handed except for Ethan, holding a large cooler out in front of him. I step away from the two zombie-obsessed individuals at my sides, let them ponder over the gory idea of whether or not we'd be food for the living dead that only exist on TV.

"You guys are fucking weirdos," I say, taking a seat on one of the blankets.

Michael chuckles before copping a squat on the blanket beside me. "Think about it."

"I don't want to."

They both crack up before throwing their opinions back and forth. Michael believes our kind would be immune. Kennedy is hopeful that we'd be a special breed of super strong, more intelligent zombies. I just want the others to hurry down and change the subject, to distract these two wackos from their random, ridiculous thoughts.

"Was my rant too much for you, Mike?" Ms. Housley asks, moving her chair closer to his blanket.

"I wasn't trying to be rude. I just wanted to finish setting this up so you could get back to your happy self. You're on vacation, Ms. Housley. I don't want you focused on shootings and death. I want everyone here to relax, laugh, and have fun. Who knows when you'll get to do this again? You and Moms need to enjoy this break. You both work hard. Really hard."

Ms. Housley chuckles quietly, touches the top of Michael's head, briefly looks around at each of us, then the scenery. She smiles, looks Michael in his eyes, and nods. "You're right. It's the wrong thing to be focused on right here and now. Positive talk only." Her beautiful hazel-brown eyes light back up with the happiness I'm used to seeing in them.

I smile, though I'm not a part of their conversation.

"So, what's the topic? What were the three of you down here talking about while we…" She stops speaking. She scoots to the front of her seat. "What's that on your finger, Jaylen?

Give me your hand."

I lift my hand up, stretch my arm out in front of Michael so she can lean in and take a closer look.

"What is this?" she asks again. "Michelle, have you seen this?" she holds my hand up even higher.

"It's a promise ring," I answer.

Ms. Reed walks over to where I'm sitting and squats down in front of me. "What's the promise?" Her eyes move from me to her son.

As Michael restates the promise he made to me, I stare at Ms. Reed as she looks over the ring I received this afternoon. Ms. Housley remains on the edge of her seat as she listens in.

"This is expensive, Mike. You better not have blown through all of your graduation money. And you sure as hell better not have bought this with your untouched credit." Her chest rises and falls as she seethes inside.

"Ma, calm down. I didn't," he tells her truthfully, following up with an explanation that details which part of the ring is real and which part isn't.

As he speaks, she listens attentively, occasionally glancing down, turning my hand from side to side to better look at the beautiful ring on my hand.

"It's just a promise ring. It's just a symbol." He throws a fast glance in my direction. "Not a symbol that our relationship is fake. I got what I could afford."

"And I love it," I say in front of his mother, Ms. Housley, and everyone else. "Only a selfish, greedy person would expect you to blow everything you have. I love what it represents. It means a lot to me."

Ms. Reed sighs. Her face doesn't hold any particular expression. I can't read it or that sigh.

"Ms. Reed, we're not about to run off and get married. I promise. Neither of us believes that'd be the right thing to do until after college."

"I like you for my son. I really do. I like you as an

individual. I like that you're respectable and that you take your education seriously. But both of you are young and want to shack up together. That's an easy way to become distracted. Spending time together will be the perfect reason to not feel like going to school on certain days or finishing up a paper. Making a fast buck so that you guys can do things sooner rather than later will be the perfect reason to push school off and work a dead end job now. I don't want your relationship to be what hurts you in the end. I know you're both adults, but listen to someone who knows. Don't move too fast. You've got a lifetime ahead of you."

Michael and I look at one another. Ms. Reed still has my hand.

"We're not rushing, Ma. This is just me letting Jaylen know that she's not in this alone. I know her plan, and she's going far. Now she knows mine. We're moving forward together. I'm showing her that I'm the man you raised me to be."

Ms. Reed eyes her son. Her expression is still unreadable. The kind, nurturing expression that usually covers her face when she's speaking to me hasn't shown up at all during this talk.

"I want the best for the both of you. I want to see you both succeed. I want you both to make it, and I'm not just referring to your relationship."

"We will," I say. "Let's us show you that we will."

Ms. Reed offers me a half smile. I guess I can understand her concern. Her son just graduated from high school and has already put a ring on his girlfriend's finger. Not only that, but he's left home to live with his girlfriend. She needs to know where his focus really is. I get it. I'm important, but not more important than him educating himself and being able to support himself as an adult.

"I'm happy for you both. It's beautiful."

"Thank you, Ms. Reed," I say softly.

With one head nod, she stands, and moves back to her seat. The hand she held on to throughout our short talk is now in Michael's. He kisses my ring. We exchange smiles, share a little moment of our own, though we're not by ourselves.

"Congratulations," Ms. Housley whispers. "Sorry I put you on the spot, but I'm Team Mother." She offers us a playful wink.

I nod, not even the teeniest bit angry. I have nothing to hide which is why the ring is on my finger and my hands are where they can be seen. Sure, people will doubt us. We're fresh out of high school and to the outside world, we're playing house. What we're not playing is love. I cannot wait to show everyone that we're not only going to make it, but we're going to make it big. Big and happy.

Around the bonfire, us Quisis sit, all with a bottle of water nearby. Ms. Eden shares tales of growing up in Cameroon, of her ability to control the minds of others once upon a time. That ability has trickled down the family line and is now Kesia's to use. What Ms. Eden once used on her teachers and even random strangers, she no longer owns. It became her son's once she birthed him and he passed it on to Kesia, but it wouldn't have become her gift if she weren't the first born of her parents. What Kennedy shared with me once before, Ms. Eden has now reconfirmed. Our gifts came from our parents, but if more than one child is had, the eldest is the only one to luck out.

I laugh until tears nearly fall as Ms. Eden shares pieces of her life with us, as she takes us through her childhood mischief. I laugh until my eyes are pulled in the direction of movement, of others. I blink several times in an attempt to erase what I think I see. But what I'm seeing is real. The movement down the stairs toward us doesn't stop. With each step they take, the feeling of our kind intensifies.

I hurry to my feet. So does Kennedy. So does Michael. Jackson and Mrs. Everly jump up as well.

Ms. Everly asks her son, "Friends of yours?"

Five individuals walk behind her, and at her side is her thin, long-legged, blue-eyed protector. With a water in each of her hands, her long black hair secured in a high ponytail, she heads down to where we are. In Michigan, not in Virginia, but hours away from her home, their home, she's here.

Indigo's here.

Chapter 14

I move closer to Michael. So close, our arms touch. My heart punches against my chest in a hard, loud, slow rhythm. As Indigo heads our way, fisting two bottles of water, all I can think is that she's here for a fight and she came with back up. I've seen *20-20* documentaries, shows on ID Discovery that focus on families that stick together to carry out unthinkable crimes. I never thought I'd be face to face with a family of crazies, a family who lacks morals and will partake in anything necessary to protect a member, no matter how wrong that member may be.

"What the hell is she doing here?" Michael asks Kennedy.

Kennedy shakes her head. "I never told her where we were. I swear. I told her I was going to Canada."

All of us are on our feet, even Ms. Eden. Ms. Housley takes a step closer to Michael, nearly steps in front of him. Ms. Reed moves closer to her son. I take a small step to the side, allow her to be next to her child, to whisper calming words to him.

"What are you all doing here? This is private property," Mrs. Everly says.

"And it's beautiful. It's a lovely place to sit around and

plan someone's murder."

"Nobody's planning anything, Indigo," Kennedy says.

"Indigo?" Ms. Eden repeats, earning squinty-eyed, fearful glances from Indigo and Avery. "This is the young lady who stirred up all the prom night chaos?"

Kennedy nods. "Why are you here? How'd you even know where we were?"

"You told us," Indigo says coolly. "Remember our talk in Virginia?"

All eyes move to Kennedy. The stares make tears build in her eyes. My hammering heart beat begins to hurt. The sudden, unexpected feeling of betrayal is the painful rhythm my heart is pounding out. Pounding out more quickly and harshly.

"She's lying. I swear she's lying. I told her I was going to Canada. I would never bring this kind of craziness to someone's home, let alone my friends. My family." Kennedy cries and shakes her head. "She's lying. I never told her anything."

What the fuck did I do? Did I put my trust in the wrong person again? Did I really give Kennedy the power to hurt all of us? Should I have listened to Michael and watched out for Kennedy the same way I should've better watched out for Indigo? I feel blindsided, disgusted with myself for being so naïve, and scared because I don't know what's about to take place and who's about to get hurt. I know for sure they didn't cross several state lines just to talk.

"You can wipe those damn tears. If you helped these nuts find this house, you're standing next to the wrong people," I tell her. "Go stand next to your friends, to those who have your loyalty. You said you weren't picking a side, Kennedy, but it's looking like you're Team Indigo. You don't believe in violence, but you let seven people roll up on us?"

Ethan rushes to Kennedy's side, eyeballs me. "Calm down, Jaylen. Don't let this girl turn you against your friend. I didn't have to go to school with her to learn that Indigo is clearly a psychopath. It's a good chance she's lying right now."

"Then how did she find out where to come?" Lark asks. "Kennedy openly admitted that she talked to Indigo before coming here. I don't even know this girl. I didn't know coming here meant I may end up in a fight for my life."

Indigo's eyes show calmness as she stands quietly with her squad. Her people look prepared, holding and gulping water, eyes filled with threats and rage. She looks like she's chilling, like what we're seeing, she's not. Like where we are, she isn't. Who is this girl? How was she able to hide deep inside the Indigo I once loved and enjoyed spending my free time with?

"Don't speak. Nobody else speak. Let me address her aunt," Ms. Reed says, briefly looking at me and then Lark. She makes strong eye contact with Michael. "Don't you move. Don't open your mouth unless you think about your words."

She takes a few steps away from her son, steps toward Indigo and Avery. "I'm Michelle Reed, Michael's mother. I've met Indigo many times in the past, and to my understanding, you raised her from birth. So I'd like to speak to you, mother to mother. You guys didn't run in and attack us, so you must want to talk or hear something from us."

Avery stands still. Silent. Her long, thin frame doesn't look like it'd be capable of hiding super-human strength, but somehow from within, this woman, like me, can be a demolisher. I hope Ms. Reed can remind this woman that most of us here are adults, and only one of us for certain, Indigo, wants to see others get hurt. I don't know what Kennedy told Indigo, don't know if I've befriended a wild-card, but I do know I don't want to fight this out. I don't want Avery to ever put her hands on me again.

Avery doesn't speak, just eyes us viciously through those intimating, electric-blue eyes. Her frightening stare moves across all of us. There's absolutely no way of telling who she hates most, who she wants to go in for, who should be most fearful.

"I can't imagine a grown woman, let alone a mother, flying, driving, or bussing herself and six others to Michigan to kill teenagers. I can't believe you would be okay doing something like that," Ms. Reed says, her hands quivering. "My son almost lost his life, but he's willing to move past this, to let this go so life can move on. Is that what you needed to hear? No one has been here plotting. No one has snuck up on your family. Indigo is not in any danger. We're on vacation. I need you to understand that. I brought my family out here to clear their minds of Indigo, to finally feel safe again, to breathe again."

Avery throws her niece a quick glance.

"No matter what thoughts you pulled from Jaylen's mind, you must remember what has pushed these kids to feel like they have no choices. Indigo snuck around my house countless times. She reported Jaylen's car stolen on prom night in an attempt to get them arrested. She left Michael..." Ms. Reed's head falls. She clears her throat, doesn't look back up. "My son. She left my son alone in the woods, without water, to dry out and die." She slowly lifts her head, looks at Indigo. "I don't know how someone could do that to a person who was once their friend." Ms. Reed shakes her head, looks away from Indigo and refocuses back on Avery. "Jaylen and Ethan tried to end things. They made it clear to me you didn't want to hurt teenagers. They told us everyone wanted to walk away, to never see each other again. Everyone, but Indigo."

Again, Avery throws her niece a quick look. Indigo never looks back at her, doesn't show care for the unbelievable situation we're all in. Like Ms. Reed, I can't begin to understand how a teenager could convince their guardian, their parent, to gather others to carry out any kind of violence. We've been feeling like we're on the defense. How did Indigo convince others to join her on the offense?

"That child of yours needs help," Ms. Reed says. "No one here thinks death is the answer. She needs help that no one here is capable of giving her."

Ms. Eden clears her throat loudly. "She can't be helped. Maybe that's why her aunt would rather stand by her in a fight. Maybe she knows her child is broken, irreversibly damaged. Maybe she knows, but loves her too much to allow her to be hurt, though we all know she would deserve it. She almost killed someone. Just a boy she liked in high school who liked someone else. What happens when she meets someone in college, feels love for them, but he or she doesn't feel the same for her? If she does the same thing to them that she did to Michael, or worse, do you stand by her and attack them as well? Do you cover for her? You are the reason this child is here. All of you are the reason," Ms. Eden says, pointing to those who walked in behind Indigo. "She wouldn't have come here alone. She'd have no way to. She'd have been too afraid to." Her deep accent, her unique pair of eyes, the sternness behind each of her words keeps all eyes on her and all mouths closed.

I look at the five others that walked in behind Indigo and Avery. Most of my focus has been on Avery and Indigo. The culprit and her bodyguard. I scan the others, look over each of their faces. Three of them are males. Two look Dominican, but neither is Raphael, the guy who showed up at the park when Ethan and I met with Indigo and things went array. One has a beautiful head of curly, black hair, and the other has fallen in with the growing trend of men wearing buns and beards.

The other male is as pale as Avery, though shorter. His black, wavy hair is slicked back old-school style, the way rebels wore their hair in older films. The two ladies standing amongst them are eyeing Ms. Eden. One has a pixie-cut, is standing with her legs spread, and her arms folded. She has large, amber, wide eyes. They almost look round at first glance. If it weren't for the look of revulsion covering her face, she'd probably look like a doll. My eyes then move to the other female. Her red hair forces me to believe she's the one who went with Indigo when she met up with Kennedy. I look over her face, her very familiar face. I stare at her through squinted eyes, take a step forward trying to make sure she's who I think she is. Then I step back.

I look at Ms. Housley, then Michael. I whisper, "That redhead is Scarlett, the mind reader. She must've dyed her hair."

With Scarlett eyeing Ms. Eden, I assume she's browsing her brain, reading her thoughts.

I turn to Kennedy. Her sad, pink eyes look into mine as I say in a low voice, "I'm sorry. Redhead is Scarlett. She read your mind when you met up with Indigo. She changed her hair color so you wouldn't know it was her. You didn't get a good enough look at her at graduation to realize who she was when you saw her up close."

Ethan eyes Scarlett, narrows his eyes as he inspects her face from where he's standing. He nods once, agrees with me silently.

Indigo nudges her aunt. "They're over there whispering. They're lying, Auntie. They've been here scheming. You remember what we got from Kennedy. Kennedy wouldn't lie."

"But you would," I say.

Ms. Reed holds up her hand. "Jaylen, stop!"

"Indigo took Scarlett with her to meet up with Kennedy. Kennedy didn't tell them anything. Scarlett was in her head, taking information that wasn't hers to take. They're the ones plotting. Why else would she dye her hair? Why would adults take part in this if they weren't as sick as Indigo? I mean, think about it. If you knew Michael tried to kill someone, would you become his new partner in crime? You're trying to reason with the unreasonable. With sickos!"

"Jaylen, please."

"Ms. Reed, I'd never disrespect you and I'm having a hard time watching this woman do that very thing. You're doing what any rational parent would do. You're trying to bring light to the situation, to get everyone to see this logically. You're talking to another grown woman who won't even respond to you. We're standing in front of one sick family."

"I want to believe the mother in you is the only reason you're here," Ms. Housley says to Avery. "I love my son more than I love myself. I can't say for sure how far I'd go to save his life. The only thing we need for all of you to understand is that Indigo isn't in danger. You're here to save her from nothing at all."

Avery finally breaks her silence. "Kennedy was under the impression that your only reason for being in Michigan was to gather as many of our kind as you knew to sneak up on and kill my niece. At that meeting, we only wanted to know what was going on. Scarlett was only there to read quietly, and I honestly was hoping to find out…" Avery shakes her head. "I don't know what I was hoping to find out. I knew things wouldn't quietly go away based on how the meetup at the park went. I just didn't expect to find out that you all were really grouping together to savagely murder her." Avery turns to Ms. Eden. "You're right, she may not be able to be helped, but I don't want her killed. I raised her. I wiped her every tear. I've worked my ass off to put her through private school because I wanted her to have the best. She made a mistake. She shouldn't have to pay for it with her life. Every day, we've spoken about this. Every day," she repeats. "Yes, I can admit that all isn't right with her, but there's no way in hell I'd ever sit home just waiting for a mob of people to walk in on us and kill my child, which of course means killing me too, because I'd never not fight for her. There's no mother here who would sit by and let something like that happen. It was either we wait for you to come to us, or we come to you all. I figured the best thing to do would be to get out here as quickly as possible. Do I want to fight? Absolutely not. Do I want to kill anyone? Not in a million years. Would I kill to protect my child? Like you, Michelle Reed, and like the rest of the mothers here, I'd protect my baby at all costs."

Indigo is the biggest damn liar I've ever known. This woman loves Indigo to death. She's willing to fight for her, even die for her. No way is she the ice-cold monster her niece described her to be. This level of love and protection can't be a newly learned behavior.

I look around, try to get a read on the faces of those who didn't ask to be a part of this, but are standing with us. Kesia is at her grandmother's side. Jackson, the jokester couldn't look more serious standing at his mother's side. Lark, petrified, stands next to Ms. Ava, both eyeing Avery. Ethan is still at Kennedy's side, supporting her through what's probably the greatest nightmare of her life. She never wanted to be on any side, let alone be the reason we were caught off guard. Ms. Housley is still at Michael's side. Lastly, I look at my boyfriend as he hasn't spoken at all. His eyes are on Avery before they're on me.

"I love you," I whisper.

"Love you, too," he says aloud before stepping up to stand at his mother's side. "I'm Michael. Ms. Avery, I can't look at your niece without wanting to knock her head off. There's no point in me acting as if I like her. Scarlett will know the truth. The truth is, I despise Indigo. Do I want to kill her? I did. I did when all I could think about was prom night, which is a memory I wish I could erase. Do I want to hurt her now?" He shakes his head. "I just want to move on with my life. If you can keep your niece in Virginia, away from my mom's house, and make sure she never steps foot off her college campus to harass us, I'll never bother her. I want nothing to do with her."

My eyes move to Scarlett. *Give the damn head nod. Give the damn head nod. He's telling the truth.*

Scarlett turns to Avery, nods her head.

I exhale. I can hear Kennedy exhale as well.

"Me and my family don't want trouble, Ms. Avery. I get why you're here. It's unbelievable that y'all would come this far, but I get it." Michael nods as he speaks. "You'd rather sneak up on us than be caught off guard. Makes sense. Now, you've heard it from me. Scarlett can confirm that it's the truth. Scarlett can read us all, as a matter of fact. We don't want to fight."

The swooshing of the waves and the fire crackling and popping are the only sounds filling the space so many bodies are sharing. I don't know what's left to be said. We've made it clear that a fight is not what we'd like to partake in. It couldn't be more obvious that the only, and I do mean the only, problem standing amongst us is Indigo.

"Well, what more can we say? Can we get back to our evening? Can you all leave my property?" Mrs. Everly asks, though her questions weren't asked in a conversational way. She doesn't need an answer, nor does she seek to further discuss. She wants them to go. Now. We all do.

Avery's electric blue eyes aren't intimidating at this moment. In this moment, with her eyes darting from her niece, to the ground, to us, to the ground again, she just looks lost. Sad. What do you do when you're parenting a troubled teenager you can't get professional help for? It's true that Indigo has an obsessive personality, but she's grown now. Can Avery really force her into therapy? If Avery did want her locked away somewhere, Indigo could easily get herself out of that. All she has to do is vanish and slip out of an open door. Prison is what I want for her, but getting her in would be equally as difficult as keeping her there. Pouring out water is laughable to humans. Not a charge. And keeping someone behind bars who is capable of becoming an invisible woman is just another joke just waiting to be laughed at.

Suddenly, sadness overwhelms me. I feel for Avery. The thought of losing the child she raised is a devastating one. She can't stomach the idea of someone hurting her baby, so she's forced to stand in a position of possibly having to hurt others. This is a lose-lose situation for her.

"Please go," Mrs. Everly states firmly. "There is nothing

more to discuss and frankly, I would like for you to leave while things are still calm. I heard about the last time Ethan and Jaylen met up with you all. I don't want that to happen here at my home and I don't want my son involved in this any further."

I watch Indigo closely. I stare at her oh-so-calm face. I don't know what's going on in that wicked mind of hers. I take a quick look at her aunt. Avery looks defeated, not relieved, which is how she should feel. The people she was so sure were planning to kill her niece, her child, are anxious to end things peacefully. Our minds have been invaded. She knows violence isn't on them. I wonder if she's asked Scarlett to raid Indigo's brain. Time and time again, it's been proven that the true threat is the one she resides with.

Avery slowly turns away from us, her head slightly lowered. My eyes move back to Indigo. Indigo's eyes now looking over at the angry-faced, pixie-cut tagalong.

Your turn. Turn your ass around, too. Walk away, Indigo. End this. Move on with your life, so we can move on with ours.

Before our eyes, the one thing none of us wanted to see happen, happens. The unpredictable, unstable Indigo vanishes. Lark gasps loudly.

"Go inside, grandma!" Kesia orders.

I rush to move in front of my boyfriend, Ms. Housley grabs on to him, and Ms. Reed stays at his side as the others are hit with shock. Their eyes frantically search around, completely unsure of what to expect next. I keep my eyes peeled, remain in front of Michael as I know he's the one she hates the most. Half, if not all of her resentment is held for him.

"I don't need y'all to block me. Let me go. Let her come at me. I'd rather it be me than any of you."

I ignore him, stare down at the sand in search of her footprints. I don't know what exactly her plan is, but there's only two people here she definitely feels betrayed by. That's

Michael and me. I don't know what Indigo's feelings are when it comes to Kennedy, but I don't feel as though Indigo holds hate for her. Michael and I aren't in the possible safety zone Kennedy is in. With Indigo unable to be seen, we're in grave danger. We're her targets.

Indigo's squad moves in closer as I stare at the sand, as I look at jumbled footprints that aren't cluing me in to the direction she plans on running in to attack one of us. She may run straight at me, may run around the fire to strike me or Michael from behind. I want to run forward toward the mess of prints, but if I charge toward her invisible frame, Avery is going to react.

Behind. Backstab. Indigo's style. I turn around. I move from in front of Michael, quickly coming to the realization that Indigo's more likely to sneak up behind him. She's more likely to attack him as she hates him more and his physical strength is nowhere near the level of mine.

My heart slams against my chest. A chill runs up my spine, forces me to twitch. I blink rapidly as I look for her footprints to take direction. My hands shake uncontrollably. My eyes briefly find Kennedy's. Like me, she's searching the sand, looking for the invisible girl who can't be trusted, who's incredibly feared at this moment. Everyone here knows we've done all we can do to prevent any escalations. Our efforts were noticed and I believe appreciated by everyone on her side. Everyone, except her. Now, my newfound family is in trouble. The moment I get my hands on her, and I will to protect those I love, Avery and those who tagged along with her are going to jump in. I don't know their capabilities, but I'm sure they're powerful. Lethal. Otherwise, Indigo wouldn't be comfortable enough to start a fight. She knows she'll be defended. She knows they have a great chance of dominating and destroying us. And that's what she wants. She wants to break us down, ruin this family, kill the happiness Michael and I share all because life hasn't unfolded before her in the exact way she wants it to.

A growing trail of impressions comes toward me. As expected, a behind the back, sneak attack on Michael is what she's going for. She hurried around the fire, even passed by Ms. Eden, Kesia, Mrs. Everly, Jackson, Ms. Ava, and Lark.

"Jackson, stop her!"

Jackson stands in front of his petite mother, tells Lark, "I have to see her. I have to be able to lay eyes on her."

I'm shoved by a force I can't see. I stumble back, fall into Michael's back. Quickly, I find balance, reach forward, and grab one of her invisible arms.

I hear those around me, so many voices, so many jumbled words that are hard to make out due to the loud drumming of my heartbeat. I feel arms trying to pull me away from her. Enraged, I push their hands away and get my other hand on Indigo. Still unable to see her, each of my hands holding each of her arms, I throw myself forward and into her, forcing her down on her back.

Her legs kick wildly, but she's unsuccessful in getting me off her. I need to get my hands around her neck again, only this time, I need to hold on and squeeze until she exists no more. I tried to be reasonable, tried to be as human as possible about this situation, but she won't stop. She never will.

"Andrew!" she hollers out. "Get her off!"

I don't look around to see who's coming to her rescue. I'm surrounded by family. They've got me covered. Jackson can pause one of them and Kesia can mind control another. Michael and the others can combine their abilities and find a way to keep Indigo's people off me. I just need to end Indigo, to destroy the poison.

I get my hands around her neck. I take hits, scratches, and pushes from her as I squeeze as tightly as I can. With Indigo beneath me for the second time, with my hands stopping her from breathing, the darkness I felt before returns. It burns me to have to be this person. It pains me to have to kill. But I have to. I have to end her to save us.

I don't look nor move toward the chaos I hear around me. I commit to what I'm doing, to ending someone who is hell-bent on ending my happiness and the life of someone I love.

I grip even tighter, pushing her head further down into the sand. The mix of voices around me doesn't make me loosen my hold. The loud cries from Kennedy don't stop me. If I don't end her here, we'll be faced with this same situation again at another time. Sooner or later, Indigo is going to sneak back up on us again.

She viciously claws my arms. Tears begin to form in my eyes, clouding my vision. I came here to vacation, to take a break, not to take a life.

Her nails dig into my arms. With both hands still secured around her neck, the body reappears. I gasp, release my hold. I look down at her pixie-cut, her round eyes, her sweat-soaked face. I watch as she chokes, rubs where my hands just were. I look down at who isn't Indigo.

Another one capable of vanishing. *Oh no. Oh no. Oh no. I almost killed the wrong person.*

I climb off her in a hurry. I look down at who isn't the person I wanted to harm. True, she did vanish, did attempt to attack us, did come along with Indigo with the same thoughts as her in mind. But I'm not this person. I'm not Indigo. I can't comfortably hurt, let alone kill a complete stranger.

The necklace clasped around her neck that I couldn't see when my hands were there reads Luna.

I step back from Luna, look around for the others, try to locate all of my loved ones, tune back into the fact that Indigo is the greatest threat and she's somewhere on this beach. Everyone is scattered. While focusing on who I thought was Indigo, I missed a lot, but just as expected, my family held me down. Avery is as still as a mannequin. No question, Jackson is why she hasn't ripped my head off or anyone else's. He's keeping her in place. Ethan is far down the shore. I had to have been focused completely on my attempt to not feel the wind result of him zooming by. Kesia is briskly moving toward Ethan, toward the others who came with Indigo.

A shriek forces my eyes to the right. On the other side of the bonfire, Michael is lifted completely off the sand, water dripping from his body. Mid-air he's being pulled toward the fire. Fright flings my eyes open as wide as they can spread. In quick bird-like motions, my head moves in fast twitches as I try to eye everyone close by, as I try to figure out who has Michael's ability, the ability to move something or someone without being hands on. Indigo's crawling back onto the shore. Ms. Reed, wet as well, is only feet away from her, trying to reach out and grab her. Ms. Housley and Kennedy tug at Michael's legs, trying to pull him back down, get his feet back on land, stop him from reaching the fire. Avery's still frozen. I look back down at Luna, at who I just assaulted. Her head is slightly lifted, her round eyes glued on my dangling boyfriend.

Her. It's her. "No!" I scream stepping forward, toward her, reaching out, trying to pull her eyes, her focus, her thoughts from him. A snap of the head in my direction, Luna's wide-eyes now on me, I don't see, but hear Michael's body slam into the sand. A half a second it seems, and she's on her feet. Luna rushes me with a strength I don't expect, a strength much like my own, a strength that forces me back at such a speed, with such might, I fly back several feet, tumble, causing a split second blackout, and then crash face down in the wet sand at the shoreline.

Before I can lift my head, disoriented, I'm grabbed by my ponytail, pulled up to my knees. With my hair being tugged, I use one hand to try to remove Luna's hand from my hair, and the other to try and rub sand from my face, to prevent grains from getting into my eyes and killing my vision.

I don't know who the hell this chick is, what Indigo told her to make her so aggressive, so dead set on taking us out, but her actions have directly asked that she be eliminated. And I plan to do just that.

I reach back, grab her wrist, grunt loudly as I snatch her body so that she's pulled in front of mine. Still on my knees, I release her wrist, hurriedly reach around to the back of each calf, and pull as hard as I can. Both feet temporarily off the ground, she smashes in the sand, landing on her back. I don't wait, don't care anymore that she isn't Indigo. Her hair is too short to grab, so I can't return the favor. I grab a hold of her neck, use the strength I've mostly only needed for animals, and drag her further into the lake, until the water is waist deep. Her legs kick wildly as I submerge her, as I force her into the one thing our bodies can't live without, while robbing her of the ability to do the one thing we all need to do as humans or aliens. Breathe.

She resurfaces, pierces my ear drums with her scream, fights her way out of my hold. She tries to get away, to escape this horrible death, but I can't let her get back to shore. She's used three abilities already. Either one of her parents had two powers, or she's had the most amazing, but dangerous ability of them all passed along to her. Power mimicry.

Unwisely, she gives me her back, allowing me to lock her in a choke hold. I pull her further back into the lake. Her wild kicking is much less effective while being held this way. With my eyes on the shore, on my family, searching for the ghostly Indigo, with Luna's eyes likely doing the same thing, I keep moving back until the water level hits my chest. From here, an enormous blaze catches my eye, the high flames reacting as though gasoline was poured onto the once small bonfire. I cover Luna's eyes, take away her ability to focus on anything and change it. I submerge her again, use my strength to keep her held, to keep her beneath the surface.

With her securely locked in my hold, painfully breathing in water, terror escapes me in a loud wail. I scream, I cry out for Michael from the lake as I see Indigo reappear, charging at him, running for him when he's so close to the overwhelming blaze Luna caused.

Avery is still frozen. Jackson has yet to let her go. He knows about her strength, knows she's stronger than me. But in this moment, he needs to free her. He needs to stop Indigo.

"Jackson!" I scream, attempting to break his gaze, the others still down the beach, huddled in a way that I can't make out what's happening.

She goes invisible again, at the sound of Jackson's name. Jackson turns my way, let's Avery go, allows her to enter the lake. A loud groan, one I can hear clearly from this distance, over the sound of the water, escapes Michael as her unseen body rams into him. His body falls into Ms. Housley. Ms. Housley's body is caught by the flames.

I screech, let go of lifeless Luna, let the lake swallow her until her dried out remains wash to shore. I try as hard as I can to get back to dry land. As Michael tries to smother his burning arm with one of the blankets, I wade through the water as quickly as I can toward Ms. Housley's burning body.

No sight of Indigo. Avery on the loose. Michael badly burned. A life taken with my hands. Ms. Housley, my friend's sweet, freckle-faced mother covered in flames.

Chapter 15

*P*etrified at the sight of Ms. Housley's condition and the frightening sound of her silence, I'm unable to budge. I stand, feeling so heavy in my drenched clothes, so heavy-hearted as I witness Ms. Reed, Kennedy, Mrs. Everly, Jackson, and Michael surround her. They work to smother the flames burning through her human exterior, incinerating her insides, frying what makes her a Que, what makes her Ms. Housley.

I fall to my knees as Kennedy lays hands on Ms. Housley. I make silent wishes. Wishes for her to fully recover, to no longer feel the heat, the excruciating pain of the fire cooking away her flesh. I wish for Kennedy's power to prevail, to save Ethan from being parentless, to save him from an emptiness one can only feel when they exist in this huge world without the needed support of a parent.

Please, Kennedy. Work your magic. Save her. Save her for Ethan. Save her for all of us. For all of those who love her.

Torn from my thoughts, my silent wishes brought to an abrupt stop, my head snaps back. It feels as though I'm being scalped, like my head is being pulled off and may fully detach from the rest of me.

I'm ripped from the ground and thrown from the shore by my hair. I soar above the ground, above the lake, like a lightweight rubber ball. Loud air whooshes by my ears, deafens me until I drop, until I land harshly into the large body of fresh water. Face down, disoriented again, bolts of pain shoot through my body as my world suddenly becomes black.

Get up, Jaylen. Get up before she gets to you, before Avery ends you for ending Luna.

I don't move. Can't move. Mental coaching is failing me. Being thrown so far, my body plummeting into the water and smacking against the surface, feels more like I hit solid concrete instead. Avery has a strength that far exceeds mine, that undoubtedly could kill me. Will kill me if I don't get up.

Face down, I breathe in a hefty amount of Lake Michigan. The burn of the water entering through my nose as opposed to air helps evaporate my bewilderment. How close Avery is, the thought of someone coming into the lake to help her hurt me, the terrifying thought of my family not reaching me in time, the deep desire to live gives me the needed drive to find air above the surface. I don't want to die. Not today. Not like this.

I cough violently. Lake water and saliva spray out of my mouth. I blink repeatedly, try to clear away the blurriness, as the slam against the lake left my brain feeling completely discombobulated.

A firm grip around my neck, Avery dominates me with the power inside her and shoves me back beneath the surface. I immediately swallow more of the lake.

Like Luna, I react wildly in a panic, kicking and trying to squirm out of her hold, away from a painful ending.

With both hands, I'm able to pull her hand from my throat. The moment my head breaks through the surface, I cough again, blinking rapidly, and backing away into deeper depths.

"Ethan!" I shout as loudly as I possibly can, forcing myself to cough more. "Lark!" I scream her name as loudly as I did Ethan's, needing them both. He's the fastest, will get to me in seconds. She's our mermaid, my fish-like sister, the only one who can survive beneath the waves. Michael's telekinesis would be helpful, but he's burned, injured by the fire. He needs to stay on land and recover.

I change direction, move sideways away from Avery as my eyes regain focus. I try not to move too far back. I need my head to remain above water while my feet are still planted in the sand beneath. If I'm forced to swim and fight, I'll drain myself much sooner and likely never leave this lake again.

With loud splashing, moving through the water like a speed boat, Ethan hurries to help me. Lark swims as quickly as she can behind him and then I lose sight of her as she dives farther down. Kesia, Jackson, and even Michael with a bad arm, move through the water urgently in my direction. Following comes Indigo's squad, but no Indigo.

I never stop moving away from Avery. Her intense, heart-stopping, vicious, electric-blue stare gives me all the strength and motivation I need to move faster than her. She wants to kill me, not because I came after her niece, but because her niece somehow convinced someone equally as psychotic as her into attacking perfect strangers. I was left with no choice but to eliminate Luna. Like Indigo, our promises to leave things alone, our interest in moving on with our lives in as peaceful a way as possible, proved ineffective in making Luna turn around and walk away. Like Indigo, she wanted to fight no matter what. I don't know what their relationship was, what lies Indigo may have told her, but she matched Indigo's hate for us and her determination in taking our lives. Luna left me with one ugly choice and I took it.

Ethan reaches me, stands at my side, makes me feel a little safer than I did a half a second ago. Though I'm physically stronger, I'm not in tip-top shape at the moment. I didn't prepare for a fight like Indigo and her people did.

"Avery, think about what you're doing!" I continue to move away from her, my body aching, worn out, needing to guzzle fresh water, needing to rest, take in, and release normal breaths, not fast, frantic ones. "You said before that you never wanted to hurt teenagers." I cough again. "We're kids to you, Avery! We're the same age as your niece!"

No words from her, just fast movements in my direction. Fire in her eyes. Death in her stare.

"Avery, please," I beg, thinking about what I've already done to Luna. "Please don't make me..." I correct myself. "Us. Don't make us do anything else we don't want to do. Remember, we didn't come to you. Everything that's happened, you made happen!"

She continues to move toward me, her long, thin frame still in pursuit of someone begging for this to end without more pain.

"Leave me the fuck alone!" I scream. This is a fight for my life. One I don't want to have, but must.

I lower my head, take a large gulp of Lake Michigan, swallow, try to take deep breaths, build some more strength, and quiet these aches. I take in more water, silently hope what's left of the day's sunlight gives my body enough fuel to get me through this battle, to come out victorious, to stay alive.

I stop moving, stop running, stop exhausting myself. This fight is going to happen. Tiring myself out will only increase the chances of it ending horribly for me.

Only a few feet away from me, Avery grunts loudly and is suddenly sucked into the lake.

That was no hidden sink hole, no mysterious predator. That was my sister. Our mermaid. Lark.

Ethan and I swim toward where Avery went down, trying to get to her before her squad gets to us.

Avery resurfaces briefly and is taken back down again. Her arms splash wildly above the water and then the rest of her pops back up. Unsurprisingly, Lark is having difficulty keeping her down. Not only because of Avery's strength, but also because of her height. To take this beast down, we're going to need to outnumber her, pull her further back into the water so she's easier to keep submerged, combine our abilities, and cross our fingers that nobody she brought with her has the ability to poke us with a magic finger and completely annihilate us.

Avery steps back, dips under the water, and tries to see who's attacking her from down under. A second later, she comes up again and takes a step toward the underwater threat.

With her focus on Lark, I lower myself and swim past Lark, around Avery. I become the predator.

Like I did when I was attacked by the bear on prom night, the way I'd treat any other ferocious animal, the way the hungry go after their prey, I come up behind her. I grab her shoulders and use them as support as I climb onto her back, locking both arms tightly around her neck and both legs around her small frame.

Out here, in the lake, my best bet is to let what we're standing in be my greatest weapon—not my super strength. I'd rather Avery exhaust herself trying to fight me off, to breathe in lung-fulls of water each time she goes under in an attempt to free herself from my clutch, to do the damage to herself with each passing second of the struggle. Choosing to fight this out wouldn't make sense. I'm not only unrested and in pain, but kicks and underwater hits won't hurt her as much because the water resistance won't allow my strikes to cause the amount of pain I want. On the up side, the resistance works against her, too. Still, if I pretend to be Wonder Woman, she has the greater chance of doing more damage and keeping me held underwater than I do her.

I suck in a chest and two cheek-fulls of air just as she begins her fight for my release.

We go under. Eyes closed.

Both of her arms pull at mine. I struggle to hold onto her.

Struggle not to release this air, this oxygen, just to inhale what'll kill me.

She does an animalistic barrel roll followed by another, trying her damnedest to shake me off while pulling us further, deeper into Lake Michigan.

I squeeze, holding on as tightly as I can, though I can feel myself losing the security of my hold. I can feel her power, her fight to get me off, her determination to see above water, to breathe in air again.

Avery roars. Bubbles formed of her pain escape her mouth, rise above us to where we're both desperate to get to.

Lark tries to help me keep her down, pulls at Avery as she fights for me to let go, as she throws her body around.

I lose my air. Both cheeks deflate.

Don't breathe in, Jaylen. Don't breathe in.

Unable to fight without oxygen, without the ability to breathe, I forfeit the short battle. I redirect my focus. At this moment, beating Avery isn't going to happen unless I'm willing to lose too. Both of us need air. Depriving her of hers is the equivalent of depriving myself.

With my right foot, I push off the sand at the bottom of the lake. My head breaks through the water, tears back into the land of free oxygen, and immediately a series of fast, deep breaths begins. Every breath hurts. Every breath is exhausting. I need to get out of this lake. I need the safety of dry land, yet my body is calling for what's all around me. I've never not needed water and needed water so badly at the same time.

I pull in a mouthful of water. Mid-swallow, mid-breath, I choke. It flies out of my mouth, ends up right where it was a second ago.

Avery pops up right beside me. The second her face clears the water, she begins choking. Water comes out her mouth and air enters every short second it has the opportunity to. Tears fall from her eyes as she hacks loudly and deeply.

I look for Ethan who was at my side and is now so far

away from me, much deeper in Lake Michigan. Jackson is facing the shore, standing several meters away from me. Kesia's now beside me. Lark's somewhere underneath me, okay I hope, as Avery made it back up, but she hasn't yet. Michael's backstroking toward me with his eyes fixated on the bearded guy who entered the water behind the friends I called in for help. How tired everyone is, I'm not sure. What they've been experiencing while I've been in the middle of my own battles is unknown to me. If I had been watching their every move, I'd exist no more. I'd be pulseless, a woman of the past, a victim of Avery's first attempt to drown me. I'd be dead. Like Luna.

"I'm so tired," I say to Kesia, trying to use the little energy I have left in me to move away from Avery, away from the retaliation I know is coming. "So tired and so thirsty."

"You go. I'll keep her here. I'll make her believe underwater is peaceful and desirable. I'll make her calmly, effortlessly, end herself."

Short, uneven breaths make it hard to speak. "You shouldn't have to kill, Kesia. That's not why I invited you here. That's not what I want you to have on your heart for the rest of your life."

"Go, Jaylen," she states sternly, her accent strong and authoritative.

I take a gulp of the lake again. This time, I get the water down. It doesn't make me feel better even slightly, but I know it's what my body needs. It's what it's begging for.

I take in more water. Avery's choking can still be heard. Ethan's fast swimming and hard splashing pull my eyes his way as he races toward us.

Avery goes down again.

"That you?" I ask Kesia.

She shakes her head. "Must be Lark."

"You okay?" Michael asks, his question rushed. "Can you swim back to shore?"

I don't get to answer. Avery pops back up again. Lark with her.

"I need help!" Lark tells me. "I thought she'd be worn out by now. I thought all the water she'd be forced to breathe in would make this fast. Easy. But she's tough, and the longer I use my ability, the longer I struggle with her, the faster I'm going to tire out."

"Kesia, get in Old School's head," Michael says, speaking of the shorter guy who came with Indigo. His hair is straight and weighed down by the water while his eyes are wide and on Avery. "He's got telekinesis, too. Don't let him pull Avery to shore. Don't let him throw anyone else out into the lake the way he just did Ethan."

No wonder Ethan was so far from us. No way in hell would he just swim away and leave us in the middle of a struggle. Lucky me, my fight was mostly underwater. Without being able to lay eyes on me, he wasn't able to throw me a great distance. I'd be too weak to swim back.

"Got it." Kesia nods and turns her attention to the other telekinetic Que, immediately invading his mind, taking over his thoughts, and stopping him from dragging Avery his way.

"Lark, me and you," Michael says. "Me and you are going to take Avery down. Jaylen, I love you. Swim to shore, to Kennedy. Get water."

Lark is back under the water. Michael swims a few feet in the direction of Avery before stopping. He stands, watches Avery.

I backstroke toward shore, trying to get to a point where I can stand and my head remain above water. As I move, my eyes dart in all directions. I look all over for Indigo, the one who caused all of this, the one who has learned how to manipulate and control those who surround her, the one who can become unseen at any given moment, the one who can be impossible to track down because of her ability. I look at Michael, at Avery, at Kesia eyeing Old School as she drifts his way, at Ethan heading straight for Indigo's bun-haired, bearded friend. The friend now heading for Avery, likely to defend her, to partner with her since it's Lark and Michael against one.

I watch as Ethan swims faster than an Olympian right for the bearded guy who he looks to collide with. Each stroke and each kick bringing them closer to one another.

I fear them smashing into each other, heads clashing at such a speed, irreversible injury resulting, and my friend getting hurt in a way that his body cannot heal itself.

Only a couple of feet from him, Ethan, still moving briskly, bounces back mid-stroke. He hits something. What, I don't see.

Indigo. Maybe that's Indigo. I flip over, abandon the backstroke, gulp down some water, and swim much less impressively toward Ethan. Legs tired. Thirsty. Body aching. Head still a little shaky from being thrown, hitting the water, and scuffling in the deep.

Mid-swim, I swallow down more of the lake. Though it's a fresh water source, it sure as hell doesn't taste like what I drink on the daily. Nonetheless, it'll do the same. Keep me hydrated. Alive.

"Stay there!" Ethan yells. "I'm good."

I stop swimming, tread water, and look around again for Indigo. No sign of her. My eyes return to Ethan. "What happened?" I ask him before glancing at Indigo's bearded friend who's no longer swimming. He's treading to stay afloat.

Ethan reaches out in front of him, both hands trying to feel what he swam directly into, what neither of us see, but he felt.

He pushes out in front of him, and slowly I paddle his way, just in case I'm needed, even if just to be the one who gets harmed so he doesn't leave here with a scratch.

"Something's here. I can feel it. Some kind of blockage. Not a person."

I look at the bearded guy, scan his calm face, notice how

casually he's floating though someone's trying to attack him. There's no panic, no fear, no preparation for an attack of any sort. That's because he's protected. He's in his own little bubble. What Ethan swam into, is pushing against, and what neither of us can see, is a force field. A protective barrier making him as untouchable as the invisible Indigo.

I swallow more water and try to take slow deep breaths. "Force field, Ethan! That's why…" Another deep breath. "That's why he's so chill!" I speak loudly so I can be heard.

And that's why he was trying to get to Avery. He could probably wrap her in his bubble too if he were close enough to her.

I look down at the lake while sucking in more water. Swallow after swallow, I pull more in. My body absolutely needs it to get out of this lake.

As I lift my head, Avery's body lifts as well. Held above the water, just as Michael was held when Luna tried to fry to him, she dangles. Lark resurfaces and drinks some of the lake as she watches.

Michael's head tilts back, his eyes on Avery's floating body as he bends her. Her long, thin physique becomes a U shape in a backward bend. She coughs while dangling, likely still trying to get water out of her lungs. No screaming, no begging, she doesn't speak.

My stomach sinks, feels as though it may fall completely out of me. My heart throbs. I want to turn away, not sure of what I'm going to see if I keep staring, but I have to look. I have to know what he does, have to keep vigilant watch for Indigo who couldn't possibly stay invisible much longer.

There's a sudden, loud crack, and the U flattens. The bearded guy who came with her gasps aloud from within his safe zone. Lark lets out a short scream, covers her mouth. I shake at the sight of Avery's body. I tremble at the sight of the back of her head against the back of her calves, her spine snapped. He bent her backwards in a way no flexible trainer, yoga guru, or dancer would ever bend themselves, especially in such a rush. He broke her back and folded her in half like a sheet of loose leaf paper.

Avery's body drops, and Lark instantly dives down to keep her under, to make sure there's no more life left in the strongest of the Ques here.

Michael turns and faces me. My overtired brain, eyes, and limbs are making it more than a chore to stay above water. I can't stay out here much longer. Physically, I'm worn. Mentally and emotionally, I'm damaged. Damaged because of what I've done and seen today, because of what else I may have to find the guts to do.

Michael rushes to me and turns so I can climb onto his back. With Avery under the lake, Lark down there to ensure that she doesn't find the strength to unfold and resurface, my eyes move to Kesia. Her eyes hold Old School's gaze as she slowly allows herself to sink. He becomes hidden beneath Lake Michigan as well, goes down calmly with her. Through the power of her mind, the control of her thoughts, Kesia convinces him to drown himself, to spend his last moments in the unbreathable world beneath Michigan's calm waves.

I know he'll never come up again. Neither will Avery. Just like that, two more people who were alive just minutes ago are now people of the past.

Lake Michigan was a stunning paradise when we first arrived. It's now become nightmare territory. A graveyard. A graveyard with a ghost still lurking around.

Chapter 16

hile I was terror-stricken, screaming for Ethan and Lark to save me from Avery, many rushed into Lake Michigan. Ideally, only my family would have entered and come to my assistance, but Avery was important to those who came with her which is why they ran in as well. In the moment, with so much going on, fear roaring out of me, painful currents shooting throughout my insides, I had thought Avery's whole group came in. Now, with my fear no longer alive, I see Scarlett never entered. She remained on shore along with the curly-haired guy who came with them. The two of them are kneeled down beside Kennedy, Ms. Reed, and Ms. Ava. All have their backs to the water.

Still holding on to Michael, I look around and try to spot unnatural movements in the water, obvious ripples that may show me where Indigo is. No signs of her.

Michael struggles to swim with me on his back but doesn't ask me to get off, doesn't huff or fuss about the difficulty. He doesn't holler ahead to Jackson who's still in the water, meters in front of us, facing the shore. In water that his head just barely clears, Jackson stands, focused, not struggling to swim as we are.

I didn't have time to wonder why he didn't pause Avery, why he didn't make it easier for Lark to take her out, but now I see. His eyes are on his mother. Mrs. Everly is perfectly still, mid-step, on her way into Lake Michigan. She was more than likely on her way in to help, to do whatever she could to keep her son safe. Jackson must've turned, taken a quick look behind him and noticed her. Though Jackson ran into the water because I was in need, he did what any of us would've done if faced with the same choice. He did what he could to keep his mother out of harm's way.

I hang on to Michael as he moves toward shore, puts forth great effort to get me back on dry land. But why? True, I won't drown there, but we're still too vulnerable with Indigo unable to be seen. In addition to that, Indigo's bearded friend is still in the water, protected in his bubble. There's no telling what he may do, what other powers he may have. Jackson, Ethan, Lark, and Kesia are in the water. Family. Maybe Indigo is, too. The greatest threat. Michael and I are not leaving our family. We're not swimming all the way to shore to possibly watch one of them get hurt from a distance.

"No," I say. "Not the shore. There's still a threat in the water. We're not leaving the others in here with him." I let go of Michael, drink in more of the fresh water lake. "I mean it," I tell him after a large swallow. "I'm not leaving this lake without them."

"I'll take care of him and I'll make sure they get out. Just go, Jaylen. You're weak."

"I'll be okay. Really," I say, not one hundred percent certain I can make it through another fight, even a short one. I'm tired, can typically experience quite a bit before any pain sets in, but I've had a long day. Though most of it was pleasant, I'm not fully hydrated, I'm worn out, and I need a few bottles of water and a long night's sleep. My body is telling me to do as Michael instructed, but I love these people, and loving them isn't something I had to teach myself to do. It was almost immediate. We're connected, we're the same, and we're getting out of Lake Michigan together. I don't know how exhausted they are. I'm not sure how much fight they have left in them, but whatever they feel or think they have, I want them to know for sure that they have me. I'm not going anywhere without them. If one of my family is intended to be hurt, it'll be me instead. They don't even know Indigo. They won't be causalities of the war she started.

"I'll take care of him from here," Michael says, treading water, eyes on our bearded enemy as he draws him away from Ethan, toward us, using only his mind.

"Stop, stop, stop! Listen!" Our enemy holds his hand out, his eyes wide and filled with terror. "Listen, please. I didn't come here to die!"

Michael stops dragging him when he's only a few feet away from us. Kesia, Lark, and Ethan move in and position themselves so he's surrounded, so that whenever he runs out of the strength he needs to keep his protective shield up, we can close in and end him.

"I'm Matias." His hand is still out. "Please hear me out. Please," he begs. "I didn't come here to die." He works his legs vigorously underwater to keep his head above.

"Just to kill us, right?" Ethan pushes forward and bounces back again. Matias's protective barrier is still up and keeping him safe.

Matias shakes his head. "I came here as protection. To save Indigo and Avery from people they said were gathering to kill them over a silly high school misunderstanding. I've never killed anyone. Never even wanted to," he explains in a rush through frantic breaths. "But they said they couldn't even go home, that you all were gathering as many friends as you could to sneak up on them and kill them. They said they can't go through the cops or courts because of what we are. Me, my brother..." He points toward shore. "We just felt bad for Indigo. She was terrified and crying. We thought this was a group of high school bullies incapable of letting some drama go and taking things to an unimaginable level. I didn't know she started anything. I didn't know you guys tried to end this without violence. I didn't know we were walking in as the villains. I thought she was saving herself by taking you guys out before you guys could get to her."

We all work our limbs to stay above water.

"I was here to offer a safe barrier for them. I thought they were in danger. Not causing it."

"How do you know her? Indigo made it seem as though she didn't have others."

He shakes his head, answers me. "I don't know her. I only met her because of this. I knew Luna."

My stomach drops at the mention of her name.

Matias continues. "Luna's family had some kind of distant relationship with Avery. Luna brought me into this. We tried to walk away. Run, actually. You all saw." His eyes run across Ethan, Kesia, and Lark. "When Luna went invisible, Scarlett, Andrew, Diego, and I ran off. It was clear this wasn't self-defense. We wanted to go. You guys followed us, threatened us, and didn't let us leave. Why would we run so far down the beach away from you all if our plan was to attack you and kill you?"

"I don't know you. Why would I believe anything you say? You came with a group of nutty ass killers. I wasn't letting you off this property, and I said what I had to say to stop you from getting close to my people." Ethan's face is expressionless, shows no sympathy, no care for the position Indigo and her family put Matias in.

Now it makes sense. That's why I saw Kesia running to catch up to Ethan. They took off and Ethan had to stop them from leaving, said whatever he could to keep them at a safe distance from the rest of us. Speed and agility are all he has, but he didn't let that stop him from using the right words to keep a handful of their group far down the beach. Only, I know for sure his words weren't enough. Scarlett has not only seen Ethan use his abilities but has the gift of invading minds and reading thoughts. My eyes briefly go to Kesia. No need to ask how he got over on Scarlett, how he was able to keep her from revealing his lies. Kesia had to have been in her head, controlling everything, likely encouraging nods which led Matias and Diego to believe Ethan's threats.

"I don't wanna die. I tried to go. I didn't come in this water to do anything except help Andrew and Avery. To protect them. I came to offer a shield."

"A shield? So they couldn't get hurt, but they could still fuck us up?" Michael asks loudly.

"The fight had already started. I would rather the people I came with stay alive. If they all die, what's most likely to happen to me? Of course I came in here to protect Avery and Andrew. Right or wrong, having the numbers increases my chances of leaving here breathing."

"Or you could've just ran off when Jaylen called for us instead of rushing in to help Avery. Stop playing the innocent victim-without-a-choice. You came to hurt people you didn't know, you tried to run and got caught, and when you had another chance to run off, you ran into the fight." Lark breathes unevenly as her body shakes from an upsetting mix of emotions.

"I wasn't thinking. You're right, I could've taken that opportunity to run, but I wanted to save those I came with. Really, I wanted to help sooner. We heard screams, but we didn't wanna get burned. Your friend said he had the gift of creating fire." He throws a quick look at Ethan. "He said she could control our minds so that we wouldn't be able to move away when he starts burning us," he explains, pointing at Kesia. "We didn't wanna get fried, so we stayed put. When so many of you ran in to attack Avery, I just felt the urge to save her. Regardless of how scared I was and still am, I wasn't willing to run off and leave her in here alone. I'm not that guy."

Clearly, Andrew, the old school lookalike, was only trying to protect Avery, not murder us. If he were as crazy as Luna or Indigo, he wouldn't have thrown Ethan. He would've used his telekinesis to hurt him, to end his existence, just as Michael used his ability to kill Avery. They came to protect the wrong people. Andrew is dead because of that. I'm not letting Matias die because he's been woven into Indigo's web of lies.

"Leave him alone," I say before gulping down more water. "If they wanted to hurt us, they would've, especially Andrew. All he did was throw you, Ethan, even after you threatened to set him on fire. Andrew could've killed you from a distance just as Michael did Avery. He didn't. They just got involved with the wrong people. They thought they were helping someone. They got sucked into Indigo's bullshit."

Michael drinks some of Lake Michigan as well. The others don't speak. We all tirelessly work our bodies to stay above water.

"Seriously, guys!" My achy body shakes all over. "He's not Indigo. He's not Luna. He's not Avery. He's not trying to attack us. We're not bad people. We defend ourselves. We don't maliciously kill. Maybe if we had time to really look at the situation, really had time to think about why Ethan was thrown and not brutally harmed, Andrew would still be alive."

Kesia's brows arch outward, she bows her head, tears fall as she treads water. I know the idea of killing someone who wasn't the threat we thought they were is shredding her heart. None of us came here to kill, especially her. She's only here because we coincidentally bumped into each other at Princeton. Other than coming from the same extraterrestrial line, we have no other ties. It feels shitty to know I lied to get her here simply to learn about our alien background, and she ended up being pulled directly into the mess we took this vacation to escape.

Michael turns, briefly holds my gaze with those forest-green eyes, then looks back at Matias. "Swim to shore," he tells him. "Take your brother, take your mind-reading friend, and get the fuck off this property."

"Mike," Lark calls out. "Calm down. It does sound like he got caught up with the wrong people. I don't think he's a bad guy."

Michael shakes his head. "I don't care. He's not one of us. He's not my family. Don't let your guard down yet. He came with a lunatic that I'm not letting off this property. You hear me?" he asks Matias. "I'm not letting Indigo leave here just so she can run up on us again with another group of people. She's going down today. If you try to intervene, if you're playing Mr. Innocent right now just so you can get back on dry land and try something, I'm telling you, I will personally take you out myself. You touch, even breathe wrong on any of my family, I'm not going to snap your spine, I'm not going to fold you in half, I'm not going to take you out quickly. It's going to be slow. It's going to be painful. I'm going to slowly twist your head, twist it like it's a bottle cap, and I'm going to break your fucking neck. So, let me make it clear to you one more time. If you try to play me, if you lay hands on anyone, you're done."

"I just wanna go home," Matias says, his voice almost that of a child. "I just wanna leave here with my brother. Alive."

Michael reaches out, pulls me over to him. "Hop on."

"I'll swim. I'll be fine."

"For me, please, hop on. Let me at least get you to a point where you can walk. I don't want you to exhaust yourself too much more."

Again, I climb onto my boyfriend's back.

"You first. We'll be behind you," Michael says to Matias, unwilling to take any chances. "You guys keep an eye open for Indigo. She has to be getting tired. She's been invisible for a while."

As we head for shore, I look around, my mind suddenly questioning if Indigo saw her plan falling to pieces, stood by, watched her family and friends have their lives taken, and simply took off. She sure as hell didn't help me during the buck attack. She didn't use her ability to remain unseen and help me take down the animal. She vanished and let me fight on my own. Though she was close by, she still left me. Left me to possibly be killed. Looks like she's done the same thing here today. Indigo is the most manipulative, self-absorbed, unpredictable individual I've ever personally known. Though Michael's threats to Matias made him sound like an insensitive monster, I understand why he wants little to no interference. He's done guessing, done having to walk around with his guard up. He's ready to close the horror-filled chapter known as Indigo today. So am I.

I let go of Michael when we get closer to Jackson. I know we're at a place where I can actually stand in the water, walk, and still breathe. We all head for shore, Jackson included, his mother now free to move. Able to see her son is out of danger, Mrs. Everly turns and rushes back to the huddle.

With my breathing still sporadic, my body sore, feeling like 300 pounds of dead weight, I move sluggishly. I see the shore, can't wait to step back on it, but my mind and eyes are still trying to find Indigo. My brain is trying to think like her, figure out what move she's waiting to make, but we're nothing alike. I can't warp my brain to even come close to hers. All I can do is hope that we see her before she's right up on one of us, before she's right up on Michael. I try to spot her, but somehow she's remained invisible. Or maybe she's hiding. I look up toward the house, squint, try to spot her figure around the outdoor seating area. Nothing. *Where the hell is she?*

Just feet from dry sand, my eyes are pulled to my left. A water bottle is lifted, tilted back, but the contents aren't being emptied onto the sand. They're pouring into something. Someone. Her.

I nudge Michael, nod my head in the direction of the bottle, pulling his attention that way.

"Ethan," I whisper. "Water bottle. Ten o'clock."

Far from covertly, we all hurry that way. The half-empty bottle falls to the ground as we charge for her invisible frame. She reappears for a split second before we lose sight of her again. I keep my eyes on the sand, watch the direction of her footprints. All of our bodies are probably sore and we definitely need rest, but knowing where Indigo is, knowing she's the reason we've had to kill, knowing she's the reason we'll never be the same after this evening, has ignited us with the necessary fury to battle it out once more, to finish what she both started and tried to end in the worst way.

Still no sight of her body, my eyes follow her footprints leading into the water.

I shake my head. There's a small chance I could still overpower her on land, but there's no way I can battle it out in the water. I can't be pulled under again. Fighting for air and fighting to keep my hands on the hollow girl will kill me. Not her.

Lark asks, "Should I go in? Should I go after her?" Her eyes are on the ground, on the path of footprints that end at the shoreline.

I shake my head, trying to remain as clear-minded as possible. "No. She's gonna have to come out sooner or later."

Further up the shoreline, she briefly reappears, then goes invisible again. Right away, I get exactly what she's doing. She's waited too long, should've left when she had the chance, when we were all in the water, but now she's trying to escape, however, she's used her ability for too long. Her body is tired, too worn out to keep her hidden, so she's trying to sneak away. She tried to lead us back into the water, to give herself an even greater head start, but none of us rushed back in.

She reappears again in a flash, further away than before, and then, just like that, she's unable to be seen again. She's remaining at the shoreline so her footprints are incapable of being followed, so they're erased as they're made. She's hoping to create a great enough distance between her and us so she can get away unharmed. Get away and leave behind her irreparable mess.

"Ethan, how are you feeling? Got enough energy left in you to catch her?" I ask as I can hear him taking deep, ragged breaths. He's been thrown, too, had to experience his body slamming into Lake Michigan. He may not be able to zoom down the shoreline to grab her, meaning one of us will have to try our luck and possibly be outrun, allowing her to maybe get off the property.

"I'll keep her in place."

I turn to Jackson. "How? She's blinking and every time we see her, she's farther away."

"I just need to see her for a second and I'll hold her in place."

Ethan grabs the half-empty bottle Indigo started, chugs it, and throws the empty plastic back in the sand. "I'll find the energy. I wanna be done with this shit."

"Just grab her for me, bro," Michael says. "She's gonna fight for you to let go, but don't. When I see her, I'll drag her ass back down here, and I'll finish her."

We stand, wait for just one more glimpse of her, wait to see where Ethan needs to run, wait to see if she left the shoreline.

I take a quick look behind us, at the burning fire, where our evening was supposed to be spent, where relaxation was supposed to happen, and laughs were meant to be shared. Still huddled together are Kennedy, Ms. Reed, and Mrs. Ava. I don't call out to them, don't pull them away from what they're doing, don't break their focus which is likely on Ms. Housley who needs to be saved for Ethan. I don't want them to worry about what we can finish.

I'm worried, though. Worried about the whereabouts of Scarlett and Diego. Just because they tried to leave before doesn't mean they won't attempt to hurt one of us when they see what happens to Indigo. Us rushing in her direction was enough to get them to drop their care for Ms. Housley and move toward the danger. Not away. *Where the hell did they go?*

I spin my body completely around and find them right beside Matias. Standing behind the three of them is Mrs. Everly. Her right brow wings up. Her nostrils flare. She stands shorter than the boys, but there's no fear in her face. No kindness. No weakness. If they were to turn, make the assumption that she's ungifted, her expression alone would make them feel differently. Her face bluntly states, *Don't try me.* No smart person would.

Kesia stands before the three of them, speaking faintly, her eyes on Scarlett. I don't speak to any of them. She's in Scarlett's head and she needs to stay there so that whatever she says is believed. The boys need to be kept in line. We don't need anyone else to play hero and run to Indigo's defense.

Ethan darts off without warning. Sand kicks up in his path. Wind blows past my body, giving me a chill, making my body shudder. Jackson takes off, too. A turtle when compared to Ethan.

Indigo appears in a flash again, her back to us as she's trying to scurry away. Ethan not at full speed, but still moving at a rate that would win him prey in the wild, jumps, both feet off the sand, agile, not needing to pause for even a second. He lunges forward, arms stretched out, and catches Indigo in seconds.

Together, they hit the sand, roll over a few times, grunting loud enough for the rest of us to hear from where we're standing, before they land in a deadly position; Indigo face down in the sand and Ethan on her back. Both of Ethan's hands hold the back of her neck as he forces her face deep into the unbreathable grains.

I start toward them and immediately Michael steps in front of me. "You don't need to see that."

I don't look away. Can't look away. From here, I can see both of her hands digging into the sand. Clawing. Her legs lift and kick against the beach. She's fighting a hopeless fight to survive. Her position puts her at the greatest disadvantage. She's going to die and I'm going to watch it happen. It's the sort of thing no one ever wants to witness, even hear about, and it's a darkness that's going to be marked in my memory forever. Indigo, the first Quisi I was ever in the presence of since the mysterious disappearance of my biological mother, is about to take her last breath on this beach. The girl I shared laughs with, so much of my free time with, and cared for so deeply is being suffocated.

I don't stand by anything Indigo has plotted or done, can't ever forget her attempt to take Michael's life, but I'm struggling a great deal to stand by this. I bend over, grab a hold of my belly, squeeze myself, try to stop the tightening, the unbearable pain festering inside me. I groan. Squeal. It hurts. Everything about this burns. Everything. Being Indigo's friend, her love interest, her ex-friend, her enemy, her target.

Michael bends down, matches my posture. "Sit down, babe," he whispers. "It's done. Sit down."

Done. I stand up, my eyes shoot back to Indigo and Ethan. He's on his feet. She's still face down in the sand. Motionless. Perfectly still and Jackson's eyes aren't on her at all.

I grab my chest, try to breathe more evenly, try to calm the erratic drumming of my heart beat, try to ease the unexpected amount of pain flooding into me at the sight of her unmoving body.

"You have to breathe, Jaylen. Breathe," Lark encourages.

"Indigo was wrong. Dead ass wrong for all she did, all she caused, but this still hurts. It hurts so fucking much. It hurts more than everything else that's happened here today." I say, a crushing pain in my chest, my eyes full of tears that are desperate to fall, my throat too tight for screams to come out.

"She was your friend," Lark says. "A very close friend. I understand why you're in pain. I'd be disgusted if you weren't."

I grab Lark's hand, keeping the other over my chest, over

my aching heart, as I watch Ethan and Jackson come back our way.

"Jaylen, please sit down."

I ignore Michael. I squeeze Lark's hand and try to get a grip on my newfound reality. Try to take in, to accept what's happened in front of me. So many horrific acts. None of which we asked for.

"Mike," Jackson calls out.

I look up, look down the beach, then direct my attention to where Jackson just forced Michael's.

On her hands and knees, her hair messy, hanging past her face, she's alive. Indigo's still alive. How? Her face was pushed into the sand. With every breath her body made her take, I'm sure sand was inhaled. Unless, after breathing some in, she held her breath and played dead, so Ethan would get off her. Regardless of how, there's still life in her. There's still more to be done. More that I don't know if I can see happen.

Michael turns to me. "I love you. I'm sorry. I have to."

He takes a few steps away from us, steps in Indigo's direction. No longer moving, eyes aimed straight at my ex-best friend, he uses the power of his gifted mind, the strength of his thoughts, and begins to drag her.

Loud screams, desperate claws into the sand, she tries her hardest to stop him from pulling her our way. Still in the crawling position, she's being forced within our reach, brought right into the hands of danger, right into the hands of the person she tried to kill, caused to be burned, and who now has the power to do just that to her.

"Help me! Scarlett! Matias! Kennedy!"

My stomach twists in a sickening way the moment she calls for Kennedy, the moment I know she's placed my friend, my sister, into the one predicament she tried her damnedest to avoid.

Arm's length from him, Michael stops moving her, never reaches out to grab her, to even pinch her.

Indigo looks around frantically, realizes no one plans to help her, then shakes her head fearfully, in disbelief. "You're going to let them kill me?" she cries, on her knees now, her teary eyes peering into Kennedy's.

"Stop talking to her. You came here to kill us. People you and your friends don't even know. Don't you dare make her feel guilty!" Lark points, her eyes blazing, anger coloring her cheeks.

Kennedy stands, never takes a step forward, and cries with her eyes on her ex-girlfriend. She never wanted to see any of us hurt, definitely never wanted to be the person looked to for saving.

I move to Kennedy's side, place my arm around her, and give her support, give her a real friend. It's all I can offer now. I'm still in pain, still feeling a bit rattled. Should my strength be needed, I'm likely to disappoint. My body is begging for rest, liters of water, and calmness. Not this. Not more fighting, more chaos, more trauma.

Indigo continues to shake her head. Sobs. "Kennedy, don't…"

She goes silent. Her body becomes perfectly still. Nothing is moving. Her eyes aren't even blinking. I know why. I've seen this many times since I've been in Michigan. It's been done to me. That's Jackson. He's stopped all movement, taken away her ability to run, to even speak. She's not going anywhere. She's glued to that spot, stuck in the same position, unable to defend herself from what's to come.

Michael cocks his head to one side, gazes into her unblinking eyes, then puts his mind to work. I don't watch him. I watch her. Watch to see what he makes happen to the girl who once tried to kill him, who saw him in a similar position. A position of being incapable of running off or helping himself. A helpless position in which she decided to make an unimaginable choice.

Indigo's head turns slowly. Her eyes are still open, but

never move. They stay centered like a possessed doll.

I cringe and pull Kennedy closer as I feel her entire body shiver. It's disturbing to see Indigo in this way, to watch Michael do to her what he threatened to do to Matias.

Her chin slowly moves past her shoulder, past the point of normalcy, comfort, stretching.

I shake too, clenching my teeth together, listening to my throbbing heartbeat in anticipation. I wait to hear the pop, the snap of her neck, the sound of her life ending. A sound I'm not likely to forget, that'll probably haunt me and give me a lifetime of nightmares.

"I can't!" Kennedy screams, pushing away from me. "I can't!" She pushes Michael, breaks his gaze. "I can't stand to watch you do this. I don't know what I feel, what she deserves, if it's up to us to punish her. But if it is, it's not meant to be like this. Not slowly! Not torturously! You're acting like a sadistic maniac!"

I grab Kennedy. Seeing things play out so slowly, I understand her horror. It does seem monstrous to slowly twist someone's head. It's one thing to kill because you have to. It's another thing to go about it in as painful, and as hideous a way as possible.

"This is who you are, Mike?" Kennedy asks, briefly looking over at Indigo who's still on her knees, held in place by Jackson, her head in a disturbing position, sand still on her face.

Michael places one hand on each of Kennedy's shoulders. "None of this is who I am. It's who she made me become. I didn't follow her anywhere. She came here, Kennedy. I'm not the crazy one. I'm not the monster."

"It's *how* you're doing it, Michael." I say, my voice low, my heart still in a hardcore race, my body still jittering. "I understand you threatening Matias. I understand your feelings toward Indigo. But slowly twisting her head around, Michael? *Slowly?*" I shake my head, completely taken aback by his capabilities. I haven't forgotten what I did to Luna, but I didn't prolong it, didn't look into the eyes of someone I was hurting and draw it out as long as I possibly could.

My eyes leave Michael's, run across the seared, blackened flesh that wasn't burned completely off his arm, then focus in on his chest. Its rising and falling brings my attention back to his face, to his mouth, to the deep inhales and exhales I'm just now hearing.

"My fucking arm hurts. I'm feeling this," he says, looking at his burn before making eye contact with Kennedy again. "I'm missing skin. I'm tired. I'm thirsty. I wanna do it quickly, but I'm struggling. I don't have as much in me as I thought. I have to do it, though, Kennedy. She can't leave here just to try this again."

I take my hands off Kennedy, step back, cup my hands, and scoop up some of Lake Michigan. With as much water as I can hold, I bring my hands to Michael's lips. He hastily takes the water down. I cup him more water, bring it to his mouth, and he slurps it down.

Indigo gasps, backs away on her knees.

"I need some, too. I need water. I can't hold her all day," Jackson says.

All of us are so drained. We expected to have fresh bottles nearby throughout the evening, expected to sip them while conversing. We didn't rest up, drink up, and prepare for this battle. We treated this as a regular day. Not a day of war.

Indigo stands, rubs her neck, and backs away. She becomes invisible, then becomes viewable almost a second later. Like us, she's exhausted too. Exhausted and scared.

Our eyes are glued on her as we stand, waiting for her next move. All of us are probably moments from collapsing, hitting the sand, but none of us want to show just how spent we really are.

Indigo takes one more step back before trying to flee, her chosen route around the side of the fire where no one's huddled. Her short sprint is quickly halted by Ethan. Before I can blink, he's in front of her on the other side of the fire. She steps away from him, turns, notices the rest of us moving in to surround her. She stands, her back to the fire. She takes no more steps, throws her head from side to side, tries to watch Ethan and all the rest of us at the same time.

I remain at Kennedy's side, only feet from Indigo who's positioned in front of the small bonfire that's nowhere near the blaze it was when Luna fueled it with her wicked thoughts.

My eyes stare into Indigo's. It's still hard to believe that such darkness, such trouble, such viciousness could lie behind such beautiful eyes.

Tears pour from those eyes as she uses two fingers to sweep away sand from her face. The crushing pain in my chest becomes sharp, cuts deep into my heart. I grab my chest, never take my eyes off my ex-best friend. I fight with myself to not cry with her. I fight the urge to try to save a person who refused my first attempt to keep them unharmed. I fight with my body to even stand here on legs that feel so unstable.

The fire grows in an instant, reacts as though it's been heavily fueled. Flames higher than Indigo make her jump forward. The rest of us jump back in surprise. Even the moms who were huddled on the other side jump up, release short screams and gasps, loudly revealing their shock and fear. Kesia, too, hollers out, pulls my attention her way. The blaze broke their strong eye contact, pulled Kesia out of Scarlett's mind, briefly ended the control she had over her brain.

An icy ripple runs through me. *I know you're tired. I know you're tempted to look everywhere, but stay on Scarlett and the boys. Focus on the potential threats. Keep them close. Get in whoever's head you have to. Make them believe the worst. Make them act foolish. Do whatever. Just don't let them draw this out longer. Don't let the three of them team up with Indigo in her moment of desperation and begin a new fight that we're too weak to survive.*

Mrs. Everly and Kesia stay right on Matias, Diego, and

Scarlett. With Scarlett's eyes on Indigo, Kesia moves in closer, waits for her to move in any way so she can grab her. Stop her.

Mrs. Everly maintains her threatening stare. Her eyes never leave the boys. The boys, like Scarlett, keep a close watch on Indigo.

I look at my boyfriend, notice the lack of surprise on his face, then follow his green eyes to the flames.

I bite down on my bottom lip. A tear escapes my eye. He's using the last of his energy to burn her up. I'm going to watch the guy I love incinerate Indigo. I'm going to watch him kill her in one of the most painful ways. I'm going to witness Michael throw her into high flames that are going to burn through her skin, destroy everything human and alien about her, gruesomely end her existence. The existence of the first Quisi I met when I transferred to Trinity High.

I eye Indigo again. She stands, her face completely flushed. Her pain-filled eyes now on Kennedy. Kennedy's crying can be heard, her agony felt.

From Kennedy, to me, then back to Kennedy again, Indigo's eyes travel. More tears fall from her eyes. She nods once, her eyes still on Kennedy.

I reach over, take Kennedy's hand as I question the meaning of the nod. Indigo takes a short step back, bringing a core-shaking, ear-popping scream out of Scarlett.

Scarlett rushes toward Indigo with an open hand reached out. I grab her and yank her toward me, away from Indigo, never releasing Kennedy's hand from my other.

Indigo lets her lids cover her sad, defeated eyes. Out, at her sides, she extends both of her arms.

Scarlett reaches for Indigo, pulls to get away from me, but I use what's left in me to keep her held.

One deep breath, one that I can hear and see Indigo take, and then silently, she falls back.

Kennedy and I scream in unison. I free Scarlett as Kennedy nearly pulls me down with her as she falls to her knees. I watch the sparks escape the blaze, breathe in the horrid smell of her body cooking.

My hand still in Kennedy's, she squeezes it tightly, lets out blood-curdling screams, and questions repeatedly *why* and *how.* That's something I'll forever ask myself. Is there something else I could've done, that we all could've done? Why did it have to come to this? How did we let it get this far?

I watch the flames rip through Indigo's flesh, blackening and shriveling her stunning exterior. I stand, unable to move as she twitches, kicks a few times, and dies a slow, inhumane death I couldn't have wished on her or anybody else.

Mrs. Everly and Ms. Ava kneel beside Kennedy, whispering to her, and rubbing her back. Scarlett and Matias try to pull Indigo's body from the fire without getting burned. Diego uses blankets in an attempt to smother the flames, but because of Michael, because of how much he made the fire blaze up, the blankets are catching fire instead of bringing it down.

I stand with my hand still in Kennedy's. Michael, now behind me, wraps his arms tightly around my body. I look down at Kennedy who's still hysterical. I look around at my family. At Ethan standing with his head lowered and his hand on his forehead. At Ms. Reed who's back on her knees on the other side of the fire with Kesia at her side. At Jackson who's sitting in the sand chugging water. At Lark who's sitting and re-hydrating as well.

My eyes then move to the survivors of Indigo's squad. I watch as they attempt to save her fire-covered body. I watch the girl who used to be my best friend become more and more unrecognizable as she burns. As I stare, I wonder silently what was going through her mind. What was her final thought? Was she terrified of what we may have done next and felt that suicide would end things faster, or did Indigo remain in control right up until the end? Did she choose how she'd go out, end herself on her own terms, as opposed to letting someone else do it? No one will ever know for sure, but I'm more inclined to believe the latter.

Indigo didn't always fight for the right things, but she was a fighter nonetheless. She carried this out until there was nowhere left to go. She could've allowed one of us to finish her, but someone else would've won, would've beaten her. She surely wasn't going to go out like that. She wasn't going to let Michael, of all people, be the one to end her. She fought to maintain control from start to finish. Things started by her hand and ended the same way.

I see her. I see her face, her stunning Latina features. I see her seated in my homeroom, Ms. Noonan's class, her almond-shaped, brown eyes staring at me as I enter on my first day at Trinity. The same day, I see her walking alongside me toward Ms. Ward's house, bright-eyed as she goes on about a crush I hadn't yet realized was me. Another image of her surfaces, her dancing, laughing, making my birthday so memorable at the Spring Theatre Dance. Then, I see her on prom night, the last time I was moved by her physical appearance. She walked in, stole the eyes and attention of everyone in the room with her beauty. The last time I saw her that night was in the woods. I had realized she had been stalking us throughout the evening, but I didn't have enough time to fully process just how unbalanced she really was.

I blink a few times, try to blink away the images of Indigo. I look up at the sunset, orange sky. An orange so stunning, I'd take a picture under different circumstances. With my head tilted back, my mind unexpectedly revisits the day I hung out at the lake with Indigo after only being at Trinity for a few days. I remember the topic of death coming up, her admission of fear surrounding what would happen to her after her life ends, if she'd even remain a part of people's memories. I recall her words. *We may not even be remembered after we die. We don't know what happens after death.* I hope to live for many more years before I know for myself what death feels like and if there is anything that does happen after my last breath is taken, but I don't need to overthink her other statement. Indigo will be remembered by many. To our classmates, they'll forever remember her flawless beauty, likely question down the line if she remained as gorgeous after high school, if she went on to marry a super-hot athlete. My family, those on this beach, will remember her as psychotic, as a monster. I will, too. For a while, I'm sure. Hopefully, one day, at some point, I'll be able to focus more on the laughs, our happy moments as best friends, and not the horror. Not tonight.

"Mom!" Ethan turns in a full circle. "She went in?" He looks all over, seeking answers, waiting for her to shout back.

I look to where I last saw Ms. Housley, where she was accidentally knocked into the fire by Indigo, into the overwhelming blaze created by Luna. Right in that location, Ms. Reed is on her knees sobbing. Kesia is consoling her, wiping her tears.

"Mom!" Ethan calls out again, his brows furrowed, his eyes shooting in every possible direction.

Michael slowly takes his arms from around me.

"No," I say in a low whisper. I shake my head, step toward Ms. Reed. "She's okay," I whisper to myself. "She has to be."

Michael hurries to his mom's side, drops to his knees, wraps arms that were just around me around his mother.

Ethan stands. The fear, the uncertainty of her location, her well-being, turns his face red, forces an intimidating grimace to take over his face as no one answers him.

I look at Kennedy, think of her place throughout the entire fight. She never left this area. She was trying to save Ms. Housley. Ms. Reed never left her friend's side. I remember the others, the huddle, the attention to this particular location. Their focus was on something right here, someone right here, the person we're all looking for.

"Wait!" I say loudly. "Ms. Eden isn't here either."

Kesia looks up at me. Teary-eyed, she replies, "She's fine.

She's inside. I sent her in. Had to play with her head a little, but I got her to go inside so she wouldn't be my focus."

"Then my mom went with her," Ethan says.

Ms. Reed stands, looks to Ethan, her eyes so red, they almost look as though they're bleeding. She shakes her head, opens her mouth to speak, but nothing escapes.

Not one or two, not a few, but streams of tears fall from my eyes. Just now, I notice a bunched up blanket on the ground near Ms. Reed, a blanket that is laid to look as if it covered something long that is no longer under it. Sandals with no feet in them are at the end of it.

I know why they never left the huddle. I know what held their attention, what kept everybody gathered around this area, kneeled so close to the ground. The sweet, freckle-faced woman succumbed to her injuries almost immediately. She fell into a high fire, had to have been burned severely, and died surrounded by people working to save her.

Ethan nods surely, though his face doesn't match. "She's okay, Ms. Reed. She's okay. I know it."

"She's not, baby." Ms. Reed mouths words I can barely hear, but read coming from her lips.

In a millisecond, Ethan's by the blanket. He's down on the ground beside his mother, the only parent he had left. With his hands on top of the blanket, he slowly rocks back and forth. His mouth falls wide open. His face flushes so red it looks sunburned. His eyes close tightly. Every vein in his neck becomes visible, looks as though they may pop as he releases a grief-filled, silent scream. He's so consumed with pain, cut so deep by this loss, it's impossible for him to get the sound out.

Ethan takes a balled up fist and strikes himself in the chest repeatedly. Sound never comes from his stretched open mouth.

Ms. Reed lowers, blows in Ethan's face, tries to get him to catch his breath. She grabs his fist, stops him from hitting himself, from losing total control.

Water is pulled from the cooler by Diego. It's uncapped and handed to Ms. Reed. She doesn't shove the bottle in his face. She speaks lowly to him, encourages him to breathe, to let it out.

Loudly, startling me, he lets it out. He roars, breaking me down completely in a spot I can't bring myself to move from. Surrounding cries can be heard from the others as watching him, as hearing him, is excruciating. Heartbreaking. His anguish, his devastation, his tragedy is shared amongst all of us, though no one's heart and no one's life will be as affected as his.

Ms. Reed cries with him, tries to talk him into drinking a little, but he doesn't take the water, doesn't stop wailing.

Michael reaches out for the bottle and his mother immediately hands it to him. With both hands free, she immediately wraps her arms around her friend's son.

Still inconsolable, one hand still on his mother, Ethan's body shakes. His tears pour onto Ms. Reed. This loss, this unimaginable, senseless loss, knocks me to the ground.

Lying on the sand, I blink slowly. I can't take anymore. My body is too weak to keep me on my feet. I'm dehydrated, emotionally shattered, heartbroken for my friend, my brother, and crushed having to accept the loss of such a compassionate, loving woman.

Slow blinks don't make it easy for me to see whose hands are on me. My eyes aren't seeing clearly. Blurred, distorted faces are all I can see.

"Jaylen, drink it."

I hear Michael's voice, feel cool water slip down my throat.

"Look at me, please," he begs.

Eyes open, I try to see him more clearly, try to see who else is at my side, who's squeezing my hand. I can't. I can hardly blink, can barely find the strength to swallow the water he just poured into my mouth.

My eyes slowly close. The sound of cries can be heard everywhere. I can hear sniffling and sobbing right above me. My name is still being called out by Michael. Louder than everything else my ears are taking in, I hear Ethan's misery. I can hear his cries, his loud screams, his unbearable pain.

I don't reopen my eyes. Can't. My body isn't asking for rest, for an emotional break. It's taking one.

On the sand, I hear my friend suffering through a loss no one should have to experience, especially unexpectedly while on vacation. To the gut-wrenching, tragic tune Ethan is singing, with my eyes hidden behind their lids, I lie in my own darkness with nothing but horror all around me.

Chapter 17

arkness.

I feel around, feel the soft grains. Still on top of the sand, where everything happened, where death occurred, I lie on my back. My body's still incredibly weak, feeling unrested, sore, and devoid of energy. There's a pulling in my gut, a nauseating pull that's most definitely there because of what I've done and seen here this evening.

My mouth becomes full. Cool water.

I swallow it, hear myself gulp it down. Eyes still shut, keeping me in blackness, I exhale softly.

"Drink more," the voice whispers, the accent still recognizable even when spoken at such a low volume.

More water pours into my mouth. I take another swallow before whispering my boyfriend's name.

"He's fine. He's resting, too. Take some more water, then get some more rest."

Ms. Eden just barely lets the word *rest* leave her lips before she's pouring more water into mine. I cough some of it out before I somehow manage to take the rest down.

She rubs my head. "Rest."

Might be easier to do that if you weren't pouring all this water down my throat without allowing me time to prepare for it.

Eyes still closed, hands gripping the sand, I slip back into sleep. Sleep that I hope proves to be more restful than the sleep my uneasy stomach wouldn't allow me to get the most of. Sleep that was constantly disturbed by the nightmare images my mind keeps producing.

* * *

Darkness.

Overheated, I kick out of the thick covers. I push my hand out, try to feel my surroundings, run my open palm against warm, soft fabric. I open my eyes, blink a few times, try to understand where I am, if I'm really awake. Still darkness.

I struggle with shaky arms to push my body up. I groan and quiver all over as I use the little strength that's left in me. Upright, I release a dry cough, feel around for water, something my body is aching for.

My searching hand hits something. The warmth, the feel of skin, and the sound of breathing that my ears are just now registering make me pull my hand away. I'm in bed with someone in a pitch black room. Possibly one of the girls or maybe Ms. Eden. Last thing I remember is lying outside on the sand and her at my side giving me water. Regardless of who it is, I'm sure they don't want to be felt up in their sleep.

I nudge the mystery person, need them to wake up and help me. They don't make a sound, don't move, remain in their deep sleep. Another nudge, followed by shaking. They're breathing pattern remains the same. They don't move.

I use my other hand to feel around on the other side of me. My hand hits against plastic. Immediately, I grab the bottle, use my trembling hand to uncap it, and waste no time chugging the entire thing. I feel around once again on the same side of the bed, hoping to hit another plastic bottle. I do. I grab the other full bottle someone left here for me and drink the whole thing as quickly as I can.

I place both empty bottles back on the bed. I attempt to lie down gently, but my body falls hard back into the same spot, in the same position I was in when I awoke.

Once more, I try to wake the person beside me. I poke them with my trembling finger, pat them in an attempt to get them to make a sound. Still, they lie in their deep slumber.

I shut my eyes. The darkness behind my lids is equally as dark as the room. So dark, I'm not sure who I'm in bed with. So dark, I question if I'm really awake.

* * *

The penetrating sound of my scream and Kennedy's.
The sight of Indigo falling back into the flames.
The smell of my ex-best friend's body burning.
The devastation cutting through my heart.

The scene replays repeatedly, tears through my senses in a horrifying way, pulls me out of my sleep, springs my eyes open.

I squint at the unexpected brightness of the sun. It's morning, but what's good about it?

Drenched in sweat, I kick out of the heavy comforter. I turn to my right. No one's at my side. I turn to my left. Two fresh bottles of water lie right next to my pillow amongst sand particles that likely fell from my hair.

Someone has been checking on me, has covered me up with this heavy blanket for a second time, has opened the blinds to let in an unwelcomed brightness.

I push myself upright. My arms are unsurprisingly still shaky. I haven't slept well at all. My body is forcing me to constantly return to dreamland, but the nightmares are kicking me back out.

I uncap a bottle, rehydrate myself in a hurry, trying to ease the pain still covering my body. Bottle number two is gulped just as quickly as the first.

I look around the space, want to call out for help, want someone to come to my side and tell me the lie we all need to hear at some point in our lives; that everything will be okay. But I can't scream, can't even hold my body up any longer.

My body collapses back onto the pillow. My throat tightens. That dagger in my heart twists viciously. Flames burn inside my belly. Tears well up in my eyes. I hurt immensely from the inside out.

My eyelids lower, block the tears from falling. I yawn as my head falls slightly to the left.

Drifting. I can feel myself drifting back into a haunted place. Sleep.

Alone, I lie in this bed. Alone, I lie suffering with neither of my hands held. Alone, I try to appreciate the fact that I'm breathing this morning. After all, after last night, many aren't.

* * *

Still resting on the left side of my face, I open my eyes and take in the daylight. Quickly, I shut them tight. I reopen them just a smidgen, give my eyes time to adjust, to welcome a wider view of this new day. The sun doesn't bring a smile to my face, doesn't make me want to get up, though at this point, physically, it feels as though my body is finally able to.

I lie quietly, look at the two full bottles of water beside me. Bottles likely brought up by Michael. The presence of our kind covers this entire property, but after moving in and out of unpleasant sleep sessions, after experiencing a whirlwind of emotions while trapped inside my nightmares, I'm awakening to a whole different feeling. Michael. I can feel his presence, the only presence I can fully separate from the others. He's close, maybe in the room with me, but I don't turn over. I stare at the bottles of water, move my hand up to them.

"Want me to help you?"

I don't look Michael's way, don't want to make eye contact

just yet. I don't even want to look at myself after everything that's happened.

Michael places his hand over my abdomen. "You've been sleeping for a long time," he says, rubbing me gently. "Almost twenty hours. Looks bright, but the sun will be setting in a few hours."

His touch brings back heartache. I'd briefly forgotten about my pregnancy scare, my worries of becoming a parent and living a life I have no desire for. Now, I worry that perhaps a baby had been forming inside of me, and the horrific events that happened right here on Mrs. Everly's land ended the short life of mine and Michael's child. After all that I did, after all that I experienced at the hands of Luna and Avery, I couldn't imagine a fetus surviving. Still, a definite answer is needed. I need to know what's going on inside my body, and I haven't had a chance to speak to Jackson's father yet. It's a confidential conversation that must be had as soon as possible.

So much. There's so much to process, to be hurt by, to worry about, to have to get past and work through. So much.

His hand remains on my belly. "Say something."

"Ethan," I whisper.

"He's still out on the beach. He doesn't want to be bothered, spoken to, touched, or anything. He wants space and to be alone."

Not alone. He wants his time with his mother, assuming she's still out there under that blanket.

His hand moves up to my hair. "We're giving him his time and his space. We've been making sure he has water."

"Kennedy?" I ask.

"She's okay. As okay as she can be. She's been crying a lot. Everyone's taking care of everyone."

Except me. I haven't been supportive. I've been in and out of sleep, leaving those who have been keeping an eye on me to deal with their feelings and pain without my shoulders.

"I'm sorry," I say in a low voice, the guilt making me want

to cry. "I should've been up."

"No, you should've been asleep, just like you were. You didn't walk away from us to take an afternoon nap. You fell out. Your body took what it needed. And if it needs more, close your eyes and go back to sleep."

"I don't want to sleep. I don't want to see it happen again, over and over again. Me drowning Luna, Ms. Housley hitting the fire, you…" I pause, shudder at the thought, at the mental image of what he did to Avery.

He sighs, caresses my cheek, speaks, though my eyes still haven't met his. "I know," he says. "I know what I did, what you saw, what everyone saw will change how I'm seen and how you all feel about me. I know it was brutal. I couldn't stay asleep either. Nightmares don't begin to describe what I've had to keep re-watching. I don't even know how I feel about myself. After what I did, what I felt I had to do, but could've done differently, less viciously, I feel like maybe I'm a monster."

I grab his hand, but don't turn his way. "My hands aren't clean either, Michael."

"You can't even look at me." His volume drops a great deal, but the pain behind his words delivers a gut-punch.

"Because I'm dealing with my own demons," I explain. "I felt like I was forced into a corner, that I had no choice but to do what I did. But that doesn't make it easier to accept. I never wanted any of that to happen. I'm forced to question who I am now. I can't look at you because I'm worried about who you might see."

"You're the same person," he rushes to tell me.

"Really? Then why are you suddenly a monster? A monster didn't put this promise ring on my finger. I didn't fall in love with, and still love deeply, a monster."

The room becomes silent. We're both attacking ourselves, beating ourselves up because our vacation was intruded upon and we were forced to fight for our survival. We are changed, no doubt about it, but in any other situation, in a fight where our lives weren't put on the line, neither Michael or myself would've made the same choices. We both wanted to end things before anyone got hurt. We're not the monsters. Our hearts are still good. We have to live with what we did, we aren't proud of what we're capable of, but that's proof enough. Our feelings at this moment tell me a lot about myself and a lot about my boyfriend. We're decent. Decent alien beings.

Slowly, I turn my head. Immediately, my eyes move to Michael's wrapped arm. Somehow, it slipped my mind that Michael was burned when Indigo rushed him in an attempt to knock him into the fire.

I lightly place my hand over the bandage. "Who wrapped this? How bad is it?"

"It's bad. It's not healing like most of my other wounds have, but pain-wise, it's tolerable at this point."

That's one of the greatest things about being a Quisi. Our pain tolerance exceeds that of humans. What would knock them to their knees, have them crying out in pain, we can typically withstand. What humans require extensive medical treatment for, our bodies usually repair on their own.

"To answer your other question, Jackson's dad is here. He came up here and checked on you multiple times. He's the one who wrapped my arm."

My eyes leave his wound dressing, travel up to his face, reach his forest-green eyes. His normally, bright, white sclera are pink, likely from exhaustion and crying. Both of his lower lids are red, swollen. His thick, curly hair is messier than usual, one side smashed flatter than the other. His skin isn't radiant at all. His cheeks are flushed. To a stranger, he'd look ill, but because our kind doesn't get sick, and I know what he's done and been through, I know his appearance is due to his emotional state. His appearance reflects the regret that's burdening him because of how he chose to end Avery. It reflects the worry he feels for his parentless friend.

I push myself up. "Oh, Michael."

"I'll be okay," he says quickly, not wiping away a bit of my concern. "Just a lot to process."

"Tell me about it."

"I just feel so bad for Ethan. I feel so bad for my brother from another..." He begins panting, grabs his chest, holds back the word *mother* as tears fall from his swollen eyes. "She never left my side because she knew Indigo wanted to hurt me more than anyone else."

I grab his hands, squeeze them, and try to offer him support while silently encouraging him to let it out.

"Indigo wanted to kill me. Not just kill me, but burn me alive. That's not anger. That's blackness. That's emptiness. Soullessness. Hate. Indigo wanted me to see her. That's why she reappeared before charging me. She wanted her face to be the last thing I saw before dying. That's evil. No other word for it."

More tears fall from his eyes. He sniffles, turns away, tries not to look me in the eye as he breaks down.

"She killed Ms. Housley on accident. That was supposed to be me. Ethan should still have a fucking mother! He... he..." Michael chokes on his words, squeezes my hands as though he's holding on to them for dear life, bites down on his bottom lip, and cries so hard, animal-like squeals escape him. Unrecognizable sounds that rip through my entire body bring about a nauseating feeling in my stomach and carve through a heart I'm surprised is still beating after all of the hurt it's been forced to endure.

I wrap my boyfriend in my arms, pull him close to me, and hold him tightly. I let the few tears I can no longer hold in fall into his hair.

"She's still supposed to be here. I'm not," Michael cries.

I hold him close and whisper, "I love you."

Not thinking any less of him for releasing his emotions, not questioning his manhood, not guilting him in any way for what he did, though his methods were shocking, I hold on to my love. I feel the pain within me intensify with every tear that falls from his eyes, with every sniffle I hear, with every short, ragged breath I feel him take. Holding him is like palming an uncovered razor. His heartache slices right into me, makes my hidden emotion run out like blood from a fresh cut.

My body begins to shake all over. The arms I have wrapped around Michael vibrate against his body.

He pulls away from me, looks over my face, looks down, over my body. He takes my hands. They still jitter inside of his. "I didn't mean to upset you like this." He grabs a water from the bed, twists the top off in a hurry, and then holds the bottle to my lips. "Drink some."

"You first," I insist.

"Never."

I take a few sips, my hands still quivering. He moves the bottle from my mouth, allows me time to swallow.

"Your turn. Drink some. And then finish letting it out. Say whatever you need to say. Don't hold it in. This is too much to deal with on your own."

"Practice what you preach," he says. "You have to let it out, too. You have to say whatever you feel. Scream if you need to. Cry. Whatever. Just do what it takes to make yourself feel a little better."

"Believe it or not, even though I'm shaking, even though I'm crushed, even though I'm not sure how to move forward, this is helping me. I hate, and I do mean absolutely hate seeing you like this, but I'm so relieved to know you're struggling with all that's happened. That's proving to me that you're not even close to a monster." I shake my head. "You're not even a bad person."

"I just wanted to see this end differently. I was waiting for the Hollywood ending."

"Which would've been?"

"Everyone surviving. Avery knocking some sense into

Indigo, and her realizing she was going nuts over some high school bullshit. Indigo going to college, falling in love, and getting distracted by some new guy or girl." He shrugs. "I just wanted everybody to be okay. When the anger in me died down, this whole thing boiled down to a very simple fact. Indigo needed help. I didn't think the help she'd receive would be from a group of family and friends willing to help her kill a family." He shakes his head in disbelief. "You hear isolated stories about demented families like this and you ask yourself where the fuck those kinds of people come from." He takes a quick sip of water. "I still can't process this. What did she say to them? How did she persuade people to travel across state lines to carry out a murder plot? Why did she walk right up on us instead of just rushing in to attack us? Why was it so important for her to try to end my life? It wouldn't have fixed y'alls friendship. It wouldn't have repaired what was broken between her and Kennedy. It would've only ended my life."

All the questions he's rattling off, I have as well. So much of this makes no sense, but it happened anyway. So many of the things Indigo was determined to see happen, we were struggling to even think about. We couldn't even bring ourselves to create a plan. We never spoke one into existence. All we were able to determine was that Indigo needed help, that she was a broken individual, hollow on the inside. We didn't stop to think that she may be able to find others like herself, be able to convince them to travel, and…

My train of thought stops immediately. My mind shifts back to the horror-filled evening. There were three left alive from Indigo's group. Matias, his brother, Diego, and Scarlett.

"What happened to the other three?" I ask. "After Indigo…" I stop, don't finish the sentence, pull the bottle from his hand, take a loud gulp, then ask, "After I passed out, what did you all do with Matias, his brother, and Scarlett?"

"Let them leave."

My eyes bulge. "How did that final conversation go?

What'd they promise?"

"They never wanted to fight after hearing our side of things."

I nod, already aware of that fact.

"But they did what we felt like we would've done. And that's try to save the people they came with. Scarlett and Diego stayed on the shore and tried to comfort my mom after she watched her friend take her last breath. Matias wasn't an aggressor. There was no reason for us to believe they were secretly plotting anything else. They were desperate to leave and we wanted to see them go. They apologized, all seemed legitimately sorry for what they saw happen and had a hand in. They promised to stay away."

I exhale. I'm relieved to know more lives weren't taken or lost after I blacked out. I hope they keep their promise. It's the only way we can really move past this. Without them on our minds, without another surprise visit, we can grieve, and down the line, grow. Hopefully.

"Finish that bottle."

I do so without putting up a fight. He grabs the other water and gives his body what it needs. Together, we sit on the bed. Silence brings me a moment of comfort. No screaming, no sobbing, no questioning. Just quiet. Finally.

Michael breaks that silence. "I love you. This hurts, but I know we're strong. I know we'll get through this. We're going to be okay."

I nod. *We have to be.* We have to be because so many who were okay yesterday, aren't today. We have to be for Ethan. We won't be able to support him and keep him together if we're a bunch of scattered pieces ourselves.

Chapter 18

A few more tears, a lot more hugging, and countless *I love yous* are followed by a long shower. Finally, I'm free of sand and a bed I couldn't find the strength to get out of for many hours. As I move down the stairs, an overwhelming feeling of dread falls over me. I know I won't be walking in on a group enjoying themselves, curled over laughing, chatting about good times. I'm walking into the aftermath.

I enter the living room. These faces don't look like they're on vacation. They look like they've been through hell. And no matter how you define the word hell, whether or not you believe it's a place, hell is universally thought of as horrendous and frightful which is the best way to describe the things we've all been through. There's so much sadness filling the space. I don't know who to go to first, who to hug first, who to first tell that I'm here for them.

Ms. Reed sits on the end of the sofa, fisting a bunch of Kleenex held up to her nose. Michael's right at her side, where he told me he'd be before giving me the privacy to shower and dress alone. On the love seat sits Ms. Eden and Kesia. Kesia's head is resting on her grandmother's shoulder. Ms. Eden's cheek is resting against the top of her granddaughter's head. Ms. Everly is collecting empty water bottles, her hands visibly unsteady. Jackson is right beside her, placing full bottles where the empty ones are being picked up from. Jackson's father is standing by the window, speaking softly on the phone, eyes focused on a view that may still look like paradise to him, but will never look the same to any of us. Lark and Ms. Ava aren't in the room. Michael didn't mention that they left, so I'm sure they're around. Maybe resting downstairs or talking in the sunroom. Maybe supporting Kennedy who isn't present either.

I walk over to Ms. Reed, kneel down in front of her, and touch her knee with my left hand. Dangling from my wrist is the charm bracelet she gave me. I clear my throat, take a deep breath, look her in her red, teary eyes. "I am so sorry about your friend. I wish I could say something, anything, to take your pain away, Ms. Reed."

She shakes her head and closes her eyes as her despair pours from them.

Michael rubs her back, pulls his mother close to him, and holds her in a snug hug as she cries for her friend. A friend she just recently became reacquainted with after life pulled them in separate directions. A friend she watched die, watched leave this world before being given the chance to say a final goodbye to her only child.

I rub her knee before standing. I look at Michael, watch him work to comfort his mother, listen to him whisper words I'm not positive are true. *You're going to be okay. We're going to get through this.*

I step away from them, try not to make her even more emotional by doing the one thing I didn't want people to keep doing to me when I lost my mom. I didn't want people staying in my face, constantly repeating the words, *I'm sorry*, or promising to me that I'd be okay when that's something no one could guarantee.

Jackson holds a bottle of water out in front of me. As I

take it, I watch him quietly mouth the question, *You okay?*

I nod, reach out to his mother. She hands me an empty water bottle, though I was expecting her hand.

How are you feeling? I shake my head. That's a dumb question to ask her. *Are you okay?* That's an even dumber question. None of us are. So, what do I say to her? What's appropriate, but not annoying or angering?

"I can do this for you, Mrs. Everly. I can clean up."

She shakes her head. "I need something to do. I need to keep busy."

"Maybe you should rest," I suggest.

"Already done that," she says, picking up another bottle. "How are you? Did you sleep well?"

I nod, then throw the lie out before I can say it to her. "No," I say honestly, swapping that nod out for a truthful shake of the head. "Nightmare after nightmare. My head was full of screaming. Crying."

"Same here," Jackson says.

"We all struggled with the images our minds couldn't stop replaying. I could even smell..." Mrs. Everly scrunches her nose, inhales deeply, and slowly exhales loudly. "I couldn't wait to wake up."

"I'm sorry this happened here."

"No. No!" she repeats, pointing an empty bottle at me. "I don't want to hear any more of that from you or Mike. She was sick and so was her family. Sick. Psychotic. I blame them. That's it. No apologies necessary. No apologies wanted."

She pulls the empty bottle she handed to me from my grasp and walks away. My throat tightens. My body does a sudden twitch. The sorrowful feeling flowing through this house is imprisoning. I want out of this house. I want off this property where luxurious upgrades and scenic beauty no longer take your breath away, own your eyes, and erase all negative thoughts. Here, now, on this massive, lakefront property, darkness exists. Peace died along with Ms. Housley. Happiness faded the moment Indigo and her family intruded upon our vacation. A hole formed in our hearts that were forced to take lives. This place will never be the same. We will never be the same.

I stand in front of the loveseat, look at Kesia and Ms. Eden. Again, I don't know what to say, but saying something is required. *Sorry I lied to get you here and you were forced to kill.* No, that's not comforting or even mildly pleasant. *How are you doing this morning?* Already know the answer to that one.

I use my go-to method, the one that usually works in my favor, the one I only abandon on occasion, the one I pushed to the side in the hopes of getting as many of my kind together to learn more about myself and make this as memorable of a vacation as possible. I use honesty. I tell them, "I don't know what to say."

Kesia pushes herself up from the sofa, leans in, and pulls me into a firm embrace. "We don't blame you. We don't need you to say anything." Her accent pierces my heart. It took someone all the way from Cameroon to give our kind a name, to give us some sort of an identity. I never wanted to repay her in this way for her openness, kindness, and information. I never wanted her *thank you* to come in the form of a visit from my ex-best friend and her conniving band of family and friends.

"You shouldn't be leaving here with blood on your hands. You should be leaving here with a jar full of sand, a phone full of pictures, and a head full of happy memories. You shouldn't be leaving here a..." I stop, squeeze my friend. My sister. I can't call her a murderer. Kesia isn't malicious. Kesia didn't set out to kill. She didn't enjoy the act of invading someone's mind, taking over their thoughts, and ending their life. She simply did what she had to do, what she was made to do to protect those she thinks of as friends, those who became her newfound family.

Ms. Eden stands and stretches her arms around both of

us. In her strong Cameroonian accent, she says, "It will take time to heal. It will take time to fully forgive yourselves. It will take time to accept that your hands were tied, that you were forced to make a choice. You made the right choice. You chose to live."

I remain silent, trying to let her words sink in. I've seen murders committed on television. Gory murders. Unthinkable crimes. Some of them based on actual events. No matter how gruesome they were, how seared they are in mind, how differently they made me look at this world, seeing doesn't even slightly compare to doing.

I exhale, still in the arms of my friend. "I'll be sure to tell myself that every day."

"Every day until you believe it," Ms. Eden says.

I think I already believe it. I made the only choice that made sense, which was to save my life and do whatever I could to save the other innocent lives out there with me. My mind agrees with Ms. Eden. My heart struggles to, however. My heart is filled with guilt. Regret.

"I should check on Kennedy. Ethan. The others, too."

"They're in the sunroom," Kesia informs me, slowly allowing her arms to fall to her sides. "Ethan is still on the shore. Might be best to give him his time."

I nod and hug Ms. Eden before heading for the sunroom with Kesia at my side. With our arms interlocked, we step into the bright room being occupied by Kennedy and Lark. My eyes immediately find Kennedy's. She looks as though she's survived a brutal fist fight. Her eyes and the areas beneath them are raised and red. Tears are still on her face. I know she's been asleep. Our bodies have forced us all to sleep, but she hasn't stopped crying. I knew that no matter how this played out, even if Indigo and I had come to an agreement, that Kennedy's middle-man position would always burden her, make her feel like a traitor, and hurt her no matter which one of us she was dealing with at the time. She has a good heart. She's a peace seeker. She's a special, kind soul.

I briefly make eye contact with Lark, silently hope she understands the urgency I feel in consoling Kennedy first. I hurry to Kennedy, sit beside her on the coffee colored sectional, push back her brunette curls, invading her space in a way I hate mine being invaded. It's not so hard to understand why people do that to me. They care, and their concern makes it hard to stay away from me in my moments of pain, just as I can't stay away from someone I care for in a moment such as this. Kennedy's broken. I am, too, but I've had more than enough practice in dealing with grief, heartache, and loss. True, she's lost a parent too, but she's more sensitive than I am. She has a more fragile nature about her. She needs my support, and I couldn't imagine letting her down.

"I'm here," I tell her softly, pulling her head to my shoulder. "No matter what you're feeling, what you have to say, I want to hear it."

Kennedy bawls, making my eyes tear up. I blink repeatedly, take a deep breath, tilt my head back, take another deep breath, fight the powerful urge to cry with her.

"It's okay," Lark whispers, inching closer to Kennedy's other side. She grabs my hand. "You should let it out, too. Let it all out. This was ugly for all of us."

Kesia stands in front of the three of us. My eyes go to hers. Upon contact, Kesia's tears fall. Lark's grip on my hand tightens. My body shakes. My insides become a furnace. I need to let it out, to fully cry it out, to relieve myself.

Kennedy's head rests on my shoulder. Lark holds on to my hand, keeps it firmly locked inside of hers. Kesia kneels, touches my free shoulder, and I break. I break down with my friends. I cry with my sisters. I give in to my emotions, something my body and the weight of my world has pushed me to do before, but I'm still not fully comfortable with allowing to happen.

"How is this our lives?" Kennedy sobs. "I feel like we all

tried to do what was right. Where the hell is our happy ending?"

Together, we gather closely as our internal struggles push through us. As the four of us hold each other, support each other, and bond through our pain, I recall a line I once heard somewhere. A befitting answer to Kennedy's question.

Happy endings are for stories that haven't finished yet.

Chapter 19

I take each step as slowly as I possibly can. The closer I get to the end of this forty-step staircase, the more wrong my words sound in my head. I want to say so much to Ethan, want to do what I feel can't be done—comfort him after the loss of his mother. The reality is, I'm taking on an impossible task. There will be no soothing him this soon. This is simply an act of friendship, just me saying *I'm sorry* and likely repeating what everyone else has already said. A bunch of words that he's probably tired of hearing because he already knows. After all, he's out here away from everyone for a reason, the same reason I purposely detached myself from others and became a stone during my roughest patches. Because sometimes people make your struggles feel heavier when their goal is to do the opposite. Sometimes, people accidentally bring out anger because all you want is your time to grieve. So if I know this, if I've been in his shoes, why the hell am I still walking down these stairs? Why am I disturbing a person who has requested time to their self?

I stop. I stand still about halfway down the staircase. I look down at my friend sitting feet from his mother, feet from a pile of scorched wood where a fire was burning yesterday evening.

He's sitting in the location where Ms. Housley took her last breath. He's sitting feet from a blanket covering whatever is left of his beautiful mother, covering everything I don't want my friend to see.

I wipe my face and continue to step down toward Ethan. I can't imagine how I look, the face that's about to stand in front of him, the face I neglected to wash after crying my eyes out with my sisters. I'm sure one good look at me is going to tell him that the support I'm offering, I could use myself.

A water bottle in hand, my ducts depleted of tears, I take the final step and sink into the warm, soft sand. Ethan never looks my way. His eyes stare straight ahead. Not at the beauty of the lake stretched out in front of him, but at the blanket. The laid out, scrunched up blanket doesn't look as though it's covering a thing, but it certainly has what's left of Ms. Housley hidden beneath it.

With my eyes on the blanket, my memory recreates the unpleasant image of my mom resting lifelessly against the steering wheel with blood pouring from her head. No matter what I remember about my mom, somehow that image pops up. No matter what small details I forget, I can't erase anything from that scene. It's an image I've wished to forget. It's a way no child, no matter how old, should ever have to see their parent.

I move toward the blanket, toward my friend's mother. Beside her, I stand with my eyes on Ethan. I try to find the right words to say, but the thoughts swirling around in my head just don't sound right. Nothing sounds right.

With his eyes still on what's covering his mother, I stop, scan his reddened skin. His freckles aren't even recognizable as his face is so flushed. His face looks hot, like he's running a deadly fever. The rising and falling of his chest can be seen. Both of his hands are balled into tight fists.

I prepare to speak. My lips part, but I pause. Nothing I say is going to bring a smile to his face. Nothing I say is going to erase any piece of yesterday's tragedy.

My heart sinks as my eyes fall back down on the blanket. Underneath it could be anything. Burnt bits of Ms. Housley. Dried remains in a shriveled up cocoon. Who knows? What I don't want is for Ethan to see her like this. Whatever *this* is. The recollection of the last time he saw his mother should be a memory that brings forth a smile. He should immediately see her hazel-brown eyes, her adorable spatter of freckles that he was lucky enough to inherit, and her warming, oh-so-welcoming smile. He shouldn't see what's left behind of her body, charred pieces of her, or anything else scarring. Yesterday will never be a forgotten day for any of us, but when Ms. Housley crosses her son's mind, I want her life to flash before his eyes and dance in his thoughts. Not her death.

I need to do this for Ethan, assuming he hasn't lifted the blanket already. I need to move Ms. Housley. I need to save him from seeing something he can in no way prepare for. I need to save him from the disturbing images and thoughts that sneak up on me at the most inconvenient times, and bring out the hardest, most uncontrollable emotions that one couldn't imagine actually exists inside of them. Though I struggle with showing my feelings, they come out in one way or another, never leaving a good mark, and I don't want Ethan to feel like me. I want him to do things the right way. The hard way, but the healthy way. I want him to have a proper memorial for his mother, to cry, to hit a bag until the anger subsides enough for his fists to unclench. I want him to talk it out, to repeat himself until he feels as though everything that's on his heart has been dealt with. I want my friend to take his time, to be brave enough and strong enough to face his emotions, and for him to deal with this loss. I want him to be something he's not, that we're not, but our emotions sometimes make us feel like we are. Human.

I step closer to Ms. Housley, prepare to ask Ethan to let me be the best friend I can be for him at this time. Before I can speak, like a gust of unexpected wind, he's from his seat, mid-leap when I panic, retaliate, and rush him, meeting his chest with both of my hands.

His back crashes through the chair he was just sitting in. It breaks into pieces as he lands on his back causing particles of sand to fly up, creating a theatrical effect, though none of this is entertaining to me.

Before he can move, I quickly position myself on top of him, grab each of his wrists, grip them tightly, hold them down with my gifted strength, mash them down into the warm grains.

"Get the fuck off me, Jaylen. I wasn't going to touch you."

I stare down at his face. He's not kicking, squirming, or fighting to get me off. With a fiery rage burning through his eyes, he uses his words, and scares me with the tone of his voice.

"I said, get off me."

"Why did you come at me?"

"Because I don't want you to touch my mother. Of all people, your ass should understand that."

Still holding him down, my eyes piercing his, I shake my head. "I would never have touched her without your permission. Never!" I repeat. "I wanted to ask you to please let me move her for you. I want to prepare the memorial for you, in whatever way you'd like it prepared. I just don't want you to lift that blanket and see something you'll never be able to release from your mind. Ethan, I miss my mom every day. Every fucking day. She was one of the most beautiful people I've ever seen. When I think about her, I think about her youthfulness, her drive, her humor, her warmth. I see her smile, her hair tied up in a bun, her natural, flawless beauty that glowed more and more every year. Know what else? I see her dead. Not in a casket, not made up to look like she's sleeping peacefully. I see her bleeding from her head, lying dead against the steering wheel. I smell her death, Ethan. I see it and smell it when all I'd like is happy memories." I shake my head. "I don't want that for you. I don't want you to have those images of your lovely, beautiful, perfect..." Tears fall from my eyes as I choke on my words. He cries too. "I just don't want you to suffer inside your own mind like this. That's it. That's all I want. I want to apologize for being in your life which invited Indigo into it. I want to tell you that I'm here for you. I want to move your mother with your consent. I want to be your *friend*."

I let go of his wrists, climb off him, and lie beside him in the sand amongst broken pieces of chair. I cry with him, let tears fall. Tears I'm surprised my body can even produce after all the crying I did with the girls.

On Lake Michigan, on this beautiful property, we lie beneath the sun in our own darkness. Two motherless, two fatherless, two broken individuals with unfillable holes drilled into our souls.

"Not yet," he whispers.

"No rush," I say, my voice as low as his. "Take your time with her. Just don't allow yourself to believe you're alone when you're not. Don't carry even more pain throughout your life if you have a friend right here begging you to let her carry it for you."

Side by side, atop the natural blanket of soft warmth, I lie beside Ethan. As one who can fully appreciate the art of silence, I feel an overwhelming urge to say something to him. Where does this come from in people who are trying to comfort others? I've offered my support. He's even accepted it, though he needs more time. What more do I need to say? Why do I have this urge stabbing at me to keep talking to him? Just being here should be enough.

"I'm not sorry," he says, pulling me from my self-questioning session.

I turn to him. "Not sorry?"

"That you're in my life. Just sorry that all this shit

happened. Sorry that my mother…" His voice shakes, trails off. He shakes head, pounds his fist against the shore.

My insides burn. My shattered heart bleeds out for him. The Housleys are the definition of good people. In this situation, they're innocent. Ethan went with me to meet up with Indigo in the hopes of quieting this whole mess. Never did he want violence to ensue, and when it did, he did the only thing a loyal family member would do; protect their own. Ms. Housley died trying to protect her dear friend's son. Her motherly instincts, her protective nature, her selflessness didn't allow her to consider herself or her own safety. Indigo's hate was directed at Michael first and foremost. Ms. Housley knew that, knew her son could jet out of any situation, knew that the main person who needed people at their side was Michael. And that's who she remained beside.

"What the fuck do I go back to? An empty house that has my mother all over it?"

I remember asking myself the same thing. No matter what my house on Elm street means to me, walking through the front door is the hardest punch, cut, happiness killer I could ever receive over and over again. The houses our moms decorated and helped to make safe places will never feel like our homes again because the most important part is missing. Them. Our moms.

"Come back to Jersey with me for a while. Michael will be there. Or we can all go back to Virginia and stay with Ms. Reed. Wherever you want to go, I'll make the arrangements to be there for you. You're my brother, Ethan. I love you." I shake my head, question if I'm saying too much, coming across as too overbearing, too annoying for him at this moment. I should be listening, just allowing him to say whatever is on his mind and heart. *Shut up, Jaylen. Give him what you wanted. Space, quiet, and the time to make decisions for yourself.*

"I don't know."

Nobody knows what they want to do after they lose

someone. It hasn't even been a full 24 hours. *Stay quiet, Jaylen. Just listen. As much as you want him to know that you're here, that you'll be wherever he is, that your shoulders and your home are available to him whenever, he doesn't need to hear the broken record replay.*

He punches the beach again, growls. "A family. Not a crazy girl and one of her friends. Adults. She got adults in on this." He places his hand over his forehead. "How is that even possible? How do you convince people to cross state lines, fill up on water, and prepare to kill off a family on vacation? One of them had to have snuck onto the property yesterday, seen us having the bonfire, and realized how few us were here. That's probably why they were so calm and why they felt so confident that they'd defeat us. Why else would they walk down the stairs so calmly and face off with us? This girl got people to stalk us, spy on us, and attempt to kill us. What the hell kind of power did she have?"

I can't answer that because I'm not sure. I'm sure guys are possessed by her beauty, but what about everyone else? What was it about Indigo that made everyone around her want to protect her, to see her happy even though at times she did things that would make her underserving?

I shake my head, stray away from an answer that focuses specifically on Indigo. "We're all surprised because everything that happened, happened to us. Let's face the facts. We live in a world where crimes like this aren't unheard of. There are several killer families in America's prisons right now. There are many criminal masterminds that have called together a group of seemingly normal individuals to carry out heinous crimes with them, and sometimes for them. We, the humans and us Quisis, or Ques, whichever you prefer to call us, share one hell of a dangerous world."

"You happy she's dead?"

My stomach turns before sinking painfully as if I swallowed a cinder block. His question is beyond shocking. It's difficult. It requires explanation. There is no simple *yes* or *no* to his short, cold question.

"I am," he says, answering his own morbid question. "I only wish I could've pushed her."

My heart beat takes off like a horse frightened by a gunshot. Not one part of me feels as though he's lying. That's another feeling Ethan and I can say we've both felt, an experience I understand all too well. I thought Indigo killed Michael on our prom night. Killing her and avenging his death didn't register in my mind as difficult. My heart was completely filled with nothing but pain, triggered by the temporary loss. My mind was overtaken by a level of anger that scares me to even think about. That's what's inside of Ethan. A version of himself brought out of hiding by a deranged lunatic.

Our backs on the sand, our bodies side by side, I reach over and grab a hold of Ethan's hand. "Who you are today, you won't be next week. Today, you wish you had pushed her. Once you start moving throughout the grieving process, the hate you're feeling will slowly dissipate. I'm sure you'll always be angry, but you won't wish you had taken her life. That kind of dirt can never be washed off your hands."

"Maybe you just think you know who I am and what I'll feel because you're comparing me too much to yourself."

"I knew your mother. Briefly, but I knew her. I know you, too. It hasn't been long, but it's long enough to know you're not that guy. You're a good person, Ethan. Like anyone else would be, you're fueled by your emotions at this moment. These feelings will change."

He pulls his hand from mine, pushes himself up into the sitting position. "No they won't. Stop comparing my situation to yours. Your boyfriend is still here. My mother is not."

I push myself up as well. I knew I should've kept my mouth closed and simply listened. No one wants to be told how they feel or will feel, especially when they've only been allowed less than a day of often interrupted grieving.

I look at the blanket, at what's covering Ms. Housley. I

look out at the lake, at the new, unmarked grave for Indigo's people. I then look at Ethan. I look at him and I see myself. A human lookalike. An alien. A Que. Lost. Angry. Shocked. Broken. Terrified. Parentless. Alone.

"I'm sorry," I say. "Of course you know how you feel."

"So do you. You've lost your adoptive mom and your biological mother. You know what I'm feeling," he states surely.

"I do. At least, some of what you're feeling. I also remember how I felt when people tried to console me. I didn't wanna be told shit. I'm wide open, Ethan. Say anything. Hit me with anything unexpected. No judgement. If you still feel this enraged a week from now, that doesn't suddenly make you evil. You need your time. I'm not here to rush your healing and I didn't come down here to further piss you off."

I begin to push myself to my feet when he grabs my wrist. My eyes go to his. More tears fall. No words. I lower myself back down on the sand. I don't speak, but do take my friend's hand again.

He brings my hand to his face, a hand that trembles as his tears run down the back of it.

My friend, my brother, shouldn't be in this much pain. His mother's remains shouldn't be feet from us. That Great Lake stretched out in front of us shouldn't be a crime scene. We should all still be alive, smiling, only upset about one thing, and that's having to return home and separate from one another. This shouldn't be our lives. This shouldn't be our new reality.

"Who the hell are we now? What are we?"

His questions bring about another sick twist within my belly. They're questions that force you to realize how much you've changed, force you to realize you have the ability to become an entirely different individual, even if just for one evening. That's disconcerting for me.

Ethan. He was a driven, funny, warm, non-violent, peacemaking guy. He's still that guy no matter what he thinks or says. Today, he's shattered. Understandably so. He's a bunch of pieces I'm determined to get back together.

Me. I was adjusting to being a part of an extraterrestrial family. I was learning, slowly, but still learning how to exist in my house on Elm Street without my mom. I was looking forward to college. I was looking forward to living alone with Michael. I was almost whole for a minute. I was growing, finding my place. *Who am I now?* I'm a high school graduate, a Princeton Tiger, a devoted girlfriend to a guy who's going places. I'm a homeowner at 18. I'm a gifted genius, a super-strong feminist. I'm an alien, unknown for what I really am to every human who surrounds me. I'm a lot of things. I'm also Luna's killer.

What are we? I turn toward my friend, my hand still in his, tears still rolling down his face. We may be aliens, may take long looks at ourselves and question just about everything because of what separates us from humans and because of what makes us immediate threats to animals. We may be from another place, somewhere we'll never learn anything about, but we're in the right. *What are we?* We're conscience having, good-hearted Quisis trying to fully process what happened so we can determine what's next.

What are we? I make eye contact with Ethan. "We're survivors."

Acknowledgements

There are so many people who played an important role in helping me publish this novel.

Each of you mean so much to me.

First and foremost, I must thank God for all the blessings he has bestowed upon me. Last year was one of the hardest years of my life. I was sick for most of it, my anxiety was at an all-time high, and for months on end, I was too stressed to write. This year already looks brighter and I owe all thanks to my Heavenly Father. Thank you for strengthening me, helping me through such a dark year, and helping me find light again.

Kayla and Kaden, you are mommy's motivation. You push mommy to work harder. While I aim to inspire and guide you both, you two inspire me. I work to better myself daily, I relentlessly pursue every passion of mine, and I refuse to accept failure because I have to be a mother you both can look up to. I am so proud to be your mother, and I will forever work to make you proud.

Andrea Childers, Temecka Evans, and Ella Fleming-Christie, you three supported *Outsiders* from the very beginning. Your encouragement and support are fully appreciated, and though you may not realize it, you've inspired me to keep going, even on my darkest days. I appreciate your open-mindedness and your enthusiasm about my story and characters. You all mean so much to me.

Joe Beckett, thank you. Thank you for proofreading my blurb and for supporting *Outsiders*. In addition to that, thank you for being a friend. Your support, encouragement, and kindness helped me through a very difficult time, and I am so happy writing brought us into each other's lives.

Holly, I really appreciate your detailed critique. *Outsiders 2* needed your set of eyes and I appreciate your attention to the overall story. You were amazing to work with, and I'm certain we'll work together again. You rock!

Dominique, I am so glad I found your line editing service. I appreciate your time and attention. *Outsiders 2* was a mess when you received it. You did an amazing job cleaning it up. I also appreciated your overall thoughts. Everything you provided was helpful. Thank you so much. You're awesome!

Laura Barone, you are one hell of an editor! I am so glad we got to work together again. Thank you so much for proofreading *Outsiders 2* and for proofreading my blurb. On a personal note, thank you for reaching out to me when I wasn't feeling so well. I really appreciate your support. You're an exceptional editor and a truly beautiful woman, inside and out. Thank you for everything!

Cindy Draughon, I am so glad we got to work together. Your eagle eye caught a lot of errors we all missed. I can't thank you enough for your help and quick turnaround time. I know for sure we'll work together again. You're fantastic and so encouraging!

Lorraine Morlock, I can't fully express how great it was to work with you. I believe in following my gut, and deep down I knew a mistake or two was left behind. When I hired you to do the final read through/ oops detection, I expected you to only find one or two lingering errors. You caught several of those annoying little mistakes we all missed. I really appreciate your help and kind words. You were a joy to work with, and I'm sure we'll work together again.

Ilsie Omareva of The Woodsy Fawn (www.thewoodsyfawn.com), working with you for the second time was another awesome experience. My cover is perfect and everything I wanted. Again, the marketing materials were stunning, and I appreciate all of your hard work. Thank you!

To all of you who have read, reviewed, purchased, or simply added my book to your lists, thank you. Whether you enjoyed my work or not, I appreciate your support. Thank you for giving me and my work a chance. I appreciate and thank you all.

I have to thank all of my family and friends. I love and appreciate you all. Thank you for the love and support.

Thank you all for helping me make my dream come true!